HARD FALL

BRENDA ROTHERT

KAT MIZERA

SILVER SKY PUBLISHING, INC.

PROLOGUE

HADLEY

Seven years earlier

"You're going to LOVE him," my best friend, Lauren, gushed. "Seriously, Hadley, Wes is the total package. Hot, smart, funny *and* he's a professional hockey player. If Ben wasn't already the love of my life, I'd go for him."

I gave her a skeptical look. "You're always telling me how different the two of them are."

She waved a hand. "Not in any of the important ways. Stop being difficult. My point is, he's great, you're in a major man drought *and* you've got a hotel room all to yourself tonight."

I suppressed a sigh. Lauren had been my best friend since we met at orientation our freshman year at UCLA. She was the peanut butter to my jelly, and I'd have done anything for her.

Which was why I was pasting on a smile as she ushered me across the crowded lawn of her parents' Naperville backyard. They were hosting an engagement party for Lauren and Ben, who were getting married in two months. After their three year, extremely long-distance relationship—her in LA and him in Boston—they didn't want a lengthy engagement. We'd graduated college a couple weeks ago and Lauren was knee-deep in wedding plans.

It was all happening so fast. A few months ago, our biggest worries had been passing our final exams and finding the cheapest prices on our favorite wine and frozen pizza. Now, Lauren was getting married and moving to St. Louis with Ben, where he would be playing pro hockey, and I had just started my new job as a writer for *Willow*, a lifestyle magazine in New York City.

"Oh! I think I see him!" With a squeal, Lauren grabbed my hand and led me through the clusters of people drinking and eating mini cucumber sandwiches.

My stomach churned nervously. I'd been hearing Lauren talk about Wes Kirby for the entire three years she'd been with Ben. I knew he was hot—I'd seen pictures. And Lauren had assured me he was more than just that.

She was right about the drought. It'd been almost a year since I'd had sex, and seven months since I last went on a date. I wished I could chalk it up to being too busy with finishing school and graduating, but the truth was, I just hadn't met anyone I liked very much. I was hoping Wes and I would have good chemistry. He was the best man in the wedding, and I was the maid of honor. We'd be seeing a lot of each other that weekend, and also the weekend of the wedding in August.

"Crap, Ben took him to talk to someone," Lauren said, groaning. "He knows I want to introduce you two."

"Let's go eat," I suggested. "I haven't eaten all day, and I'm starving."

"Okay. Just don't spill food on your shirt." Lauren gave me a stern look, very familiar with my tendency to spill a little here and there.

"I try not to," I said, rolling my eyes. "It just happens."

"You need a bib."

I shrugged. "It sure wouldn't hurt."

She just sighed and put an arm around my shoulders as we walked over to the food line. "Maybe that can be your first story for the new magazine." She put a hand out in front of us and waved it in a horizontal line, mimicking a headline. "Essential supplies for the woman who is forever spilling food on her shirt. You could include cute bibs, Tide wipes and bags big enough to hold extra shirts."

"You're an asshole," I muttered, laughing.

"But you love me anyway."

"I do." I sighed and met her gaze. "What am I going to do without you, Lo? We've been best friends for four years and roommates for the past three years."

Her light blue eyes widened as she gave me a serious look. "*Nothing* will keep us from being best friends, Had. Not ever. Even when I'm raising babies and you're the executive editor of *Vogue,* we'll still talk every day and see each other as much as we can."

Lauren reached the front of the food line and picked up a plate, passing it to me before grabbing one for herself.

"I'm so glad Ben likes cookout food as much as I do," she said, grinning. "We're not prime rib and caviar people. Give me a burger and some orange-powdered Kraft mac and cheese any day. I don't even need the fancy kind with actual cheese."

I laughed and said, "Remember that time we were studying for finals and we hadn't eaten all day and we cooked that huge pan of frozen mac and cheese in the oven and we both burned our mouths on it?"

"Oh shit." She laughed. "That was the worst. I seriously thought I might never regain feeling on that part of my tongue."

"We binge watched rom-coms the next day with a big bowl of ice between us, just putting new cubes on our tongues after they melted."

Lauren loaded her plate up with pasta salads and a cheeseburger, and I went for a hot dog, mac and cheese and some fruit. She was one of those naturally thin women—a size four who stayed gorgeous no matter what she ate, while I had to work out every day just to stay a size ten.

She got stopped by an aunt and uncle who wanted to congratulate her, and ten minutes had passed before we finally sat down at a table to eat. Lauren was an only child, but her parents had multiple siblings and her extended family was big. They'd always included me in their holiday get-togethers, because the only family I had left was my brother, a Navy SEAL who was never in one place for long, and an uncle in Florida.

I was so hungry that I immediately shoveled a spoonful of mac and cheese into my mouth, following it shortly with a bite of my hot dog. If we got called away to have pictures taken again, I wanted to at least get a few bites in so I didn't get hangry.

"Hey babe," a deep male voice said.

I turned to see Ben approaching us, Wes right beside him.

Fuck. He couldn't have gotten a less flattering first look at me, my mouth wide open. I chewed as quickly as I could, wiped my mouth and smiled up at Wes as Lauren stood to hug Ben.

"Hey, Wes," Lauren said, hugging him next.

I nervously ran a hand over my face, praying I'd gotten all the leftover crumbs. My heart hammered as I stood and met Wes's very blue eyes. He was tall, with dark hair, a handsome face and a smile straight out of a toothpaste commercial—perfect and pearly white.

Images of the four of us double dating flashed through my mind, and obviously, I was in his lap as I imagined it.

"Hey, Hadley," he said, grinning. "I see you like to put wieners in your mouth."

My heart sank and I gave Lauren the side-eye. This guy had so much potential until he opened his mouth. He grabbed a potato chip from his plate and popped it into his mouth. In addition to chips, his plate was loaded up with a hamburger, a hot dog, and at least a cup of every side dish on the serving table. It was a wonder the mountain of food wasn't spilling all over the ground.

"Looks like you do, too," I said, giving him a tight smile as I nodded at his plate.

"Heh, yeah."

"Hey guys, we need to go talk to some people," Lauren said, giving Ben a conspiratorial look. "Just visit for a little bit and we'll be right back."

I gave her a wide-eyed *are you fucking kidding me right now* look, but she ignored me.

Wes plopped down in the chair Lauren vacated and gave me a shit-eating grin.

"What's this I hear about the best man and the maid of honor hooking up at weddings?" he asked.

"It's news to me," I said, focusing on my plate and mentally composing the rant that would be directed at Lauren later for leaving me here alone with him.

"You want to meet up for a drink later, after we all go out?" Wes asked.

I narrowed my eyes and gave him a skeptical look. "I think we're already going out for drinks after dinner."

"Yeah, but I mean after that…you know, just you and me."

I couldn't stand men like him. He didn't care who I was or what I was about—he just wanted to get laid later.

"I think I'll be pretty tired after we all go out," I said.

"Tired?" He laughed. "I think you need to loosen up."

"I'm good."

He shook his head like he couldn't understand why I turned him down and exhaled hard. "Come on, Hadley. We're both single, might as well live a little. Give it a chance and you might even end up liking me."

I laughed, unamused. "You don't even know me."

"I know enough."

I rolled my eyes. "I have too much self-respect for your taste, trust me."

"What's that supposed to mean?"

"It means I have no interest in having sex with you."

He put his hands up in mock surrender. "Hey, I wasn't asking you to. We're all going out tonight. I just thought you and I could spend some time together after."

"Yeah, while already drunk," I said sarcastically.

"Nothing wrong with having some fun."

"You seem like the type of guy who likes to *have some fun* with a different woman every night."

He shrugged and looked down at his left hand,

holding it up and meeting my eyes. "Ring finger looks empty to me."

"Ugh. Do you still live in a fraternity house?"

"I would if I could."

"Living in filth, partying every night and being irresponsible. I bet you'd love it."

He grinned. "You'd love having some fun, too, if you'd…you know, unclench a little bit."

I balked at that. "*Unclench*? Did you seriously just say that to me?"

"I think I like you better when you have a wiener in your mouth, just saying."

"*How* are you and Ben friends?"

"How are you and Lauren friends? She's about the sweetest, coolest girl I've ever met."

"*Woman*, actually."

Wes cringed. "Whatever. You're one of those people who corrects everyone's grammar, aren't you? And alphabetizes their shit. Are your spices alphabetized?"

My cheeks warmed, because *yes* my spice cabinet was alphabetized, but I wasn't giving him the satisfaction of admitting it.

"Clearly we aren't compatible," I said.

"Yeah, clearly." He widened his eyes and took a bite of his burger.

"Hey, how's it going, guys?" Ben asked as he and Lauren approached.

"Fantastic," Wes said sarcastically, standing up.

Lauren gave me a sympathetic look, and Ben cleared his throat, looking sheepish.

"Well, maybe you guys got off on the wrong foot," he said diplomatically. "Let's start over tonight."

"Pass," I said, shaking my head and getting up from my chair. "Wes might have better luck trolling college freshmen. I think I'm a little too old for him, intellectually speaking."

"Fucking ballbuster," Wes muttered.

"Asshole," I fired back, taking a step closer to him.

"Why don't you go label some shit? Or iron your power suits?"

"Go play with yourself, frat boy."

"Okay, guys." Lauren moved to stand between us. "Let's go our separate ways and not turn our best friends' engagement party into an episode of *Jerry Springer*, okay?"

I nodded, immediately remorseful for acting childish. There was no one close by, but *still*. Today was about Lauren and Ben.

"I'm sorry, guys," I said softly.

"Yeah, me too," Wes said. "I'm gonna..." He gestured to the other side of the back yard.

"I'll come with you," Ben said.

Lauren put an arm around me once they were gone. "Hadley, I'm so sorry. I never would have tried to set you guys up if I'd thought it would go like that."

"I know. I just can't see why Ben would be friends with him. He's unbearable."

"Why? What happened? He's usually such a nice guy." Her eyes were filled with worry.

"You know what?" I forced a smile. "It doesn't matter. It's your engagement party and we can talk about it another time."

"Yeah, but what about tonight? Do you think you can maybe…ignore him?"

"Absolutely."

She looked relieved. "Good. Because you're our maid of honor and he's our best man. You'll have to see each other for wedding stuff. And later on, maybe during holidays and at baby showers and such."

I gave my best friend a serious look. "Don't worry, Lo. I don't plan to ever speak to Wes again."

She bit her lip and gave me an uncertain look.

"What?" I asked her.

"I didn't want to say anything, but…you spilled macaroni and cheese on your shirt."

"What?" I looked down and saw a smear of yellow cheese sauce on my light pink shirt, a single elbow noodle still stuck there. Perfect. Wes must have been laughing on the inside as I acted indignant toward him with food plastered to my shirt.

"Fuck," I whispered.

"It's okay," Lauren said. "I have extra clothes in the house. Let's find you something to change into."

I followed her into her parents' house, keeping my gaze on the back of her head. Not only did I not plan on speaking to Wes ever again, I also didn't plan on so much as *looking* at him.

What a dick. Nothing would ever change my feelings about him—not just tonight, but ever.

CHAPTER ONE

WES

Present Day

"Wes...more!" The tall brunette, whose name I couldn't remember, was pushing her tongue into my mouth as I slid my hands under her short black skirt. She was grinding on my lap, her long hair draped all over my chest as we kissed. "Please, Wes, I need you inside of me."

"Easy, doll. We have all night." I kissed her again, trying to remember if I had a condom in my wallet because I'd left my wallet and phone on the counter when we'd gotten to her place.

Somewhere in the distance, I heard my ringtone playing Queen's "We Are The Champions" and the vixen in my lap momentarily pulled away. "Do you need to get that?"

"Nope."

Who the hell could be calling me at midnight on a Tuesday night?

Somewhere in the deep recesses of my mind, it occurred to me it might be important—why *else* was someone calling me at this time of night?

Things were just heating up again when my phone rang for the second time, but I just tugged at her top, pulling it over her head so we could continue kissing. She had a fantastic body, one I'd been thinking about seeing naked for several hours, and it was starting to annoy me that the phone kept ringing.

So when I heard the chorus of "We Are The Champions" for the third time in as many minutes, I let out a huff of impatience as she looked at me through hooded eyes.

"Maybe it's important?" she asked quietly.

"Shit." I gently pushed her off my lap and got up, walking across the room to get my phone. I didn't recognize the number but answered anyways.

"Yeah, this is Wes."

"M-Mr. Kirby?" The female voice on the other end sounded young.

"Yeah, who is this?" I tapped my foot impatiently.

"M-my n-name is…Britney. I'm, um…" She sniffled. "I'm, uh, I'm Ben and Lauren's b-babysitter."

Was Ben and Lauren's babysitter crying? Better yet, why was she calling me? I was hella confused. "Are the kids okay? Where are Ben and Lauren?"

She burst into tears. "I don't know! Please, can you come over? The police are here and I was told to call you if I ever couldn't reach them and now I don't know what to do and—" She was crying so hard I could barely understand her.

"The police are there?" I was already zipping my jeans back up and feeling around for my keys. "Okay, I'm on my way. Don't do anything until I get there." I disconnected and whirled around to the gorgeous woman I'd abandoned on the couch. "I'm sorry—I don't know what's going on. The police are at my friends' house and the babysitter is freaking right the fuck out."

She looked a little suspicious. "You know, if you weren't into me, you didn't have to get one of your friends to call like that."

I frowned. "Honey, if I wasn't into you, I wouldn't be here. Sorry, I really have to go." I ran down the hall to the Emergency Exit stairs and took them down to the parking lot. I had no idea what was going on, but my best friend, Ben, and his wife,

Lauren, had me as an emergency contact for them and their kids. Something was wrong.

Tonight was date night, according to Ben. He and Lauren tried to get a night away from three-year-old Annalise and six-month-old Benny once a month. Assuming the professional hockey team we played for, the St. Louis Mavericks, was in town and we had time off. We didn't get much of that during hockey season, but that was why he went out of his way to make time for his wife.

They were probably my two favorite people in the world. Ben and I played for the Mavericks, but our friendship went all the way back to junior hockey. We'd been friends since we were fourteen and when he'd fallen in love with smart, sassy Lauren, I'd kind of fallen in love with her too. I was godfather to their children and we spent a lot of time together, both on and off the ice. So there was zero chance I wouldn't go if they—or their babysitter—called.

———

AT THIS TIME OF NIGHT, it only took me about twelve minutes to arrive at their gated community, and I punched in the gate code since I was such a regular visitor. There was a police cruiser parked in front of the house and that scared me more than Britney's phone call. I got out of my SUV and hurried to the front door, knocking briskly.

A uniformed officer opened the door and met my gaze questioningly. "Mr. Kirby?"

"Yeah. I'm Wes Kirby. What's going on?"

Another officer came to the door and the two looked at me.

Something bad twisted through my chest, a feeling of foreboding, and I met their gazes directly. "What's going on? Are the kids okay? Where's Ben and Lauren?"

"There was a car accident," the first officer said quietly. "Mr. Whitmer died on impact and Mrs. Whitmer died on the way to the hospital."

"What?" I stared at them. "No. This has to be a mistake."

"Mr. Kirby?" Britney came to the door, her eyes red and puffy. "Is it true?"

Now that she was standing there, I remembered meeting her a few times. She was a high school student who lived around the corner and the kids loved her. She helped Lauren sometimes when we were on the road too, so she could have a little time to herself.

"I don't know anything yet, hon." I ran a hand through my hair. "Are the kids sleeping?"

She nodded.

"Do you need to call your parents?"

"I just did."

A moment later, a sleek black Mercedes pulled into the driveway and a couple who looked to be in their forties got out of the car. The woman ran forward, her eyes meeting mine in alarm.

"What's happened? Where are Ben and Lauren? What's going on?"

"I don't know." I was trying to breathe, trying to stay calm, because this didn't feel real. There had to be a mistake.

"Officers, what's happening here?" Britney's dad was trying to play the tough guy, like being a badass was going to get us answers.

"Where are they?" I interrupted.

"They're at County General," the second officer said to me. "But—"

"I need to go there." I turned to Britney's mom. "I hate to ask, but could you please stay here with Britney and the kids so I can go figure out what the hell is happening?"

"Of course, go." She nodded and then squinted a little. "You're Ben's friend. Wes, right?"

"Yes." I met her gaze questioningly.

"Lauren spoke of you often."

I didn't know what to say to that so I simply nodded, and then turned and ran back to my SUV.

———

I CALLED Ben's phone on the drive to the hospital, but it went right to voicemail.

"Hey, this is Ben. Leave a message. If this is Lauren, I love you."

Fuck.

This couldn't be happening. It couldn't be true. I refused to believe it until I saw it with my own two eyes.

Impulsively, I tried Lauren's number next, but it, too, went straight to voicemail.

"Hey, it's Lauren. You know what to do after the beep. If this is Ben, the reason I'm not answering is because I'm busy with your children. But I love you anyway."

God, those two.

My heart was practically in my throat now, and I was getting that bad feeling again. I couldn't even fathom the idea that something had happened to them.

On impulse, I called our friend and teammate Nash Reilly.

"You realize it's fucking one o'clock in the morning and—"

I cut him off. "Ben and Lauren were in a car accident. I'm on my way to County General. Can you meet me?"

"Jesus, they all right?"

"I think it's bad, Riles."

"I'm on my way." He disconnected and my knuckles turned white as I gripped the steering wheel, turning into the main entrance of the hospital. I pulled into a spot outside the emergency room and went inside.

There was a tired-looking nurse at the front desk and I approached her at a fast clip.

"Excuse me. I'm looking for Ben and Lauren Whitmer."

The nurse frowned. "I don't think we have anyone by that name…" Her voice trailed off as she typed into her computer. Then her face changed a little. "Oh. I'm sorry, who are you?"

"I'm…a friend of the family. The police came to the house to tell us there was some kind of accident." I met her gaze, losing hope with each passing second as I watched the emotions on her face. "Do you have any information you could tell me?"

"I'm afraid I can only talk to immediate family or—"

"It's all right, Jan." One of the policemen from the house had obviously followed me here. He placed a hand on my shoulder and walked me a few feet away from the desk area. "Mr. Kirby, your friend and his wife didn't survive the accident. I'm very sorry."

"You can't..." My voice trailed off and I swallowed. There was something scratchy behind my eyes and I stood there, frozen. "Are you sure?" I finally whispered.

"We're so sorry, Mr. Kirby. Do you know who we might call for them? Is there family? We'll have to call CPS for the children unless—"

"No, I'm, I'll...I'm their godfather. I'll go back there tonight. I just...can I see them?"

"I'm not sure. Let me find out."

The officer went back to the front desk while I stood stock-still. It wasn't real. It couldn't be. I didn't believe it. *Couldn't* believe it.

"Wes!" Nash came in a few seconds later and the moment he saw me, his step faltered. "Wes?"

"They're gone, Riles." I couldn't even look at him.

"Jesus, no." He stopped a foot or so away from me. "Are you sure?"

"I, uh, yeah, I think so." I looked up as the officer approached me.

"Would you like to see your friends? The nurse, Jan, said we can let you in there real quick."

"I…" My voice trailed off. I'd never seen a dead body. Not up close anyway, and definitely not belonging to my best friend.

"Once they move them to the morgue, you won't be allowed down there," the officer said gently.

"Yes. I…yes."

My feet felt like huge slabs of concrete as I followed the nurse down a nondescript hallway. We walked past all the regular rooms, to a secluded one in the back. The nurse opened the door and I steeled myself before stepping inside.

"No." My breath left me in a rush and I sagged against the wall. "Fuck, no." I squeezed my eyes shut and fought against the moisture gathering there, but it was no use.

Ben and Lauren were gone.

Ben. My best friend. My brother. Our team captain. The yin to my yang for fifteen years.

"NO!!!" The word left my chest in a guttural roar and I squatted down to my haunches because I no longer had the strength to stand. I hung my head, pain unlike anything I'd ever felt ripping through my gut.

This couldn't be real. It couldn't be happening.

But it was. Ben and Lauren were gone and I had no fucking idea how I was going to get past this.

CHAPTER TWO

HADLEY

"Miss Carrie, my mommy and daddy are in heaven," Annalise explained to the woman who just got to the front of the receiving line at the visitation.

"Hi, I'm one of Annalise's preschool teachers," Miss Carrie said to me before getting on her knees to address three-year-old Annalise.

"Yes they are, sweetie," she said, tears welling in her eyes. "And they'll always be watching over you."

"Is that true, Aunt Hadley?" Annalise asked, looking up at me while she gripped my hand.

"It is. Heaven is a place with no more hurts or sadness, and your mom and dad will be able to watch over you from there, always."

"Can't they come back, though? I miss them."

Miss Carrie gave me a sympathetic look.

"I miss them too, love," I told Annalise, willing myself not to cry. "But no, they can't come back."

Her sweet round face fell with sadness. Miss Carrie asked her if she'd like a hug and she said yes. I used the momentary break to take a deep breath and remind myself that I *could* do this.

The past five days had been a living hell. I'd hardly slept since getting an early-morning phone call that my best friend of eleven years had been killed in a car accident along with her husband.

How? That was the question I kept asking myself. How do the lives of a beautiful, young, happy couple with a three-year-old daughter and a six-month-old son just end without warning? It was unthinkable.

When I got to their St. Louis home later that day, though, and found it filled with Ben's teammates and other friends of Ben and Lauren, I went into the bathroom and fell to my knees, sobbing.

Life as I knew it was over. Even though I lived in New York City and Lauren lived in St. Louis, we talked several times a day, and we visited each other often. I was Annalise and Benny's godmother.

Seeing Annalise cry for her mother had been the hardest part. I'd been sleeping with her every night in Ben and Lauren's bed, telling her to cry as much as she needed to. She was so young, though. Even though she'd be four in a couple months, she couldn't really comprehend what was going on.

And little Benny would never know his parents. Ben's mom and dad, Patrick and Susan Whitmer, had traveled to their house from their home in Malibu immediately, and Susan had completely taken over care of Benny. She was rocking him in her arms in the receiving line, her eyes swollen and red.

Her baby boy was gone forever, and having *his* baby boy in her arms seemed to console her. Lauren's parents had come for the services, but her mom struggled with MS and her dad was her care-giver. They couldn't take on full-time care of the kids. Patrick and Susan would do it, though. I dreaded the moment I saw Annalise and Benny for the last time before they left for Malibu. They were my link to Lauren.

I wiped the corners of my eyes, my head bowed, and Annalise took my hand again.

I can do this. For Ben and Lauren, I can hold it together and be there for Annalise. I'll break down later, when I'm alone.

"Hey, Hadley," a familiar, deep male voice said.

I looked up and met the clear blue eyes of Wes Kirby. It had been disgust at first sight when we'd met seven years ago, and we'd had nothing but snippy encounters in all the times we'd seen each other since.

Christmases. Baby showers. Christenings. Weekend getaways. Annalise's birthday parties. Wes was Ben's best friend and the kids' godfather. I joked with Lauren in private that Wes was like chronic diarrhea—unpleasant and impossible to escape.

I'd seen Wes at Ben and Lauren's house in passing the last few days, but neither of us had spoken to each other. But in this moment, as he looked at me with dark circles under his eyes, his tie loosened a little like he'd been tugging on it, I felt like Wes might be the only one who truly knew what I was going through.

"Hey," I said, practically launching myself at him in a hug.

He froze for a second, probably in shock, but then his long, strong arms closed around me. I squeezed my eyes shut and pressed my face to his chest.

"Why them?" I whispered, so softly that only he could hear me. "They were the best people I knew."

Wes rested his cheek on the top of my head. "I know. I'd take his place if I could, in a second."

I pulled away and straightened myself, taking another deep breath.

"Patrick and Susan wanted me to stand in the

receiving line with the family," Wes said. "I thought I'd stand here so I can help with Anna peas if you need a break."

Annalise laughed and said, "Uncle Wes, I'm Anna*lise*."

"Anna freeze?" he asked her, expression serious.

She smiled wider than I'd seen her smile since I got here five days ago.

"No, it's Anna*lise*, Uncle Wes."

"Ah, Anna *bees*. I've got it now."

He reached down and picked her up, setting her on his hip and joining the receiving line. Annalise put her head on his shoulder as we greeted people coming through the line. There were hundreds. The visitation had been scheduled for four hours, but we were already two hours into it and there were hundreds of people waiting.

I wanted to run away and hide. All I could think about was being alone so I could cry. I'd stand here, though, for as long as it took. And tomorrow, I'd dress Annalise in the little black dress and shoes someone from the Mavericks organization had been nice enough to have sent from a local boutique, and we'd go to her parents' funeral.

Somehow I knew there was no imminent need to grieve for Ben and Lauren, because the heavy sadness would be there waiting. It would wait a long,

long time. Grief was a patient, potent bitch that I'd get to know extremely well in the days and months to come.

———

"CAN YOU HURRY THIS ALONG?" Susan Whitmer asked as she stood and rocked Benny in her arms in the crowded conference room. "We have a long trip ahead of us, and I want the kids to be able to nap on the plane. I'm trying to keep Benny on a routine schedule."

Ben and Lauren's attorney, Len Harris, peered at Susan over the dark rim of his glasses.

"The will has to be read in its entirety, Mrs. Whitmer," he said.

Rolling her eyes, she said, "Okay, if you could maybe just read it *faster*."

Benny squirmed and let out a wail.

"Want me to take him?" I offered, standing up from my seat at the large conference table.

"No, thank you, I'm fine."

I'd only gotten to hold Benny once, for around twenty minutes, in the week I'd been staying at Ben and Lauren's house. Susan was monopolizing him, and even though I knew it was helping her grieve, I was a little put off that those of us who loved Benny and wouldn't be seeing him for a while weren't being given a chance to hold him, feed him and talk to him.

Len Harris cleared his throat and continued reading.

"As to the care of their minor children, Annalise Hadley Whitmer and Benjamin Weston Whitmer, custody is to be shared by Weston J. Kirby and Hadley P. Ellis. Mr. Kirby and Miss Ellis may decide between them which will be the permanent guardian of their children. Financial—"

"WHAT?" Susan yelled, her mouth open and her eyes wide with horror.

Benny startled at the sound and his cry was the only sound in the room. I felt like someone had slapped me. I was breathless and slightly dazed. I met Wes's gaze across the table and saw that he was just as dumbfounded as I was.

"Patrick, do something," Susan begged her husband. "We're taking our grandchildren home today."

Len Harris furrowed his brow and said, "I'm afraid that's not possible, Mrs. Whitmer. Ben and Lauren left a letter for you to explain the reasons for their decision. They also left letters for each of their children and for Mr. Kirby and Miss Ellis."

"I don't care what their reasons are. We're

Annalise and Benny's family. They're our grandchildren. And we will fight this with everything we've got."

"You can do that," Len Harris said. "But in the meantime, Annalise and Benny are going to—" He looked down at the paper in front of him. "Weston Kirby and Hadley Ellis."

"The kids don't even know them!" Susan shrieked. "This is madness! I've taken care of Benny every second since I got here."

Len Harris locked eyes with Patrick Whitmer. Patrick nodded, his expression somber. He approached his wife and put a hand on her shoulder.

"Susan, we have no choice but to comply for now."

She shook her head, tears streaming down her cheeks. I closed my eyes, understanding her sadness and trying to process what the attorney had just read in Ben and Lauren's will.

I was hoping she'd left me her favorite UCLA sweatshirt. Maybe some photos of us or one of her favorite vases. When I was told my presence was required at the reading of the will, I had *no idea* Ben and Lauren were leaving their *children* to me.

I locked eyes with Wes across the table again. He looked just slightly less shell-shocked than a few seconds ago.

"Susan, we have to give Benny to them," Patrick said in a coaxing tone. "It doesn't mean we'll never see him and Annalise again."

Len Harris cut in. "There's a provision in the will that states you get the children for two weeks every summer and that you be allowed to see them on holidays."

"I can't do that," Susan said, weeping. "I can't."

Patrick managed to lift Benny from her arms, and started to carry him over to Wes.

"Wait," Susan cried. "Wait…just a second. What if they don't want them? What if Wes and…whatever her name is don't want them? Can we have them then? We'll pay if we have to."

Len sat back in his seat, looking like he hadn't even considered that.

"We'd have to revisit the issue then." He looked down at the will again. "Mr. Kirby and Miss Ellis, do you want permanent custody of Annalise and Benny Whitmer?"

Did I? I'd never even imagined this situation possible until less than five minutes ago. I lived in a small studio apartment in Manhattan. My whole world would change if I had Annalise and Benny.

But Ben and Lauren wanted me to do this. Well, me and Wes. I looked over at Wes. I still wasn't sure how this was going to work, but most likely, he would let me have the kids. He was a professional hockey player, and he didn't have time to raise them.

Wes looked up and met my stare as he said, "Yeah. I want them."

"I do, too," I said.

Susan's wail of defeat cut deep.

"We'll fight you," she said softly.

She looked exhausted. I imagined that between the loss of her son and caring for Benny, she was spent in every possible way.

"We won't shut you out of their lives," I said, the words coming out automatically. "You can come and visit them, and not just for holidays."

"Yeah, we want you to stay in their lives," Wes said.

He stood as Patrick passed Benny to him. Wes did a surprisingly good job taking over, holding Benny close the way I knew he liked to be held.

"Shall I finish reading the will now?" Len asked.

No one answered, but he seemed to take that as a yes. Wes and I found out Ben and Lauren's home was paid off and they'd both had sizeable life insurance policies and savings, all of which was left to us for the kids.

The kids. I had kids now. I'd walked into this room an hour ago without children, and now I had two. I'd never be their mother, but I was now responsible for taking care of them in every way. For *raising* them.

It was every bit as much of a shock as finding out they were gone. Grief was going to have to wait, because I was going to be busy for the next eighteen years or so.

CHAPTER THREE

WES

Some things are common sense. Making sure you hold on to a baby so he doesn't roll off a bed, not arguing when a three-year-old wants to dip her hot dog in apple juice, and putting kids in car seats. That stuff, you can figure out no matter how inexperienced you are. On the other hand, no one warns you about projectile vomiting, how many wipes it *actually* takes to clean a baby's ass after a shit explosion, or what temperature you use when defrosting breast milk.

I was now covered in puke, piss, and breast milk, Benny was naked, and Annalise didn't seem impressed with my first solo effort at parenting.

"You're stinky," she told me, wrinkling her little nose.

"Well, me and the big guy are gonna get in the

shower," I told her, scooping Benny up.

"Can I come?"

I froze. Having her in the shower with me wouldn't be appropriate, but I also realized I couldn't leave her out here by herself either. She was generally well behaved, but still only three, so she needed supervision.

Well, so much for a shower.

Christ, I was fucking exhausted and today's shit explosion had been epic. As an honorary family member, I'd changed Benny's and Annalise's diapers on occasion, but usually just pee, and certainly nothing of this magnitude. But this had been some- thing else entirely. I'd made the mistake of opening the diaper while he was still shitting and then he pissed and—I was so not prepared for this.

"Uncle Wes, I'm hungry. Is it lunchtime yet?"

Today's game day morning skate had been optional, so I'd stayed home with the kids hoping to nap when they did, but that hadn't happened. It was almost one in the afternoon and I'd barely fed them breakfast, much less lunch, and I was starting to get overwhelmed. There was no way I'd be able to nap before I left for the game, either. I was just treading water.

There was a brisk knock on the door and someone called out to me.

"Wes?" I recognized Nash's voice.

"In here!" I called back.

Thank fuck someone was here. Now Nash could keep an eye on Annalise while I showered with Benny.

"Hey." I looked up gratefully.

"Uncle Nash!" Annalise gave him a bright smile just before her eyes rounded.

Coming up behind him was our team's enforcer, a huge Swede named Lars Jansson. Six feet six inches, with long blond hair, he was a shy, quiet guy who tended to keep to himself off the ice. I didn't think he'd ever been to any of the team's family parties, and Annalise had probably never seen him in person before.

"It's Thor," she whispered, her eyes wide as saucers.

Lars stared right back. "My name is Lars," he responded in his stiff, accented English. "What is your name?"

"I'm Annalise." She walked over to him, stared up into his face, and then held out her arms, indicating she wanted him to pick her up.

There was a brief, awkward pause as Lars frowned and then turned to me questioningly. I had my arms full of baby poopsicle, so I glanced at Nash, who quickly scooped up Annalise. "Lars is one of the

Mavericks' D-men," he told her. "He has a boo-boo on his arm, so he can't pick you up. But now you can say hi face to face."

Annalise frowned. "Does your boo-boo hurt?" she asked Lars.

"I do not have—" Lars began.

"A lot of experience with kids," Nash finished for him, giving him a look. Lars looked confused for a minute but then nodded.

"Yes, this is true." He turned back to Annalise. "I am happy to meet you."

"Do you want to paint my nails? Uncle Wes said he doesn't know how."

"Er..." Lars hesitated, seemed to give it some thought, and then nodded. "Yes, I can do this."

"Yay!" Annalise wiggled to get down and ran from the room.

"You guys are lifesavers!" I told them. "I'm going to get in the shower with Sir Shits-A-Lot while you're here so you can watch Annalise. Okay?"

"Totally." Nash quirked a brow. "And I'll explain to Lars that when a little kid lifts their arms up, that means they want you to pick them up."

I chuckled as I left the room. Lars had a lot of quirks due to some mental health issues he dealt with, so while we were used to him, it would be difficult to explain to Annalise that he didn't like to be touched and was sometimes too literal. But he'd agreed to paint her nails, which would score him big points because I'd made excuses when she asked me. I'd make a mess if I tried that, and frankly, who had time? I'd been on the go since Benny woke me up just before six. Feeding, changing, making breakfast for myself and Annalise, and getting us all dressed had taken me three hours. I'd been so frazzled I'd forgotten to take her to preschool.

Benny had his head on my chest as I stepped under the warm spray of the shower. I let the water run over us and he seemed to relax under it, so we stood there for a while, letting the water do most of the work of cleaning us. He was so small and innocent, I didn't know what the hell Ben had been thinking leaving his kids in my care. How was I going to do this? Even with Hadley helping out, I had serious doubts about our ability to raise these kids. Maybe we should have let Patrick and Susan take them. Ben's parents were good people. I'd known them for years and until the reading of the will, we'd had a good relationship.

I squirted some shower gel into my hand and lathered us both up as best I could since I only had one arm free, and finally got out. Benny was falling asleep so I wiped him down with a towel, pulled on clean sweats and headed to his room to put a diaper on him before putting him down for a nap.

"How are you doing?" Nash had come into the nursery behind me and I glanced over my shoulder at him.

"You want the truth?"

"Duh."

"This is the hardest fucking thing I've ever done."

"When does Hadley get back?"

"Three days," I responded.

"How long does it take to pack?" he asked.

"Well, it's not like she's just packing a suitcase. She has to pack up her entire apartment, all her belongings, call movers, and take care of essentially everything before moving to a new state. I'm surprised she's doing it as fast as she is, but she needed to get back before we leave on the road trip."

"I still can't believe Ben's parents wouldn't stick around to help for a week," Nash muttered. "I mean, we've hung out with them more than once and they were always so cool."

"They're grieving," I said quietly, trying to hold on to Benny's legs as he kicked and wiggled, keeping me from getting the diaper on. I put my hand on his stomach as I glanced over at Nash. "We can't hold anything against them right now."

"You think they're going to fight you for

custody?"

"I'm sure of it."

Nash looked like he wanted to say something.

"Go on, spit it out," I told him.

"Are you a million percent sure you want to do this?" He made a wide sweeping motion with his hand. "I mean, this is a *lot*, man."

"But it's what Ben and Lauren wanted," I said quietly. "How can I not try? And even though I never thought about parenting them, I love these kids."

"I know." Nash put a hand on my shoulder. "And I'm here for you. Whatever you need, just give me a call."

"Things will be easier once Hadley gets here."

"You think?" He met my gaze because everyone knew Hadley and I were like oil and water. We bickered constantly whenever we were in the same room together.

"We don't have a choice," I said.

"Well, I think—dude, look out!"

I looked down just in time for a spray of urine to come up, soaking my clean sweats, my arm, the changing table, and the fresh sleeper I'd just put out. I looked down in time to see Benny give me a huge toothless grin, as if spectacularly pleased with himself.

It was going to be a long-ass afternoon.

———

I WAS GOING to be late to the wedding.

I stared at the sea of red brake lights and leaned on the horn impatiently, glaring in frustration at the ten-car pileup in front of me. Lauren and Hadley were going to kill me and this was all Ben's fault. Not that I'd throw my best friend under the bus on his wedding day, but how the hell did these things happen to us?

At the next exit, I got off the highway and zigzagged through a bunch of back roads, speeding across school zones and residential areas because I was running out of time. If they had to delay the wedding because the best man hadn't shown up, I would never hear the end of it. I pressed harder on the gas pedal.

After what seemed like an eternity, I skidded into the parking lot of the church, turned off the car, and ran inside.

"Where have you been?" Nash demanded, meeting me just inside the doors. "Ben's about to have a heart attack."

"There was an accident on the highway." I huffed out as I smoothed down the lapels of my tux and took a breath.

"You got the ring?"

"Yeah." I patted my pocket. "Fuck, I could use a bottle of water. I'm dying."

"I'll run and grab you one. I think they're about to

start everything. You literally got back in the nick of time."

"Thanks, man." I'd just started to breathe normally again when I heard her. Oh, yeah, Hadley had been waiting for me, so I steeled myself before slowly turning around.

"About fucking time." She was walking down the hall in my direction looking hotter than Hades in her skintight bridesmaid's dress, but it was the look on her face that made me start to sweat all over again. Jesus, she was pissed and since I couldn't tell her Ben was the one who'd forgotten the ring, I was going to have to stand here and take it.

"There was an accident—" I began.

"Save it. This was such a dick move, Kirby. You do realize it's their wedding day, right? And that the world doesn't revolve around you."

"I know that!" I snapped. "I can't control traffic, lady. Give it a rest, will you?"

"Lauren's been in a total panic and it's my job to keep everything running smoothly. You just about single-handedly ruined everything!"

"Well, if you have the power to control traffic, you should have!" I turned my back on her and headed toward the room where Ben and the rest of the groomsmen were waiting, but she wouldn't let up. Her high heels made a click-click-click noise on the tiled floor as she followed me.

"Okay, I get it," I said, picking up speed and hoping she'd go away. "I was late but I'm here now and everything's fine."

"I truly don't understand how someone as reliable and considerate as Ben has you for a best friend."

"And I can't understand how someone as sweet and thoughtful as Lauren has a shrew for a best friend." I opened the door to where the other guys were, stepped inside, and then closed it in her face. That probably pissed her off even more, but I needed to calm down a little before we got this party started.

Ben met my gaze across the room and mouthed, "Thank you."

"You owe me," I called to him.

"Did Hadley ream you a new one?"

"Oh, yeah."

"I'll tell her what happened and—"

"Forget it. You're the groom. You don't have to think about anything but that beautiful woman you're about to marry. I can take one for the team and handle Hadley."

Nash snorted out a laugh as he handed me a bottle of cold water. "From where I'm standing, you can't handle her at all."

"Just the sound of her voice makes my dick shrivel," I admitted.

"You two are definitely oil and water," Ben said, shaking his head. "But really, she's worked incredibly *hard to make today perfect for Lauren and I, so don't judge her too harshly. She doesn't know the real reason you were late, which makes her think you aren't taking today seriously."*

I downed the whole bottle of water and tossed it into the recycling bin.

"Look, it's over and done. Let's go out there and do this."

Ben held up his fist and bumped it against mine.

"Thanks again," he said quietly. "You saved my ass."

"That's what friends are for, right?"

"You and me until the end." Ben pulled me into a quick hug, slapping me on the back.

"Damn straight."

———

THE LOCKER ROOM is a sacred place. As a team, when we're in there, in some ways it's even more important than when we're on the ice. This was where we talked, planned, strategized, laughed, cried, and bonded. The vibe was different than when we were playing, because the one-on-one interaction wasn't just hockey oriented, but tonight it was quiet, the usual pregame energy noticeably absent. Instead of playful banter and lighthearted bickering, most of the guys were looking down, or staring out at nothing at all. It was like a freakin' funeral in here.

The league had postponed our last game because of the funeral, and even though we'd just buried our team captain, the show, so to speak, had to go on. The Mavericks' head of PR had locked out the press before the game tonight, so the public wouldn't get a glimpse into how we were handling our grief, but that didn't make it any easier.

As an alternate captain, along with Nash, a lot of the responsibility of raising everyone's spirits fell to me since Nash usually dealt with on-ice issues, like talking to the refs. The problem was that I had no emotional bandwidth left. I was battling a wave of grief so intense that it was hard to breathe some-times, and after spending the whole day putting out one child-related fire after another, I was physically and mentally exhausted.

There was no such thing in hockey, though. You battled through everything—injuries, grief, family drama, whatever it was. We didn't have the option of time off in fucking January. We were also having an incredible season, leading the league in wins, points, and goals scored. If we could win one more, we'd break Pittsburgh's record of seventeen wins in a row, but I didn't know how we'd do that on a night like tonight.

Hell, I didn't know any fucking thing right now. I didn't know how I'd survive without my best friend. I didn't know how the hell I was going to raise his two babies. And I really didn't know how I'd get on the ice every night trying to lead this team like he did—because no one could do that. Ben was the whole damn package. Smart, skilled, and a leader in every sense of the word. He could mentor the rookies, bond with the veterans, and talk a guy in a scoring slump off the ledge. Even the refs loved him.

I had neither the patience nor the people skills Ben had, so while I was a leader because of my scoring ability and experience, I didn't do as well with the serious one-on-one chats with teammates. If I were honest, I probably *could* do it, but had never been in a position where I had to. Until now.

"Listen up, boys." Our head coach, Malcolm "Grizzly" Gizzard, came in and shut the door behind him. He scratched the long, bushy beard that had given him his nickname, and looked around, letting out a long sigh. "I don't have a pep talk for you tonight. I don't have scoring tips or threats or promises. Basically, all I've got are facts. Fact one. We're on a seventeen-game win streak and we'll break Pittsburgh's record if we can win it tonight. Fact two. We're in first place overall in the league by a long way, which bodes well for our playoff chances. I don't know how to get past this game, the first one without Ben. So all I'm going to say is to play it for Ben. Play hard. Play smart. Dig deep. Don't let all the background noise get inside your heads. Now let's go."

We all got to our feet but there was a heavy weight dragging us down. I could see it in the way the guys moved, the downcast expressions on their faces, even their body language. It was a reflection of my own mood, so I understood it, but this wasn't good for team morale. We had a lot at stake both personally and professionally, and we couldn't just roll over like this. Ben would be pissed.

"All right, let's see some hustle, you guys!" I called out as we headed down the tunnel toward the ice for the warm-up. "Let's go!"

I felt a tiny spark of excitement as my feet hit the ice but as I looked around and realized Ben wasn't there, the unexpected wave of grief made me stumble.

Fuck.

This wasn't going to go well at all.

And it didn't.

We didn't just lose, we lost spectacularly. 8–0. Our winning streak was over and we were a dejected lot as we filed back into the locker room. The press was waiting for us and even though it was a shitty thing to do, I ducked out and hit the shower, leaving it to Nash and the others. I felt like a coward, but I snuck out when I finished dressing and headed home. Maybe in a few days I'd be able to handle it all, but the idea of being asked about Ben and bursting into tears on camera was more than I could stand.

I let myself in through the garage and went in search of my teammate's wife, Nina Laughlin. She'd offered to help me out this week until Hadley got here, and I found her reading a magazine on the living room couch. She looked up as I came in and gave me a knowing smile.

"Rough night, huh?"

"Yeah." I sighed. "How are the kids?"

"They're in bed. I had to read Annalise six bedtime stories and lay with her until she fell asleep. Benny's been down since eight so he'll probably be up again at midnight."

"Yeah." I gave her a weak, but grateful, smile. "Thanks again for doing this tonight."

"Lauren was my best friend here in St. Louis. She'd kill me if I weren't here for you and the kids."

"Well, I appreciate it."

"Okay, so a couple things we need to discuss." She paused. "There's only enough breast milk left for about two days. Lauren was planning to start weaning him soon, so she hadn't been pumping as much."

"Seriously?" I'd been so focused on getting through this week, I hadn't paid attention to how much was in the freezer. "That's just great. I guess now I need to grow breasts?"

She chuckled but it was without humor. "No, but you're going to have to transition him to formula. He's used to the bottle, thank goodness, so it'll just be a matter of finding the right formula that doesn't upset his stomach. I have suggestions, but you might want to call the pediatrician…"

"Jesus." I could change diapers, brush Annalise's hair, and give both kids baths, but I had no idea about that kind of thing. Formula and feeding and freakin' breast milk. This was a nightmare.

"I know it's hard," she said softly. "But Hadley will be back soon and I'm here. We've got your back. Me, Drew, the team, the rest of the WAGs. All you have to do is call." Her husband Drew was our starting goalie.

I was grateful for her and the others, but I wasn't ready to let go of the fantasy that Ben and Lauren were coming back. That this had been nothing but a bad dream.

Because I really, really wanted to wake up.

CHAPTER FOUR

HADLEY

Coffee. Coffee would make everything better.

I kept telling myself that as I changed Benny out of his wet sleeper, putting him in a dry diaper and a clean outfit before feeding him a bottle, all while answering Annalise's nonstop questions about what her parents were up to in heaven this morning.

I'd gotten back to St. Louis yesterday evening after packing up my entire apartment, working day and night while I was there and only catching a few hours of sleep a day. I sold most of my furniture, moved a few things into a friend's garage for storage, and then drove back here in Ben's Cadillac Escalade, which I'd taken to New York so I could fill it with my belongings for the trip back.

Every day since Ben and Lauren died had been exhausting and emotional. I wasn't just leaving my apartment behind when I'd pulled into the driveway of their posh suburban St. Louis home yesterday, but my life. Not a single day had passed since their deaths when I didn't cry and wonder if I could really do this. If I could really live this new life. My boss had reluctantly agreed to let me work remotely for now, but seriously…work? Even if I could find the time in between caring for two living humans, how would I sort through pitches from writers about doing your own manicures or decluttering your life? I had no focus and I was exhausted.

"Is there dancing in heaven?" Annalise asked me as we walked into the kitchen and I put Benny in his high chair, buckling his seat belt and putting a couple of toys on the tray for him.

"Absolutely. Dancing anytime you want, and singing, too."

"Anytime?" Annalise smiled gleefully.

"Anytime."

"After bedtime?"

"Yes." I smoothed a hand down her dark curls. "You can get out of bed and dance in heaven if you want to, and you can turn the music up as loud as you want."

"Are Mommy and Daddy dancing?"

I made my way over to the coffeepot, thinking about how Ben and Lauren loved to dance. I scooped coffee grounds into a filter, closed the lid and pushed the lifesaving *On* button.

"I'm sure they are. Your mommy loved dancing." A wave of sadness washed over me as the memories flashed through my mind, but I didn't let it show. "Remind me to show you their wedding video of their first dance after they got married. It was very romantic."

"What's *womantic*, Aunt Hadley?"

Wes strode into the kitchen, wearing nothing but a pair of black boxer briefs, his hair sticking up in every direction. He was all long lines and carved muscles, and even though I couldn't stand him most of the time, I had to force myself to look away. I couldn't get busted checking Wes out. He'd never let me live it down.

"Morning," he said, scratching his ass as he opened the refrigerator and looked inside.

Cringing, I said, "It's basically everything that is the opposite of Uncle Wes."

"What?" he asked, looking from me to Annalise.

"Nothing," I muttered. "And can you please put on some clothes?"

He looked down and then back up at me. "I've got underwear on. I'm just grabbing something quick for breakfast before I get in the shower and leave for my road trip."

His road trip. I was still pissed about that. Not only was he leaving for the next four nights, but he'd insisted that his body required a good night of sleep and retreated to the guest room last night, leaving me to care for both kids when I could barely keep my eyes open. Benny was teething and he was fussy, so it had been a long night.

"I want Froot Woops, Uncle Wes!" Annalise cried, racing over to him as he pulled a giant red box from one of the kitchen cabinets.

"You got it," he said, passing her the box. "You take this and I'll get us some bowls and spoons."

It took me a second to pick my jaw up off the floor and form a coherent sentence in response to what I was seeing.

"There's no way you found that box of Froot Loops in one of Lauren's cabinets," I said, shaking my head.

"Me and Annalise went shopping while you were gone," he responded, setting a gallon of milk on the table and walking over to another cabinet to get bowls.

"But...Lauren feeds..." I closed my eyes and corrected myself. "She *fed* the kids an organic diet without added sugars. She pureed and canned her own baby food."

Wes shrugged. "I fed the bananas and peas to

Benny like I was supposed to, but Annalise and I had to eat, too. Did you want us to starve or should we start eating baby food too?"

"That stuff is nothing but sugar and dye."

"Dye?" Annalise gave me a panicked look. "Like Mommy and Daddy?"

Dammit. Why didn't I think before I used that word?

"No, baby," I said, bending down so I was at her level. "It means something that makes the Froot Loops have colors."

Annalise immediately perked up and said, "I like the purple ones!"

I gave Wes a dirty look and said, "Now I'm the bad guy if I don't let her eat it."

"So let her eat it." He met my gaze, sounding aggravated.

"When are you leaving?"

"After I eat and take a shower."

"When you guys went grocery shopping, did you get a snack to take for Annalise's preschool class? Lauren's calendar in the pantry says today is her day to bring a snack for her class. Twelve kids."

"I'm the snacker?" Annalise asked, looking pleased. "I love being the snacker."

"I didn't even look at the calendar," Wes said, sounding unconcerned.

"Of course you didn't," I muttered under my breath.

"Hey, Captain Critical, I held down the fort while you were gone for four days. The kids got fed and we played and they're…pretty much clean."

"I took a bath in my swimsuit, Aunt Hadley!" Annalise said, grinning. "Uncle Wes said it's not approliate for him to see me naked."

"It's *appropriate*, squirt," Wes said, helping her pour Froot Loops into her bowl.

"Don't even think about letting Benny try that stuff," I warned Wes. "I'm going to make his oatmeal."

Benny was fussing a little bit, and I hoped eating breakfast would help. I went into the pantry and found the baby cereal I'd seen Lauren feeding him when I was visiting for Christmas, and mixed it with some of what little breast milk we had left in the fridge.

It was the small things that broke me, like running out of breast milk. The last thing Lauren had been able to do for her baby boy in this life was almost gone.

I mixed the cereal and warmed it in the microwave for about fifteen seconds, relieved that I'd seen Lauren prepare this for him before. Otherwise I wouldn't have had a clue what I was doing. I was walking it over to the table to sit down next to Benny's high chair when I remembered I'd forgotten to bring a wet cloth to clean him up afterward.

I went back to the kitchen sink to get one, and Annalise said, "Hey, Aunt Hadley?"

"What, baby?" I asked, turning around to look at her.

"I think Benny just shit himself. He's stinky."

My mouth dropped open in shock and my gaze zeroed in on Wes.

"Are you kidding me? You've been using language like that in front of her? Because I *know* Ben and Lauren never did."

He looked a little sheepish as he said, "Yeah, that's definitely my fault. I'm working on it."

I was seething inside, but I didn't want to upset the kids, so I pressed my lips together and counted to ten. When Wes and I could have a private conversation, I was going to show him how many foul words *I* knew.

He was treating this whole situation in his usual carefree frat boy manner. Seven years and nothing had changed. Just going with the flow and merging the kids with the way he did things instead of doing things the way Ben and Lauren would have wanted. He'd be teaching the kids poker and how to pop the tops off beer bottles next.

It wasn't even a contest—*I* was the one who should have full guardianship of Annalise and Benny. And in order to keep my job, I'd need to move them to New York. I didn't want to upset their routines by doing it now, but I knew it was what the future held.

"I'm hitting the shower," Wes said, getting up from the table and setting his cereal bowl on the kitchen counter, spoon still inside.

Great. So I'd be the one changing Benny's diaper. Wes could have at least offered his help. I'd take care of anything for the kids without objection, but that bowl and spoon would still be sitting on the counter when Wes returned in four days. There wasn't a chance in hell I was cleaning up after him.

———

Nina Laughlin laughed from the other end of the phone.

"Are you sure about that? Getting groceries is enough of a chore without a three-year-old and an infant in tow. Why don't you let me come over and watch them so you can take a break? Well, as much of a break as you'll get while grocery shopping."

"I appreciate it, really, but Benny and I are already packed and on the way. We're picking

Annalise up from preschool and then going to get groceries."

Nina had traded cell numbers with me after the news hit that Wes and I were getting custody of the kids, telling me I could call her anytime, day or night, for anything at all. She called me daily to check in, and so far, she was my first adult conversation of the day.

Well, I guess there'd been the one with Wes this morning, but he was only about three-quarters of an adult.

"Did they tell you how the pickup line at the preschool works?" she asked. "You don't have to go inside and sign her out. Just stay in the car and enter the line through the circular drive-through and they'll walk her out for you."

"No, I didn't know that, but thanks. That'll help because Benny's about to fall asleep."

I glanced in the rearview mirror and saw his round cheeks and tuft of dark hair reflected in the mirror Lauren had attached to end of Benny's rear-facing car seat. Genius.

"It sucks dragging a baby carrier into the school so you can pick up another kid, especially in the cold," Nina said.

She and her husband Drew had two kids who were eight and ten. It was great to have help from an experienced mom, and even better, one who had been a good friend of Lauren's.

"I did that this morning, and it did suck," I said, laughing. "Annalise is the snacker today and I bought fancy cupcakes from a bakery. I was worried she couldn't handle her backpack and the cupcakes so I carried them in."

Nina gave a little hum of concern. "Shoot, I should have told you the school doesn't allow any baked goods unless they're certified free of tree nuts and peanuts."

"Oh shit, really?" I cringed as I realized what I said and apologized. "Sorry, language."

She laughed. "Don't you worry about a thing. My husband has the mouth of a sailor, and I usually do, too. I was trying to keep it in check because I didn't know how you felt about it."

I felt slightly chastised. I'd just gotten onto Wes this morning for something I did myself. But I would definitely say it was different to swear around a baby, who couldn't understand what I was saying. At least, I hoped so.

"I'm going to have to learn to watch my language in front of the kids," I told Nina.

"Well, you're doing your best, so go easy on yourself. The school keeps extra snacks on hand in case someone forgets to bring something in, so don't worry about that."

"That's good, but Annalise was really excited about those Baby Yoda cupcakes."

"You guys will be able to take them home, though. Why don't I bring over dinner and a bottle of wine tonight? Cupcakes and a glass of wine can be our dessert. And if you need to take a shower or anything, I can mind the kids."

I smiled. "That sounds really nice, thank you."

"No problem. And are you sure you want to take the kiddos to the store? You're welcome to bring them over to my house."

"Nah, I've got it. I get groceries all the time. How hard can it be to bring them with me and have them ride in the cart?"

———

IT WAS *HARD*. Really fucking hard.

I hadn't realized that with Benny's carrier seat inside the cart and Annalise sitting in the front of the cart, I'd have no room for groceries. I had to let Annalise walk beside me, and she stopped to either ask a question about or grab every other thing she saw.

Benny spit up all over himself as I was haphazardly adding items into the cart.

"Is this fucking organic or not?" I said under my breath, straining to read the fine print on a box of baby crackers.

Fuck it. Benny was sitting in his own puke and I needed to get home and clean him up. I threw the box in the cart and headed for the checkout, where I discovered, after everything had been rung up, that I'd left my wallet in the car.

I took both kids outside with me to get it and trekked back inside to pay, sweating like I'd just completed a hardcore SoulCycle spin class. I glanced up at the cashier, who kindly took pity on me, and told me I could pull the car up to the front entrance and they would load the groceries for me.

By the time I got home, gave Benny a quick rinse and changed his clothes, fed him and got him down for a nap, I was dead on my feet. And I still had to make time to play with Annalise. I practically tore the door down when Nina arrived around five, carrying a family-sized take-out meal from an Italian restaurant. There was lasagna, spaghetti, salad and garlic bread.

"Is that your stomach?" she asked, giving me an amused grin when my stomach growled in response to the heavenly scents of garlic and meat sauce.

"I haven't eaten all day," I admitted.

"Oh, honey." She gave me a sympathetic look. "Make yourself a plate. I'll feed the kids."

"Are you sure?"

"I'm positive."

She stayed for the evening, feeding both kids and giving them baths, then reading to Annalise and putting her to bed while I focused on Benny. Then we talked over wine and what was left of the Baby Yoda cupcakes.

Wes texted after his game to check in, and I felt guilty as I texted him back that everything was fine. I'd jumped all over him about the Froot Loops this morning and then let Annalise eat two and a half cupcakes tonight.

How had Lauren done it all? I wanted so badly to raise her kids the way she would have, with healthy food and wholesome activities, but so far, just meeting their basic needs was taking everything I had.

CHAPTER FIVE

WES

Another day, another loss. We'd lost every game since Ben died and I was grumpy as fuck as I headed home. The good news was that this had been the last game before the All-Star break, so I'd have a little time to actually breathe. Maybe even grieve. The bad news was that it meant twenty-four seven with Hadley, something I wasn't particularly looking forward to. We'd barely seen each other since she'd moved in, but she was already bossy and judgmental, as if I'd scarred the kids for life or something.

I did need to watch my language, but beyond that, I thought I'd done a pretty good job considering I had no idea what I was doing. Of course, Hadley would find a way to shit on my parade, no doubt about it. She'd been busting my balls since the first time we laid eyes on each other, and while it made me laugh over the years, it was different now. We had to find a way to work together, live together, and raise these kids together. Because I'd be damned if I let her take them. I might not know all the ins and outs of raising kids, but I'd always planned on having a family someday, and I wanted to do every single thing I could for Ben's kids.

I woke up a little after seven that morning and heard noise downstairs so I figured everyone else was awake too. I felt a twinge of guilt that I hadn't set an alarm and since I'd shut the guest room door, I hadn't heard anything that would wake me either. Hadley and I needed to talk about all of this.

I left the guest room and found Hadley in the family room, walking back and forth, Benny whimpering in her arms.

"What's going on?" I asked her.

"He's teething," she said, without glancing up. "He's been miserable since last night. I've been up with him since about four."

"Why didn't you wake me?"

She shrugged. "You played and traveled yesterday. I figured you needed to sleep."

"I did. Thanks. I'll take overnight duty tonight."

"That would be great. I feel like I haven't slept in weeks."

Benny started to whine and I reached out to

stroke his cheek with one finger. "Can't we give him baby Tylenol or something?"

She chewed her lip. "I didn't want to until I had a chance to talk to the pediatrician."

"I know for sure they did it with Annalise because I used to laugh at the faces she made when Lauren stuck that thing in her mouth to squeeze it in there."

"Do you know if we have any?"

"Top shelf in the cabinet in the master bath."

She looked surprised I would know such a thing, but handed Benny to me and headed upstairs. Benny settled against my chest, sniffling a little. Hopefully, the Tylenol would help him relax and we could get some time to make breakfast. He still didn't sleep more than six or seven hours at a time, so I'd been trying to keep him up until about eleven or midnight. That way, we'd be able to sleep until around six, which was when Annalise usually woke up, but I didn't know what Hadley had been doing while I was gone.

"Have you been keeping him up a little later?" I asked her. "It really helps when—"

Hadley fixed me with one of those stares that probably made most men's balls shrivel up and recede so far north they're never seen again, but then she filled up the little squeezy thing you used to squirt medicine into the baby's mouth.

"His bedtime is seven," she said primly, handing me the medicine dropper.

I gave her a look of exasperation. "Fine. Then *you* get up for the day with him at two in the freakin' morning every day."

"What?" she demanded, narrowing her eyes.

Benny took that moment to turn his head in distaste as I tried to give him the medicine and sticky pink liquid dripped down my arm.

"Can you hold his head?" I asked. "If he doesn't take this, no one is sleeping again until he's done teething."

We finally got the proper amount into his mouth and I did my best to wipe up the medicine that had escaped.

"If you keep him up later, he'll sleep later. He sleeps about seven hours at a time, tops, so if you put him to bed at seven, he'll be up at two."

"But Lauren said he was a great sleeper," she said, suddenly looking away.

"Maybe he's reacting to the new routine, new people, new everything," I said gently. "Let's just try it my way and see what happens, okay?"

"I haven't slept since you've been gone so whatever works," she muttered.

"We might need to consider hiring help," I said after a moment.

"Help?" She looked horrified.

"We both work. Benny needs full-time care and Annalise is only in school three times a week for four hours. Lauren was a stay-at-home mom, so you can't expect to do everything she did."

She glared at me, and I figured she was gearing up for a good ass-reaming just as Annalise came skipping into the room. "Uncle Wes!" She threw her arms around my legs as if she hadn't seen me in years instead of four days.

"Hey, Princess Peas." I settled Benny in his high chair, hoping he'd chill long enough for us to eat.

"You lost last night," she announced, as if I didn't know.

I nodded. "You can't win them all, kiddo." I rummaged around in the cupboard until I found the box of Froot Loops Annalise and I had been eating the first couple of days I'd been here on my own.

"Froot Woops!" She wiggled her whole body in excitement. "I love Froot Woops!"

"Froot Loops," Hadley corrected her. "And you are *not* eating that junk for breakfast."

Annalise's face fell. "But Uncle Wes said so."

Hadley turned to give me a death glare and I arched my brows at her, almost daring her to be the bad guy. She was pretty adorable when she was mad, though, so it was fun to piss her off. Well, if I was honest, she was always adorable, but the minute she opened her mouth I forgot all about her upturned nose, full red lips or mile-long eyelashes. Even without makeup and with faint bags under her eyes from lack of sleep, she was truly gorgeous.

Too bad she hated my fucking guts.

That was okay, though. This was about the kids and she had another think coming if she thought I was walking away. I was in this for the long haul and she could stick around and help or I'd figure it out on my own. There was zero chance I would let Ben and Lauren down, no matter what Miss Prissy-Pants thought of me.

"We should talk," she said after a moment, handing Benny a bottle.

"I figured we'd make breakfast and then I'd take Annalise to school. When I get back, we can sit down and have some adult conversation."

"Fine." She turned her back to me as I poured two bowls of cereal for Annalise and me.

I HAD a feeling Hadley would be in a hell of a mood by the time I got back after dropping off Annalise, but she was sitting on the couch sipping a cup of coffee and watching Benny in his swing. The Tylenol must have worked because he was gurgling happily, a teething ring in his mouth.

"He seems much happier," I said.

"Definitely."

I sank onto the chair across from her and met her gaze over the rim of her cup.

"So, uh, how many days are you home?" she asked.

"I leave on a road trip Tuesday morning, so the next five days gives us some time to figure out what we're going to do."

"Well, there's no doubt what we're going to do," she said dismissively. "Obviously, you can't take care of the kids with your schedule, so I'm going to."

"That's why I suggested we hire a nanny," I said patiently.

She squinted a little. "I hate to use the money Ben and Lauren left us for that kind of thing, but you might be right. Once we sell the house, I'll be able to—"

"Sell the house? What the hell are you talking about? Why would we do that?"

"Because I'll need the money to buy something in New York."

"We can't move to New York." I frowned at her when she rolled her eyes at me.

"We can't, but I can. I plan to move back eventually. Once I've gotten the hang of this parenting thing and—"

"Okay, slow your fucking roll." I held up a hand.

"Watch your language."

"He's not going to repeat it, geez." I looked at her questioningly. "When did we decide that you're going to be the one raising the kids?"

She laughed, though it was pretty humorless. "I think that's a given, Wes. How are you going to take care of them with your travel schedule and practice, and everything else that goes into being a professional athlete?"

"You're here."

"My job is in New York, so even though I'm working remotely for now, eventually I have to get back to my life. And going forward, that's going to include Benny and Annalise. You and I will settle everything here and probably by summer, the kids and I will move back to New York City."

Her words were like a punch to the gut. There was zero chance she was taking those kids away from me, and I'd use every resource available to me to stop her.

"Over my dead body." I folded my arms across my chest.

She fixed me with another icy stare, but it wasn't

cute or hot this time. These kids had been left to me just as much as they had her, and I wasn't giving them up. "Surely you're joking," she said finally.

"Not even a little. They wanted *us* to raise them, not you or me individually."

"No, they wanted us to decide which of us would be best suited to raise them, and quite frankly, that's me."

"Why? Because you have breasts and a vagina?"

She flushed. "No, because you work crazy hours and travel."

"From what I've heard, you work eighteen-hour days during Fashion Week and all kinds of other big events, you travel all over the world doing photo shoots and whatever, and Lauren even said once that you work more hours than Ben and she worried about you."

"I'm single and on the verge of big things with my career," she snapped. "So yeah, I work hard. But now I've got the responsibility of these kids so things have to change."

"Yeah, you have to find a way to settle down here in St. Louis."

She blew out a breath. "Wes, how can we possibly do this together?"

"I don't know, but we have to try because this isn't negotiable. I'm not giving them up."

"Well, neither am I." She lifted her chin a notch.

Her chest was rising and falling a little fast and I couldn't help but notice that she had a spectacular rack. She'd always been such a freakin' pain in my ass over the years, I'd never even bothered to look most of the time. It was hard not to now that we were living in the same house together, though, and I figured the view was a nice reward for all the ball-busting I put up with from her.

"Wes, I haven't slept more than three hours at a time in five days. I'm tired, stressed, and still grieving. Maybe we should put this conversation on hold for a while. I just don't have it in me to bicker with you right now."

"Okay." I quirked a smile at her. "I'm really not a bad guy, Hadley."

She turned to me with wide hazel eyes, something inscrutable lurking behind them. "I never knew anything could hurt this much."

There went all the wind in my sails.

I nodded, absently running a hand through my short hair. "Me either."

"Let's try not to fight in front of the kids, okay? Mostly Annalise, because she hears everything."

"Deal."

She paused, cocking her head a little so that the sunlight coming in from outside glinted on her dark hair, giving it an auburn glow and making me imagine what it would feel like to run my fingers through it.

"You, uh, think a nanny's a good idea?"

"I do. Someone who can help out during the day and occasionally on weekends so we can both work. I have practices, workouts, team meetings, and of course games, and depending on how many hours you work, you can't do your thing all day and then take on every detail of running the house too."

Hadley looked thoughtful. "Is there money for that?"

"There's plenty of money. The house is paid for, and I'll take over paying utilities and such. That way, most of the money goes into trusts for the kids."

She nodded. "I don't make nearly what you do, of course, but I do okay so—"

"No, I've got this, Hadley. You're taking on a big portion of the responsibility when I have to travel, so let me handle the bills. Including the nanny. That makes all of our lives easier, you know?"

"Okay." She slowly nodded. "That's reasonable. How about we give this new situation a couple of months and revisit this conversation again then?"

"Sure."

"But there have to be some ground rules."

I groaned.

"No bimbos in the house. No puck bunnies, prostitutes, whatever—"

"*Prostitutes?!*" I narrowed my eyes at her. "Jesus fucking Christ, what kind of asshole do you think I am? First of all, I have never had to pay for sex in my life, thank you very much. And second, I fucking *love* these kids! You think I'd bring someone like that to the home where we all live?" I got to my feet, glaring at her. "Well, I have news for you, lady—that's some bullshit right there. You don't have to like me, but don't you ever accuse me of doing something that might negatively impact these kids!" I was hot, and not in a good way.

"Wes, I'm sorry. I—" She was still talking, but I raised a hand to stop her as I stalked from the room. A minute later, I slammed the door to the garage behind me. I needed to cool off before I said something I'd regret.

She still pissed me right off, regularly, and it never got easier to deal with her.

I stood in the garage, resting my hands on the now empty work bench Ben had used to work on little projects when he had time. And that's when the envelope caught my eye. I'd stashed the letter Ben had left me there until I was ready to read it, and if there was ever a time, it was now.

Plucking it from the table, I ripped open the

envelope and slowly unfolded the paper. This was going to hurt, but I had to get it over with. I needed my best friend more than I ever had in my life and this was essentially the last time I'd ever talk to him. Even if it was a one-sided conversation.

DEAR WES,

If you're reading this, I'm dead, and so is Lauren. It's hard as hell to even think about that happening, but at least she and I are together.

I know we shocked you by leaving Annalise (and more kids, if we have them) to you and Hadley. Lauren and I went back and forth a lot over whether we should ask you guys, or choose just one of you, but this is the only thing that feels right to us.

Do your best. You think your best isn't good enough, but it is. I know this is asking a lot of you, and maybe you'll decide our kids need to be with Hadley. If you do, I know it'll be the right decision. Just stay in their lives forever. Help them, or Annalise if it's just her, know who their dad was. Teach them how to play hockey, and how to throw a punch. Help them be happy, if you can. Walk my daughter down the aisle someday.

You're the brother I never had. I know who you really are, and that's why I know this decision is right. I want you to have a good life. Do all the things I won't be able to. Thanks for being my wingman. I love you.

Ben

FOR THE FIRST time since the night of the accident, I sobbed.

CHAPTER SIX

HADLEY

I could be too much sometimes. Several men I'd been in relationships with had said that about me. Too skeptical, too direct and too suspicious. If there were a Hadley Ellis relationship exit interview, those would be the top three reasons men cited for either breaking up with me or being at least a little relieved when I ended things with them.

The qualities that made me a less than ideal girlfriend in men's eyes, though, had helped me climb the corporate ladder at *Willow* quickly. Since starting as an entry-level writer fresh out of college seven years ago, I'd gotten several promotions and was now an associate editor.

I'd been in this role for nearly a year, and the list of responsibilities had grown longer in that time. My boss, Liz Cromwell, was…well, not very receptive to the word "no." She also left no doubt about her stance on things.

"Listen, Hadley, I need another story about organizing a fucking home office like I need a third tit," she said over the speaker on the phone in Ben's study, where I'd set up my computer at the desk to work. "Give me something fresh or don't give me anything at all."

"I totally understand, Liz. Another submission that came in through the general submissions email was for a story about making your own soaps and scrubs at home. The pitch was polished and well written."

"Ugh, fuck that. I'm trying to *sell* products for our advertisers, not encourage readers to cheap out and make their own. Next."

I moved down my list of pitches, cringing as I heard Annalise screaming and running down the hallway right outside the office, Wes making what I thought were supposed to be bear noises as he chased her.

"Best destinations for solo vacations." I recited the line from my list, not bothering to talk it up. Liz would either reluctantly accept it or dramatically pass on it, as was her style.

"Hmm…could be good," she said.

"We could make it into a package and include

lists about the best things to pack when vacationing alone, and maybe an advice column on how to ask your boss for time off when you need a break."

"I'll put it on the budget for May."

"Great."

"What else? We're doing that big photo shoot in Fiji for the July cover, so I need some stories that will fit the vibe."

"And the vibe is…?" I asked. "Tropical and exotic?"

"Right, pretty much."

I considered some ideas that I thought would play up the theme. "How about ways to channel tropical islands from the comfort of home? We can do some fun drink and appetizer recipes, maybe a piece on making a small patio into an oasis with the right plants, outdoor furniture and lighting, and some recommendations on sunglasses, swimsuits and self-tanners."

"Okay," she said, sighing heavily like it was the most horrible thing she'd ever agreed to. "But it has to be *fresh*, okay? I'm fucking tired of seeing fresh content everywhere else while we keep recycling the same old shit."

"I understand, and I'm open to any ideas you have."

"Coming up with ideas is *your* job, not mine. My job is to keep this place running."

"Well, something I'm working on is learning to make baby food at home. I could write about that."

Her hum made me think she was about to pass, but she surprised me and said, "Yeah, I like it. I'll put it on the budget for June."

The front doorbell at the house rang, and I heard Annalise's pounding footsteps as she ran toward it. The nanny Nina recommended was starting today, on a day Annalise didn't have preschool to make things a little easier.

"Hey, I have to go. I have a meeting," I told Liz.

"Okay. Send me some detailed budget notes on the things we discussed when you have time today."

She hung up abruptly, and I shook my head. I hadn't paid much attention to how bitchy my boss was before, but after getting a break of more than a week from her, I realized I hadn't missed her one bit.

So far, the people I was around in St. Louis were *nice*. Not just Nina, but everyone affiliated with Ben's team who had stopped by the house had been kind and helpful. It made my heart hurt to see how much his teammates missed Ben, but it was really nice to have so much support from people who'd loved him and his family. They were still dropping off meals and asking if we needed a hand with anything.

"Hi, I'm Wes," I heard Wes saying to the new nanny as I walked out of Ben's study.

"Hi, I'm Tori. It's so nice to meet you."

"Yeah, you too. Hadley should be here any—"

"Hey," I said, smiling as I walked into the foyer. "You must be Tori."

Her wide smile was as perfect as the rest of her. She was tall and blond, with bright blue eyes and just the right amount of curves. I couldn't hold her looks against her, but I'd been hoping she'd be more average looking, because I didn't want Wes thinking she was here for his amusement.

"It's nice to meet you," she said, shaking my hand. "And this must be Benny."

She leaned closer to Wes, who had Benny in his arms, Benny's back against his chest so he could see what was going on around him. As she gently touched the tip of her finger to Benny's nose and gave him a wide-eyed, openmouthed grin, he let out a little laugh and smiled back.

"He's adorable," she said, looking at me. "I love babies."

"Why don't we sit down in the family room and talk?" I said. "Can I get you anything to drink, Tori?"

"I'd love some water, thank you."

As we walked toward the family room, Wes leaned close to me and whispered, "Shot of whiskey for me. Oh, and maybe a meat and cheese tray. I'm kind of hungry."

I rolled my eyes, not in the mood for his humor, and said, "Get your own drink."

He smirked at me as Annalise yelled from the other room, "Uncle Wes, watch this!"

By the time I returned to the family room, Tori had Benny in her arms and Annalise on her lap.

"Do you like tea parties?" Annalise asked Tori.

"Oh, they're my favorite."

"Really?" Annalise slid off of her lap. "We could have one right now!"

Tori got down on the floor with the kids, managing to tickle Benny and make silly faces at him, drink imaginary tea with Annalise and answer our questions about her experience with children all at the same time.

"Can you put just a little more milk in mine?" she asked Annalise, holding out her imaginary cup.

"Regular milk or chocolate?" Annalise asked in a serious tone.

"Chocolate, please," Tori said. "And would you like one of these delicious cookies I made?" She held out an imaginary tray.

"Yes!" Annalise pretended to take one and nibble on it. "It's delicious!"

An early childhood education major at a local college, Tori was exactly what we needed. She could work six hours a day on Monday, Wednesday, and Friday, and evenings and weekends as needed. Plus, the kids already liked her.

"Have you ever had any traffic accidents or tickets?" Wes asked her, probably because she'd be driving the kids places on occasion.

"No. And I don't drink or smoke or anything like that."

"Okay, good." Wes met my gaze across the room and said, "Hey, why don't we step into the kitchen and find some actual cookies if we can?"

I followed him into the kitchen, and Wes gestured toward the corner of the room furthest from the family room. When we were both standing there, he whispered, "What do you think?"

"I like her."

"Yeah, I think she's really good with the kids. Would it be enough for you, since she can't be here on Tuesdays and Thursdays? Because we can keep looking if you need someone full time."

I shook my head. "She said she could do evenings on Tuesdays and Thursdays, and I could work then."

"You think we should hire her, then?"

"I do."

"Great." He took a step toward the family room, and I put a hand on his arm to stop him.

"Hey," I said.

Wes arched his brows and waited for me to continue. His forearm was warm and muscled, and it was the first time I'd touched any part of an attractive man in a long time, so I was distracted.

This was Weston Kirby. The guy who had made a lame comment about me liking wieners the first time we met. Who'd brought a date wearing a skintight tank top and stripper heels to Annalise's first birthday party. And who'd told me a couple New Year's Eves ago, while drunk, that his greatest wish for the year to come was that I'd get laid so the massive icicle wedged up my ass could melt a little.

He might be hot, with his chiseled face and blue eyes that landed him on magazine covers, but he was still Wes. Somehow, I had to ignore his looks and just spit out my concern.

"I, uh…you can't, um…" I cleared my throat. "If we hire Tori, you can't, you know…"

He narrowed his eyes in a look of complete aggravation.

"Hadley, I'm getting really sick of these comments about me trying to jump into bed with every woman I see."

I tried to whisper but it came out louder than I wanted, "She's not just any woman. She's about to become our very attractive, nineteen-year-old nanny. There are entire websites devoted to the seduction of nannies."

He furrowed his brow and whispered back, albeit harshly. "I wouldn't know anything about that, but it sounds like someone's got quite the porn habit."

"Why are you such an asshole?" I asked, groaning.

"Why are you such a shrew?"

"Just give me your word you won't lay a hand on her. The kids have lost so much already, and if they get close to her—"

Wes took a step toward me, and I could feel the heat of his body. "Fine, but you have to promise me you won't try to bone the gardener."

I scoffed. "Bob is like fifty years old, Wes."

"So what? He's got a dick and when a woman hasn't had any for, in your case, I'm guessing *years*, she might just jump on the closest man she can find."

"You're being *absurd*."

"And you're not? I'm a twenty-nine-year-old man, Hadley. It's been about a decade since I had any sort of romantic interest in a teenager. Stop insulting me because you assume I'm the worst kind of man. You don't know me."

I put my hands on my hips and said, "If it's a

given you'll keep the relationship entirely profession, you shouldn't have any problem giving me your word."

"Fine," he snapped. "I give you my word. Now give me your word on Bob."

I rolled my eyes. "Fine. I promise to keep it professional with Bob."

There was a flicker of something in Wes's eyes before he said, "And my teammates."

I recoiled. "Your *teammates*? Are you fucking serious? You think I'm trying to get with one of your teammates? I don't even know their names. I can hardly keep my head above water with the kids and my work and trying to shower every day, so the last thing on my mind is hooking up with one of your teammates."

He gave me a satisfied look. "Then maybe you know how I feel, because I'm in the same boat, Hadley. I'm just trying to keep up with hockey and the kids."

I reluctantly sighed. "Okay, that's a fair point."

He looked at his watch and said, "Let's go make Tori an offer. I have to get to practice."

"Hey." I sighed heavily. "I'm sorry. I know what you must think of me."

"Don't worry about it. I just want to do the best

we can for the kids, okay? That matters more than anything right now."

I nodded. "You're right."

"Things are gonna be better now that you'll have more help."

I felt like even more of an asshole now. I'd been bitchy to Wes, but he was still being nice to me. I squared my shoulders and smiled.

"Yeah, you're right." But the smile slid away as I said, "If I could only call her...Lauren, I mean. I think that so many times every day. If I could just hear her voice for even a few seconds, telling me that I can do this..." My throat tightened and I looked away.

"I know, Hadley," Wes said softly. "Me too."

I didn't have Lauren, though, and I'd never have her again. It still hurt like nothing ever had before. And not only did I have to find a way to get myself through this, I had to get Lauren's children through it, too.

CHAPTER SEVEN

WES

Despite the insanity going on at home, I'd been doing my damnedest to get my head out of my ass on the ice. It wasn't just me, though. The whole team was in mourning, one way or another. Ben hadn't just been our team captain; he'd been our friend. Every team had a captain, and I'd played on other teams with other captains but none of them had ever been like Benjamin Whitmer—smart, funny, and empathetic. That last one wasn't a word most professional athletes used much, but it applied to Ben in spades. It was what made him the best friend a guy could ask for, a great husband and father, and the most incredible team captain I'd ever played with.

Without his presence in the locker room, we were floundering. When it came to on-ice stuff, like talking to the refs and the mundane bullshit that was part of the game, we were fine. Nash and I could handle that. What we didn't have was the love and respect of everyone in the room. Okay, maybe that wasn't entirely accurate—there was a lot of love and respect between the majority of us in general—but we didn't command the same respect Ben had. And somehow, I had to get there. Maybe not to the same level, because I wasn't trying to replace him, but someone had to replace the role he'd played. We still hadn't won a game, and if this kept up, we'd break the record for the most losses in a row.

Tonight's game was against Washington and they were hot right now, on a badass winning streak, chasing us for first place overall in the league. We'd been so far ahead in rankings when Ben died. We were still in first, but only by two points. A loss to them tonight would mean a tie and I desperately wanted to prevent it. So though it pained me, I had to step up and take Ben's place as the leader. Nash had already said he didn't want the role, so I was going to do it unless and until my teammates decided otherwise.

"Listen up, boys." I stood up and looked around. Coach had just come in—he knew I was going to talk to them—along with the rest of the coaching staff and they shut the door behind them. "It's time. I don't know how deep you have to dig, what inner strength you have to tap into, but our losing streak ends now. Ben would be horrified. If he's looking down on us, he's cursing a blue streak. We cannot—no, we *will not*—continue down this path. So tell me what you need. If it's not me, that's okay. Let's vote on a new captain, because we're not doing this anymore."

There was silence as most of the guys fidgeted, looked at the floor, did anything but make eye contact. Finally, Lars spoke up. "No, has to be you. No one else. Ben would want this."

"Ben's gone," I said softly. "And as much as I miss him, we're still here so this has to be about what we want. All of us."

"You." Nash stood up. "Absolutely you."

"We don't have to decide about a captain tonight," Coach said quietly. "But something has to give."

"All in for Wes." Drew stood up next. "We need a captain and he's it."

One at a time, every guy on the team stood up and essentially pledged their allegiance to me. Had I been anywhere else, I might have given in to the scratchy feeling behind my eyes, but since I couldn't, I merely nodded.

"So as a team, we've decided to name Weston Kirby our new captain. I'll let PR know." Grizzly started to walk out with the other coaches but I called to him.

"Hang on, Coach." I took a breath. "I accept the vote of confidence and will take on the role in every way that matters, but I'd like to wait until next season to wear the C officially. I'd rather we finished the season with Ben still our honorary captain, and perhaps vote in another alternate. That way, we're covered behind the scenes but we continue to honor him publicly for the rest of this season."

Everyone seemed to nod in agreement.

"Tonight, we play for Ben. For real. We take no prisoners; we take no shit. Get out there and play the game we were playing before the night of January fourteenth."

We filed onto the ice and when the game started, it was like someone had flipped a switch. Nash was all over the place, passing and shooting, making opportunities to score happen. Lars was a fucking bulldog, not just defending Drew, but every one of us, every time he was on the ice. By the end of the first period, we were up 3–0 and it felt like the magic was back—the same shit we'd lost when we'd lost Ben. But a three-goal lead was the most dangerous lead in hockey, so we couldn't let up.

I skated out to the face-off circle to start the

second period and Washington's enforcer, Denby Harrowman, gave me a smirk.

"Ready to go down, Kirby?"

I smirked right back. "Give it your best shot."

"Seems to me you can't shoot for shit without your buddy Whitmer."

My grip on my stick tightened as I gave him a look. "Watch your mouth."

"What are you gonna do? Without Whitmer, I bet you can't even suck your own dick. Too bad he didn't die at the beginning of the sea—"

The next few minutes happened in slow motion, as if I were someone else, looking in from the outside. I didn't remember dropping my gloves or throwing the first punch, but there was a reason Harrowman was an enforcer and he came right back at me. I was fueled by grief and rage, though, so every time my fist connected with his jaw, his head snapped back. Hard. He got in a few good shots to my eye, but I finally got him down on the ice, my knee in his chest as I punched his face repeatedly. It took both Lars and Nash to pull me off of him and all I saw was red as the ref pointed to the tunnel, indicating a game misconduct and who knew what the fuck else.

I sat in the locker room breathing hard, blood dripping down my face, completely oblivious to our team trainer, who had to stitch me up. I didn't remember what I said to Coach when he asked me what the fuck had happened, but whatever I'd said seemed to appease him, because he grunted under his breath, patted me on the shoulder, and moved on. I was probably going to be forced to have a meeting with the player safety department, but I didn't give a fuck. No one talked about Ben that way. And sure as fuck not this soon after his death.

We won. Despite a five-minute penalty, we killed it off and went on to score two more goals, even without me. The mood in the locker room was the best it had been. I snuck out once again, but at least I'd lit a fire under their asses. Now I just had to calm down, because even after beating the living shit out of Harrowman and getting it out of my system, I was still on a tear. I wanted to rage, to yell and scream and drink and hit things. Harrowman's comment—even though I knew it was nothing but trash talk to throw me off my game—cut deep, an indication of just how much Ben's death had affected me.

Part of the problem was that I hadn't really grieved. With two kids at home and a busy hockey schedule, there was no time to breathe, much less give in to grief. The team offered counseling, but I had to be realistic, and the reality was that I didn't feel comfortable talking to a stranger about what

Ben had meant to me and how much losing him changed my life. The one person I could talk to, and would have talked to if she wasn't such a bitch, was Hadley. I tried so hard to be nice to her, to show her we could work together to raise these kids, but she shut me down time and time again. Our relationship was as exhausting as Benny and Annalise were.

I let myself into the house quietly, hoping she and the kids were asleep, but she was in the kitchen when I came in. She turned around right away, a look I couldn't quite decipher on her face.

"Hey." I stopped to grab a bottle of water out of the refrigerator.

"What were you thinking?" she demanded, hands on her hips.

I turned in confusion. "What?"

"You know how much Annalise likes to watch her uncles play hockey. You know she watches as many games as she can stay up for! How do you think she reacted to seeing you fighting like that?"

Crap. I'd never given a second thought to Annalise watching the fight.

"It couldn't be helped," I said quietly. "I'll talk to her tomorrow and explain that it's part of the game."

"It's violent and disgusting!" she hissed. "What you did to that poor guy...I can't believe you think you're fit to be a parent to anyone's kids, much less these ones!"

I whirled on her, fists clenched at my sides. "You have no fucking idea what you're talking about. You don't know the first goddamn thing about hockey, or me for that matter, so why don't you keep your opinions to yourself for once?"

"I will not. This is the kind of behavior that makes it spectacularly clear that you're not fit to be their guardian." She folded her arms across her chest, tapping her foot as if she were winning some sort of argument.

I advanced on her a bit more aggressively than I should have, but I was still hopping mad, fueled on adrenaline and pain. She took a step back but I kept going, until she was up against the wall.

"Let me explain something to you," I growled under my breath, looking down into startled yellow-green eyes. "Fighting has a long history in hockey. It's tradition. It's part of the sport. It serves a purpose. Usually to let the other team know they can't get away with something they were trying to get away with. Can you understand that?"

She swallowed, her jaw tightening in annoyance. "I understand all that," she ground out. "But what you did tonight was different. It was violent. You were an animal. You—"

"I beat the shit out of the guy who said it was too bad Ben hadn't died earlier in the season." I glared down at her, my heart racing a mile a minute.

Her eyes widened and her mouth formed an "O" but no sound came out. Then she frowned, sadness in her voice as she whispered, "He actually *said that?*"

"Yeah. He did." I still had her pinned against the wall but something had shifted. Her breath was coming in short, staccato little bursts now, her 34D's rising and falling at the same time. Her eyes blazed with—pain? Anger? It was hard to tell, but when she licked her lips, the moisture glistening on them beckoned to me like a beacon in a storm.

"I'm sorry." Her voice was uneven, her tone apologetic. "I didn't know—"

"Just this one time, can you shut up, please?" I muttered. "Because I'm going to kiss you. Unless you say no. But the window for you to do that closes in two seconds."

Her mouth opened and, once again, nothing came out.

"Hadley." I met her gaze and she gave me a barely perceptible nod but that was all I needed. I crashed my mouth to hers, sliding one arm around her waist and pulling her against me. Her lips parted beautifully, her tongue meeting mine stroke for stroke, and I didn't let up. I pillaged her mouth like a thief in the night, taking pull after pull until she was grinding against my groin, our bodies pressed together. And hers was made for loving. Slender, with luscious curves, and goddamn, those tits made me insane. I would've given my left nut to suck on them.

"Aunt Hadley? I had a bad dream…where are you?" Annalise's voice from the hallway made us jump apart and Hadley hurriedly smoothed down her top as she took a shaky breath, her eyes not meeting mine.

"I'm coming, baby." Gaze still averted, she hurried out of the room without looking back.

I watched her retreating figure with a mixture of frustration and regret. I would have done anything to follow her, kiss her some more, but I knew better. One kiss probably didn't change how she felt about me and I wasn't the kind of guy to take advantage of a woman who was feeling vulnerable. The trouble was, I was vulnerable too.

———

*"L*AUREN *and I want you to be the baby's godfather," Ben said, a smile lighting his face as he eyed me. "You down?"*

"For you and Lauren? Anything." I paused. "Wait, let me guess, Hadley is going to be the godmother."

Ben laughed, a full-on belly laugh that made me want

to knock him off the barstool he was sitting on. "Lauren said Hadley had the same exact reaction when she asked her about being the godmother. You two are such a hot mess."

"I truly have never met someone who pisses me off the way she does." I took a sip of my drink.

"I think the two of you want each other bad, but you're too damn stubborn to admit it."

"Would I have sex with her? Sure. But I can't talk to her for more than thirty seconds before I want to kill myself, so I'm going to say no, we do not want each other at all beyond maybe a quick roll in the hay. Assuming she actually even likes sex."

"Look, she and Lauren are going to be here any minute. Could you please just try to be nice?"

"I'm not the one who's not nice," I shot back. "And it kind of pisses me off that you're always defending her."

Ben sighed. "You think I don't defend you when the tables are turned?"

"I don't know. Do you?" I met his gaze with irritation. Things hadn't been the same since we'd left college. We were still tight, of course, but with me playing in New York and him in St. Louis, it was hard to stay in touch, keep up with the day-to-day details we'd shared since we were fourteen. Not to mention, he now had a wife and a baby on the way. Meanwhile, I was still foot-loose and fancy-free, sleeping my way through

Manhattan while playing hockey for one of the best teams in the league.

"Come on, you know better than that. I'm just giving you shit, and while I really do wish you and Hadley would get along, nothing comes between us. You're my brother—biology notwithstanding."

"I know." I looked away.

"What's really bothering you? Everything okay?"

"It's been weird playing without you. I love what I'm doing, and the hockey here is fucking amazing, but I don't love living here, and my teammates have been a little standoffish. I think I'm gonna get traded."

Ben's eyebrows rose a little. "For real? You have any feelers out?"

"My agent's been on top of it, but I'm not sure where we're at."

Ben looked thoughtful. "Any interest in coming to St. Louis?"

I was surprised. "You think that's possible?"

"I don't know for sure, but we could use a winger like you to round out the second line. Let your agent know you're interested."

"I will. Definitely." I was about to thank him when I spotted Lauren and Hadley coming through the restaurant toward us. Lauren looked more beautiful than ever, her tiny baby bump on display with a tight sweater and leggings. Hadley looked like a freakin' supermodel, with a *full face of makeup, wearing all black and the highest heels I'd ever seen.*

"Hey, babe." Ben got up to kiss his wife and pull out her chair and I reluctantly got up to do the same for Hadley.

"Hey, ladies." I leaned over to kiss Lauren on the cheek and Hadley used the momentary distraction to slide into her chair before I could pull it out.

"Hey, good-lookin'!" Lauren hugged me before sitting down.

"Hey, Ben." Hadley briefly smiled at him before pulling out her phone and typing something in.

God, she drove me crazy, but we were about to become godparents to Ben and Lauren's baby, so I had to suck it up and be on my best behavior. Thank God I only saw her once or twice a year.

"So did Ben tell you the news?" Lauren asked, grinning.

"Yup." I grinned back at her because I truly loved my best friend's wife almost as much as he did. "And I can't fucking wait. I don't know what a godfather is supposed to do, but I'm in, whatever it takes."

"We know that," Ben said. "That's why we chose you."

Hadley put away her phone and though she was cool as fuck to me, the four of us carried on pleasant conversation all through dinner. Lauren wasn't drinking, of course, but Ben and I were three or four bourbons in by the time dinner was over, and I'd lost count of how many martinis Hadley had ordered.

She was kind of cute when she was drunk, though, giggling a lot—even at my jokes—and constantly telling Lauren she loved her. It was obvious how close they were, despite the distance between them since Lauren was in St. Louis with Ben and Hadley worked here in Manhattan. Ironically, I had zero desire to hang out with her even though we only lived about ten subway stops from each other.

"I'm going to the ladies' room." Hadley got to her feet and stumbled a little.

"You want me to come with?" Lauren asked her.

"I'm good!" Hadley waved a hand, tottering on those stupidly high heels as she weaved in and out toward the back.

I watched her go because she had a great ass and long legs, but I wasn't the only one who noticed. At least half a dozen heads in the restaurant turned, especially one guy sitting at the other end of the bar. Once we'd finished dinner and dessert, we'd moved to the bar so our waiter could seat another party at the table, and there had been quite a few guys eyeing Hadley since it was pretty obvious we weren't together. She was oblivious, though, and I wasn't sure whether it was because she was drunk, she wasn't interested, or she genuinely had no idea how gorgeous she was.

One of the guys at the end of the bar nudged his buddy, who looked at Hadley's disappearing back, and then got up, following in the direction she'd gone.

Shit.

Did I mind my own business or did I go after her, just to make sure she was okay?

I mumbled something about having to take a leak and went back to the restrooms. Hadley was against the wall, the guy who'd followed her loosely boxing her in with one hand against the wall just to her right and the other reaching for her. Hadley swatted his hand away, shaking her head. The guy laughed, lowering his head as if he were going to kiss her and Hadley shoved at his chest.

That was all I needed to see and I reached out, yanking the guy away by the back of his shirt.

"Hey!" He swung around, poised for a fight, but the minute he saw me he stepped back.

"Is there a problem here?" I asked, leveling my gaze at him.

"Oh, hey, Kirby, sorry, I didn't realize she was yours." The guy nodded at me and headed away at a fast clip.

"What the hell was that?" Hadley demanded, glaring at me.

"I thought he was hassling you," I protested. "I was just trying to help."

"I can take care of myself," she said, narrowing her

eyes. "This isn't my first night out in the big city. Guys hit on me all the time."

"Oh, well, excuse the fuck out of me for trying to be a nice guy."

"Ha!" She rolled her eyes. "There isn't a single nice thing about you, Wes Kirby. In the future, mind your own business!"

"Absolutely," I said, throwing up my hands. "Next time, I'll be sure to let the creep from the bar assault you. No skin off my teeth." I shook my head and stalked back out to the bar. She was truly the world's biggest pain in the ass.

CHAPTER EIGHT

HADLEY

"Can I push the button?" Annalise asked, her eyes wide with excitement.

I double-checked to make sure the lid on Lauren's food processor was locked, pointed to the *Start* button and said, "Yes, it's this one right here."

"I know, Mommy always lets me push the button."

She stood on the chair she'd scooted over to the kitchen counter and pushed the button, and the food processor started to whir, running a lot quieter than I'd expected. Annalise watched as the avocado chunks in the blender swirled into a puree.

"This isn't hard," I said to her. "It feels like it's going to be a huge deal, but you just have to get organized first and clean as you go."

I'd been at it since Wes left for practice this morning, moving Benny from his stationary jumper to his swing to keep him happy, and occasionally holding him against my hip and having him sample the different baby foods I'd made.

Jars of pureed blueberries, chickpeas, green beans, kiwis and bananas lined the marble kitchen island. I was taking photos for my article about making homemade baby food, not even feeling guilty I had the Disney Channel on in the family room for when Annalise got bored and wanted a break from the kitchen.

It was Tuesday, so Tori wasn't on nanny duty today. The kids and I were in no hurry to get out of our jammies, and I felt better than I had in a while.

Here I was, actually multitasking. Accomplishing childcare and work and feeling like I actually could find a way to do it all. With an assist from coffee, of course.

I COULD ADMIT to myself that my good mood was partially due to Wes kissing me last night.

I couldn't stop thinking about it. It was so much more than just *good*. There were many words that were more accurate. *Hot. Raw. Heart-stopping.* The whole world had stopped for those few seconds, and all I'd felt was heat and muscle and the primal need coming not just from Wes, but from myself, too.

My world had never stopped turning before last night. Not once. I'd been that woman who was *always* thinking. Even during sex. I struggled to fall asleep at night, no matter how tired I was, because my mind was always on.

Last night, though, Wes Kirby had brought everything to an unexpected and mind-blowing halt. It had taken a long time to wind down from all the different emotions he'd made me feel. And this morning when I woke up, that kiss was the first thing I'd thought of.

When he'd looked at me with that swollen, stitched-up cut above his eye, I'd seen far more emotional hurt than physical. His eyes had flashed dark indigo, full of pent-up grief, anger and tension. In that moment, Wes *needed* me.

As I drained the sweet potatoes I'd peeled and boiled, I wondered what might have happened if Annalise hadn't interrupted us last night. Would either of us have seen reason and stopped the madness, or would we have ended up fucking right on the kitchen island where I was now lining up baby food?

I smiled as I thought about how much Lauren would have loved hearing about this. She'd always sworn Wes wasn't the womanizing dirtbag I thought he was and that if I'd give him another chance, we'd be a great match.

"Aunt Hadley, can I have some Froot Woops?" Annalise asked me. "In a bowl but not with milk?"

"How about if you have a banana first, and then a few Froot Loops?"

"Okay. Did you know my mommy likes to make banana cookies?"

I looked at her perfect, innocent face and dark curls and melted inside. Lauren's death still hurt so badly, but Annalise and Benny brought me comfort. Each of them had Lauren inside them, and it hurt a little less to remember she would always live on through them.

"I didn't know that," I told Annalise. "Were those your favorite cookies your mom made?"

"Banana chocolate chip is my favorite!" she said, pronouncing it "chocwut."

"Why don't we find your mommy's recipe and make some today?"

"Yeah! I can push the buttons and stir. Mommy said I'm good at stirring."

"I bet you are."

"Can I tell you a secret, Aunt Hadley?"

She gave me a solemn look, her eyes wide. I mentally braced myself for a comment about Lauren that would threaten to break me, but Annalise surprised me.

"Of course you can."

"I like to eat those baby food bananas."

Brows arched, I looked at her, waiting for the rest of the secret.

"Is that it?" I asked.

"Don't tell Uncle Wes. I don't want him to think I'm a baby."

Laughing, I set my spoon down and picked her up in a hug. "He'd never think that, and do you know what a little ray of sunshine you are?"

Benny started fussing in his swing, so I grabbed a banana for Annalise, peeled down the top for her and took Benny to the nursery for a diaper change and some cuddles. When we got back to the kitchen, Annalise asked for her Froot Loops, so I washed up and poured a few into a bowl, hoping Lauren would understand.

I settled Benny into his high chair and gave him a frozen teething ring, then cleaned the food processor and loaded the sweet potato chunks into it. This was the last batch of baby food, and then I'd arrange jars of everything I'd made for some staged "after" photos, clean up, make lunch for all of us and see if I had all the ingredients for banana chocolate chip cookies.

Benny whined and I turned around, finding his teething ring on the floor.

"I'll wash it off, big guy," I said, smiling at him as I picked it up and ran it under the kitchen faucet.

He grabbed it back, grinning, and proceeded to drool all over it. At that point, my phone rang and I walked over to glance at it, seeing my boss's name on the screen.

"Ugh." I sighed and picked it up, feigning enthusiasm. "Hey, Liz."

"Hadley. Where are the sidebar pitches for the solo travel piece?"

"I thought you liked the ones I pitched on the phone, so those were the only ones I included."

"I always want multiple sidebar pitches."

That wasn't actually true. When Liz said she was putting something on the budget, that meant it had been chosen as pitched. But I knew better than to try to win an argument with her.

"Okay, I can get some more to you late tonight."

"I was hoping for something within the next hour."

Benny squealed, dropping his teething ring on

the floor again. I picked it up and washed it off again, passing it back to him.

"I'll do my best," I told Liz. "But my nanny isn't available on Tuesdays so I'm taking care of the kids today."

"Look, I've been very flexible with this whole situation," she said, her tone laced with aggravation. "But today I need work done during working hours."

Benny started whimpering, and I turned to see his face all scrunched, winding up for an epic cry. I quickly removed his high chair tray and unbuckled him, picking him up in hopes of comforting him before he started screaming.

"And I think I can do it," I told Liz, gently bouncing Benny on my hip. "Naptime is in an hour and a half. Can I send you something within the next two hours?"

Right as I could sense Liz caving, Benny let out an ear-piercing wail, and I cringed, walking into the family room to see if maybe the TV screen would catch his attention and calm him down a bit.

"Yeah, fine," Liz said shortly. "I guess two hours will have to work."

"Okay, thanks for understanding."

Liz didn't even hear me—she'd already ended the call. Someone really needed to let her know how unprofessional it was to just hang up on people.

I took Benny over to his large baby mat and laid him down to play. I got down on the floor with him and started arranging some large letter blocks in front of him. He finally started to calm down a bit as I began talking to him.

"Should we play with these blocks?" I asked him, still lining up the ABC letter blocks. "Or should we maybe read a story?"

"Aunt Hadley!" Annalise cried from the kitchen.

I sighed. Just another day in a household with two kids. I quickly stood and scooped up Benny, hoofing it back to the kitchen. I came to an abrupt halt, my mouth dropping open as I saw orange goo splattered all over the white cabinets, the counter, the floor and even Annalise's hair and face. It had to be the pureed sweet potatoes.

"I'm sorry," she said sheepishly.

I hadn't secured the lid on the food processor before I answered my call from Liz and she must have pushed the button while I was in the family room with Benny. I didn't know whether to laugh or cry at this point. The kitchen was an absolute nightmare. Think slasher horror film but more orange and less red.

"It's okay honey," I said. "It was just an accident. We'll get it cleaned up. You aren't hurt, right?"

Annalise shook her head and I buckled Benny

back in his high chair even though he was crying again. If only I had two hands for each child.

Lauren kept cleaning cloths in neatly folded stacks in the laundry room. I grabbed several as well as some hardcore cleaning supplies. On my way back to the kitchen, the doorbell rang, and my laugh was half amused, half crazed.

"That better be Mary fucking Poppins coming to my rescue," I muttered.

Benny had stopped crying and was trying to fit his entire hand into his mouth now. At least he wasn't upset anymore. That was something.

"Aunt Hadley!" Annalise cried from the foyer.

"Yeah?" I set the cleaning cloths down and headed in that direction, praying there wasn't another disaster waiting for me.

"My Gram and Gramps are here!" Annalise said.

Oh God. In the few moments it took me to get to the foyer, I sent up a silent plea to God that it wasn't Patrick and Susan Whitmore.

It was. Annalise was grinning at me from her grandpa's arms.

"Hey," I said weakly, forcing a smile.

"Hi, Hadley. I hope you guys meant it when you said we could visit anytime," Patrick said. "We just really wanted to see the kids, and maybe help out if you need it."

"Thank you," I said, trying to think of a way I could get the kitchen cleaned up before they saw it.

"You really shouldn't let Annalise open the front door like that," Susan said, frowning at me. "It could have been anyone."

"We…she's not supposed to open it."

"It was my Gram and Gramps. Mommy and Daddy said to always open it for family," Annalise explained.

"Where's Benny?" Susan asked.

"He's in the kitchen."

"Alone?"

"He's buckled into his high chair," I said, not in the mood for her snap judgments. "Why don't you guys go up to Annalise's room so she can show you her tea party set and I'll bring Benny up so you can spend some time with both of them?"

"I want my Froot Woops!" Annalise cried, scrambling from her grandpa's arms and running into the kitchen.

Her grandparents followed, but I waited a moment, dreading the reaction the sweet potato massacre was going to get.

"What in the world…?" Susan exclaimed with pure shock as I walked into the kitchen.

"We're making baby food, and Annalise forgot to put the lid on the food processor," I said. "But everyone has accidents and I'm going to clean it up. It's not a big deal."

"Want a Froot Woop, Gram?" Annalise offered, holding out her bowl.

"What is that processed garbage?" Susan demanded. "Lauren didn't feed our grandchildren this way."

Annalise's happy expression fell away, and I despised Susan a little bit more than I already had.

"I think you should spend some time playing with Annalise," I said. "I need to clean up the kitchen and make lunch."

"That sounds like a great idea," Patrick said. "Can we take Benny off your hands, too?"

I gave him a grateful smile. "I'd appreciate that, thanks."

Annalise walked over to her brother and gave him a bright smile. "Benny, Gram and Gramps are here!" She wrinkled her nose. "Ew, I think he shit himself again, Aunt Hadley."

I needed a humongous glass of wine and a five-minute break, exactly in that order. Unfortunately, neither of those things was going to happen.

"This is the language you're teaching our grand-children?" Susan cried. "Patrick, we need to expedite the lawsuit. We can't have them around her."

"Actually," a deep voice from the entrance to the

kitchen interrupted Susan's rant, "any bad language the kids heard came from *me*, and I'm working on it. Hadley's a great role model, and she's busting her tail taking care of the kids."

I turned, so happy to see Wes I could have cried. My heart hammered with excitement as I took him in, his hair damp from a post-practice shower. He wore a Mavericks T-shirt and gray jogger sweatpants, a day's worth of dark stubble on his face.

"You need some help cleaning up the kitchen?" he asked me as he approached.

"Yeah…thanks."

Was I thanking him for sticking up for me or for offering to help clean? Both, I decided, and more. If Wes hadn't walked in just now, I would've been left alone to deal with Ben's parents, the kids and the work I somehow had to get done in the next hour and a half.

"You guys planning on changing Benny or should I do it?" Wes asked.

"I'll do it," Susan said, getting her grandson from his high chair and taking him upstairs without another word.

Wes grabbed a towel from the island and started wiping down cabinets.

"Hey, where's my lunch?" he asked.

I turned to him, ready to tell him where he could

stick his lunch, and saw him smirking. Both of us burst out laughing.

"I'll make lunch," he said. "And I can finish cleaning up if you've got stuff you need to do."

"No, I'll finish. But if you'll make lunch, that would be great. I also told Annalise we'd find one of Lauren's cookie recipes and make them this afternoon."

"I'll help with that."

"Thank you."

He moved closer, and I couldn't name the emotion in his eyes as he looked down at me. "You want to talk about last night?"

The kiss. My body warmed at just the mention of it. I shook my head, because I knew if I tried to say anything about that kiss, I'd embarrass myself and say something stupid like "it was awesome" or "you're super hot'." I'd die before I let that happen.

No, I was going to keep both my dignity *and* my cool by not saying a word about that kiss. There was no chance of it happening again as long as Patrick and Susan were here, but after that…

I didn't know whether Wes would want to kiss me again, or if maybe he'd want more, but I knew I wanted it. I've never been Team Wes, but my body had decided to join his fan club in a very big way.

———

WES LOOKED *from newborn Annalise's peaceful, sleeping face to mine, his eyes wide with wonder.*

"She's so little."

"Isn't she perfect, though?" I smiled down at the soft bundle in my arms, whispering because Lauren and Ben were finally asleep.

It had been a long thirty-six hours, Lauren's labor progressing slowly. Ben only left her side once, because he had to pee, and I felt for him during the three minutes I spent holding Lauren's hand while he was gone.

It was hard to see someone you loved in that much pain. Even with help from an epidural, Lauren was having a hard labor and she was exhausted.

But you wouldn't have known it once her daughter made her entrance into the world. My best friend was smitten with her little girl, crying tears of joy as she held her for the first time, her smile more radiant than ever.

She'd fallen asleep sitting up in her hospital bed, and Ben was snoring from a recliner in the corner. All four of Annalise's grandparents were in the waiting room, anxious to see and hold her, but Wes and I were taking our turn first.

He had been here for the whole delivery, not coming all the way in the room but occasionally sticking his head in the doorway and asking how it was going. He'd asked Lauren in the middle of a rough contraction how she was feeling and she'd just screamed, sending him fleeing.

"She looks like Ben," Wes whispered.

"She looks like a squished raisin," I countered, laughing softly. "There's no way to tell who she looks like yet."

"Nah, she looks just like her dad." He grinned. "Can I hold her?"

I frowned. "She's delicate, Wes. You have to be really careful."

"I'm not a complete dumbass. I know some things."

"Have you ever held a baby before?"

He shrugged. "Not this young, but I'll be fine."

"Hmm. Thought you might have at least one baby mama by now."

"Don't be petty, Hadley. I want to hold my goddaughter."

"Okay, okay. Hold your arms out," I whispered.

He cradled his arms and I passed the warm, sleeping baby from my arms to his.

"Make sure you support her head," I cautioned.

Annalise wiggled and wrinkled her face up as Wes took her, and he gave me a look of alarm.

"Shit, she's gonna cry," he said. "Take her back."

"Just hold her close and rock her a little. You'll be fine."

He wrapped his arms closer around her, his hands as

big as her little head. When he looked up at me, his eyes looked a little watery.

"I'm an uncle," he whispered, grinning.

It was hard to dislike him in that moment. Wes was taken with little Annalise, and I'd never admit it out loud, but he looked sexy as hell holding her.

"You are," I said, smiling back.

"Will you grab my phone from my pocket and take a picture?" He turned one hip toward me. "Phone's in my left pocket, and don't try to cop a feel while you're in there."

And I disliked him once again. I sighed with aggravation as I fetched his phone.

"Password's 696969."

I gave him a look as I entered the numbers. "Ugh, there better not be a photo of someone's tits as your wallpaper."

"I think it's a crotch shot, actually. A hairy one."

I glared at him and he winked.

"You're disgusting," I whispered.

His wallpaper was actually a photo of the Stanley Cup. I clicked the camera button and held the phone up, centering it to take a photo of him and Annalise. Wes smiled, looking as happy and proud as if he'd birthed her himself.

"Want me to take one of you with her?" he asked.

"Yes, please."

He passed her back to me and took two photos—one of me smiling while holding her and another of me kissing her forehead.

"Should we share her with the grandparents?" I asked, reluctance in my voice.

"I guess so."

Ben and Lauren had asked us to introduce their daughter to their parents while they rested; they were both too exhausted for talking or photos right now. They were in a private birthing suite with an attached waiting room.

"I can't believe Ben and Lauren have a kid," Wes said as we walked toward the door that led to the waiting room.

"I know. They're better at this adulting thing than we are."

Wes scoffed. "Yeah, I'm not settling down for a long time. Like decades."

I rolled my eyes because I knew what he probably had in mind—womanizing until he was in his forties and then finding a hot twentysomething to be semi-faithful to and have a family with.

And when he did have a family, Wes would be one of those fathers who showed up for photo ops but let his wife do all the heavy lifting. He'd probably pass out if he tried to change a dirty diaper.

I couldn't actually blame him on that one. I was over the moon to be an auntie to little Annalise, and if she needed me to, I'd change her diapers, but I was in no hurry at all to have kids of my own. I had parties to attend. Places to travel to. Corporate ladders to climb.

Like Wes, I loved my carefree, single life. Though that was about the only similarity we shared.

CHAPTER NINE

WES

Coming home to find not just a disaster in the kitchen, but Patrick and Susan giving Hadley a hard time rubbed me the wrong way. She annoyed me to no end, day and night, but we were busting our asses to take care of these kids, and no one who wasn't here with us had the right to criticize. Especially not them. They'd filed a lawsuit challenging the will, the custody agreement, the money, all of it. Like I needed Ben's money. That was laughable. The new contract I'd negotiated last year had been worth more than Ben's, and we'd laughed about the fact that for the first time professionally, I made more than he did.

There was no doubt Hadley was stressed, too. Especially since she'd totally sidestepped my question about the incredibly hot kiss we'd shared last night. I let it go because I'd noticed her hands shaking a little as we started cleaning up the kitchen, and I didn't think it was because of my question.

"You okay?" I asked her as we sat down to eat.

"Maybe?" The look she gave me was one of sheer exasperation. "My boss is being demanding and unreasonable, having Patrick and Susan here raises my stress level straight to ten, and I'm suddenly questioning every life choice I've ever made."

"Yeah, there's been a lot of that lately. But we're doing it, Hadley. Messy kitchen and the occasional curse word aside, we're taking care of these kids and making sure they have everything they need."

"Patrick and Susan don't think so."

"Patrick and Susan need a reality check," I muttered thoughtfully. "And you know what? I have an idea."

"Oh?" She arched a brow.

"We have a game tonight and the team is probably going out after. Why don't we give them the opportunity to spend time with the kids while we go out and enjoy ourselves a little? I mean, obviously the game is work for me, but afterward would be fun. We're a close-knit group and you haven't really been part of it."

"I didn't live here," she said quietly.

"Right. But you do now, and I think it'll be good

for both of us if you get to know more of the gang. We're like a family and you don't have relationships with anyone beyond Nina."

"So you think we should just leave for the whole night?"

"Absolutely." I wiggled my eyebrows. "Let's see how they do when they're a hundred percent in charge."

"That's kind of brilliant," she admitted. "I'm in. But right now, my boss is being a total bitch so I have to get some work done before she loses it."

"Go. I'll make sure Patrick and Susan are on board and then I'm going to take my pregame nap. And don't step in to help if Annalise needs you. Let them see how much work it is."

"Thanks again, Wes." She touched my arm, grabbed her plate, and left the room.

Once again, I watched her retreating figure almost longingly.

I wanted her.

There was no doubt about that, but I couldn't just press her up against the wall and fuck her the way I wanted to. Well, I could, and if I was lucky, someday I would, but not now. Not today. She probably needed it as much as I did and I was willing to bet it had been even longer since she'd gotten laid than it had been for me. I hadn't been with anyone since before Ben and Lauren died, not even on road trips, and my balls were sporting a nice shade of blue these days. But that was beside the point.

We hadn't talked about it in any detail, but we were both resolute in our desire to keep custody of the kids. Patrick and Susan were too old to start over with babies, whether they wanted to admit it or not. *Could* they do it? Probably. But why? Hadley and I were younger and had the energy and resources to give them the kind of life Ben and Lauren would have wanted. Not that Patrick and Susan wouldn't take care of them, but Patrick would be in his sixties by the time Benny was ready to learn how to ice-skate, play baseball, whatever. It was a complicated issue because plenty of grandparents wound up raising their grandchildren, but that wasn't what Ben and Lauren wanted or they would have left custody to them.

I went upstairs to Annalise's room where Susan was on the floor playing Barbies with her while Patrick sat in the nearby rocking chair holding Benny, who was squirming and whining to get on the floor. He was learning to crawl and liked to scoot around on his stomach. Patrick didn't know that, though, and I wasn't going to tell him.

"Hadley and I were talking," I said to them, pretending not to notice Patrick's discomfort. "We know you want to spend time with the kids so she's coming to the game tonight and then a group of us are going out for a late dinner. Are you guys okay taking care of the kids?"

"Of course we are." Susan looked up. "They're going to be living with us soon anyway."

I chose not to engage and merely smiled. "We'll see, I guess. But yeah, it'll be a great opportunity for you to spend time with them."

"We have to watch the game on TV, Grandma," Annalise told her. "Just like I used to do with Mommy."

Susan looked startled but then nodded curtly. "You can't stay up that late. You have to go to bed, young lady."

"But Mommy always lets me watch the first period!" Annalise protested.

I walked out just as she burst into tears.

WE NOTCHED another win so we were in high spirits as we left the locker room to head to the family lounge, where wives, girlfriends, children, and guests waited for us after home games. I couldn't explain the excitement in my gut, knowing Hadley was there with the others, but the minute I stepped into the room her eyes found mine.

She looked adorable tonight in skintight jeans, a jersey with Ben's number, and her dark hair curled and tumbling just below her shoulders. When she smiled at me, I forgot all about the impending lawsuit, how Benny never slept, and the way Hadley busted my balls all the time. Mostly, I wanted to walk over to her and kiss those sweet lips of hers and let every single guy on the team know she was off-limits. Because more than one was eyeing her, especially the new guys who'd never met her.

I settled for walking over and kissing her on the cheek. "Hey."

"You guys looked awesome out there," she said. "It's been ages since I've been to a game. Thank you for inviting me tonight."

"Anytime."

"Who's this?" One of my teammates asked, coming over to join us and holding out his hand to Hadley. "I'm Michael Boone but my friends call me Boone."

"Nice to meet you." Hadley seemed a little startled at Boone's overt interest. "I'm Hadley Ellis. I was Lauren Whitmer's best friend."

"Oh." His eyes rounded. "Wow. I didn't know that

was you. Nice to meet you, though. Welcome to the Mavericks family."

"Thanks?" She watched him hurry in the other direction and then cut her eyes to me. "What did you tell him about me that made him run off like that?"

"Nothing." I laughed. "I swear. I think he was looking for a hookup and when he realized that wasn't going to happen with the woman I'm raising Ben's kids with, he took off. The youngsters have no finesse."

She chuckled. "Probably not, but it was a good call on his part."

"So we're going to a local Italian place we like. We know the owners and they always find us space in the back room where no one bothers us. You in?"

"Absolutely." She grinned. "Annalise called for me at least half a dozen times while you were napping. And I just directed her back to Grandma. By the time I left, she and Patrick were more than a little frazzled. I don't think they remember how much work a six-month-old is."

"Not to mention an almost four-year-old."

"Speaking of which, I've got to get started on planning her birthday party. I honestly don't know where to begin."

"Doesn't she want something to do with *Frozen*?"

Hadley nodded. "It's still too chilly for something outside, so we're going to have to get creative."

"Did you talk to Nina?"

"Tomorrow."

We grinned at each other.

"All right, are you riding with me or going with Nina?"

"Oh." She hesitated. "I guess I'll go with you. I don't know if Nina and Drew are going. They were going to call the sitter to see if she could stay later."

"Cool. Then I'm ready to go if you are."

———

WE TOOK over the back room at Giovanna's Italian Bistro, a quaint place that had amazing food, good ambiance, and took care of the Mavericks whenever we came in. The owner, Vicenzo, had named the place after his wife Giovanna, or Gia to us, and they greeted us warmly.

"Good game tonight!" Vicenzo whispered to me. "Gia, she doesn't know I watch on my phone when I'm in the back."

I chuckled. "One of these days we're going to have to sneak you out to an actual game."

"From your lips to God's ears," he said, looking up to the ceiling.

"I want you to meet my friend, Hadley. She's Ben and Lauren's kids' godmother."

"The one you told me about." He reached for Hadley's hand and closed both of his around it. "We miss Ben and Lauren terribly. But welcome to St. Louis and to our little restaurant. Are you hungry? What can I get you?"

"I'll check out the menu and let you know," Hadley said, smiling at him.

We sat at a big table in the back, more than a dozen of us, and it reminded me of before the accident. This had been our favorite postgame hangout. Sometimes we came to eat, sometimes just for dessert, other times just for a few drinks and to hang out. Ben had started the tradition after home games on nights when we weren't traveling or playing the following day. It usually happened about once a month, a time for all of us to catch up, relax, and spend time together. Though the whole team and their significant others were always invited, it was usually the same dozen or so who came.

Tonight we were a rowdy but laid-back group, including Drew and Nina, me and Hadley, another veteran on the team named Ross Camden and his wife Allie, Nash, Lars, Boone, and our new Russian backup goalie, Konstantin, with his girlfriend Svetlana. He'd only been on the team a year, and mostly kept to himself, but he did come to our monthly dinners, as if trying to fit in and find his place with us. A few others were stopping by but hadn't arrived yet so we settled in without waiting for them.

"How's it going with the kids?" Nash asked. "I feel bad I haven't been by in a while, but it seems like you've got it under control."

"Well, we hired a nanny to help us out so Hadley can work and I can rest when I need to. That's made a huge difference."

"And then the grandparents arrived." Hadley picked up her wine glass and took a sip.

"Are Ben's parents still suing you for custody?" Drew asked, disbelief on his face. "I can't wrap my head around that."

"Me either," I admitted. "I used to have a pretty solid relationship with them. I've known them since I was a kid, but they're not backing down. I'm not worried about it, though. The lawyer I hired is going to chew theirs up and spit him out. There's nothing that's going to make a judge overturn the will and the arrangements Ben and Lauren left unless there was some kind of abuse involved. Which obviously isn't an issue."

"Judges make weird decisions sometimes," Nina said. "Make sure all your ducks are in a row, just in case."

"We're trying." Hadley glanced at me and for the first time maybe ever, her eyes were filled with…appreciation?

I slid my hand under the table, gently resting it on her thigh, though closer to the knee than anywhere else. I was trying to show support, not make a sexual overture, and to my surprise, she put one of her hands over mine. I almost expected her to move it out of the way but she just squeezed it gently as she took another sip of wine.

Jesus. Were we practically holding hands under the table? My heart was pounding a little harder than usual and my chest tightened with excitement. I felt like a teenager who'd just landed the pretty cheerleader and now all my friends were going to be jealous.

I didn't know what the hell was wrong with me, but somewhere in the back of my mind I recalled a conversation where Ben had confessed he didn't understand why Hadley was single.

"She's gorgeous," he'd told me. "Smart, independent, and has a huge heart. What's wrong with guys that they don't want her?"

"Well," I'd drawled. "If she busts their balls the way she does mine, who has time for that?"

"Did it ever occur to you that she likes you but you're

such a player she doesn't dare allow herself to get that close?"

I'd rolled my eyes. "Yeah, okay. If you say so. Frankly, she's hot, but not my type."

"I think she's exactly your type. You just need to grow up enough to recognize it."

Yeah, Ben had figured out there was potential there long before we did. As usual. Had Lauren had similar conversations with Hadley? I wished I could ask her, but we were exploring new territory and I didn't want to scare her off.

"Hey, guys." Van Lukather, a young defenseman on the team, came strolling in. He pulled out the chair next to Hadley's, flipped it backward and straddled it. He was probably the funniest guy on the team, always cracking us up, though he was as serious as a heart attack on the ice. He also could throw a punch, which was convenient sometimes.

Right behind him was Rory Beauchamp and a pretty young woman I'd never seen before. Rory was kind of a wild card on the team. He was young, but not a rookie; talented, but without much discipline; and, a partier without limits. Coach had sat him down a few months back, giving him a talk about all that and now he appeared to have a girlfriend. Maybe we were all growing up?

"Hey, I'm Van." Van held his hand out to Hadley. "I didn't realize Wes had a girlfriend."

"Oh, we're not—" she began, yanking her hand off of mine.

"She's not—" I said at the same time.

"Hey, it's cool. None of my business." He waved down the waiter and ordered a beer.

Hadley glanced at me and I looked back at her.

Like it or not, we had to talk about that kiss. I hoped like hell I was reading her signals right and she wanted more than just another kiss as much as I did.

CHAPTER TEN

HADLEY

"The look on his face!" Drew threw his head back in laughter. "Ben hated having pranks pulled on him."

"But he was the first one to laugh at the rest of us when we were on the receiving end," Nash added.

There was a moment of silence at the table at Giovanna's. Though there was sadness on many faces, there were also smiles. Hearing the story about the time Van had put a snake in a locker-room cooler and waited for Ben to open it in search of a drink had made me laugh. I liked finding out something I didn't know about him—it almost made me feel like he was here with us. Or at least, his spirit.

"The rookies had it worse that year," Wes said, shaking his head. "Van put the snake in bed with each of them, and we videotaped it."

"Oh shit, that's right!" Drew said. "Didn't Rory piss himself?"

Rory glared at the team's goalie. "I thought I was about to die, motherfucker. You guys are lucky none of us had heart conditions."

Wes looked at me, his expression relaxed and happy. I was feeling the same way, both of us several drinks in and full of delicious bread and pasta neither of us had cooked or cleaned up after.

"I think the poor snake was more scared than anyone," he said, giving my hand a little squeeze.

"I took him to the woods behind my parents' house after," Van said. "I'm sure he had a good life there."

"Guys, I hate to do this, but we've gotta go," Drew said, looking at Nina. "Our kids mercilessly wake up hungry and full of energy at six on the dot every morning."

"Ugh." Rory cringed. "I'd tell 'em to grab a protein bar and let me sleep another hour."

"Hadley," Nina said as she stood up. "Can I come by tomorrow, early afternoon? I thought we could catch up and hang out with the kids."

"Actually, I have both our nanny and Ben's parents helping out right now, so I could do lunch out if you want."

"That sounds great. Let's text in the morning about a time and place."

Wes leaned his face in close to mine and murmured, "Hope you don't mind, but I texted Tori and told her she can have a few days off, with pay, while Patrick and Susan are here. I want them to get the full experience."

"You're ruthless," I said, laughing. "And I love it."

The others were starting to rise from the table, gathering coats and purses. I glanced at my watch and saw to my surprise that it was after midnight.

Wes helped me out of my chair and we said our goodbyes to everyone. I'd seen Wes pass Vicenzo a credit card from his wallet a couple hours ago, and he signed for the check and got his card back on our way out.

"We thank you," Vicenzo said, putting a hand on Wes's shoulder. "Your team is always so generous with us. Bring your lovely lady back for a date soon and I'll reserve a corner table for you."

Wes met my gaze for a second and said, "I'll do that. And we'll see you next time. Thanks for staying open late for us."

"Anytime."

We walked out into the brisk night air and I put my dark purple stocking cap on. Wes grinned down at me.

"That was nice of you, to pay the bill," I said.

He shrugged. "Team captain's job. Ben always picked it up, so now I will."

"You're the new team captain?"

"Technically. But Ben will remain our official team captain for the rest of the season. If we don't start winning consistently, he might send me a message from the beyond telling me we need to get our asses in gear."

"Let's not worry about any of that tonight. It feels so good to take a night off of winning and losing and deadlines."

"You're right," he said. "And you look cute in that hat."

My heart kicked up as I touched the end of my stocking cap and said, "Thanks. Lauren made it for me."

"Yeah?"

"Yeah. She was just naturally good at things, you know? If she wanted to learn to do something, she just...did."

"You're good at things, too."

I laughed lightly. "Like ballbusting?"

Wes sighed softly as we walked in the direction of his Range Rover. "You know, Hadley, if I could do it all over, I wouldn't have made that lame crack about you liking wieners."

I whipped my head around in surprise. "You remember that?"

"Of course I remember. Over the course of exactly three seconds, your face went from interested, to incredulous, to disgusted. I'd just...had a few beers and, to be honest, I still had some growing up to do."

His humility about our first meeting caught me off guard. We reached his car, and before he could open my door, I stepped closer to him and put a palm on his chest.

"I overreacted," I admitted. "I shouldn't have let one stupid comment decide whether you were worth getting to know better."

"Can I confess something?"

I smiled and said, "Of course."

"I'd never been shot down before. I was kind of blown away when you rejected me, because I was so used to women falling at my feet no matter what I said. I once walked into a party after a game in college, drunk off my ass, and told a woman I'd just stepped in dog shit. She laughed and said I was cute. Anyway..." He shook his head, looked away and then met my gaze. "I thought you were sexy as hell. An absolute ten. And then, when you shot me down...I liked you even more."

I warmed from head to toe, pleased with the

compliments, but also trying to wrap my head around what I was hearing. "You liked me?"

"Always. I just knew I'd blown it."

He cupped my cheek in his hand and brushed his thumb across my cheekbone, then across my lips, creating a flutter of excitement in my stomach. A small snowflake fell on his dark stubble as he slid his hand around to the back of my neck and leaned down, kissing me.

It was soft and tender. His lips slowly caressed mine before I grabbed the sides of his coat and pulled my body flush against his, intensifying our kiss. His sweet words, woodsy scent and hard, warm body made me forget everything else. I didn't take the time to analyze or overthink it—I just lived in this perfectly romantic moment.

Wes groaned and pushed me against his car, his tongue brushing over mine in a kiss so passionate that I couldn't think straight. I just knew I wanted more.

When Wes's mouth moved down to my jawline, I gasped and closed my eyes, blissfully overwhelmed by his large frame and obvious hunger for me.

"Let's go to a hotel," he murmured in my ear as his lips grazed my neck.

"I want to."

"You're so goddamn sexy, Hadley. I can't wait to show you what you do to me."

Even through our coats, I felt his hardness pressed against me. I wanted to throw caution to the wind and stay in this moment, screwing Wes until the very last minute we had to return home in the morning.

The voice was back, though. That little, annoying thread of logic was telling me it was irresponsible to stay out all night, return home in the morning looking like we'd gotten drunk, fucked and come slinking back home in yesterday's clothes. We hadn't even run staying out all night by Patrick and Susan.

"I want to so much," I repeated. "But like Nina said, we have to keep our ducks in a row. I don't want to give Patrick and Susan any ammunition to strengthen their case against us. And they don't know how to pat Benny's tummy when he has gas at night. And if Annalise wakes up in the morning and we aren't there…"

Wes sighed heavily. "I get it."

"I want to." I pulled on his coat and waited until his eyes met mine. "You know how much I want to, right?"

The corners of his lips tugged up in a smile. "Yeah, tell it to my balls."

"I'm not sure a one-on-one conversation between me and your balls would be helpful at the moment."

With a low laugh, he kissed my forehead and said, "Okay, not tonight. But soon."

"Yes."

He kissed my lips a final time before stepping back, pulling me with him so he could open the passenger door for me.

How soon was soon? I wondered as he drove us home, his hand on my thigh making me so hot I was squirming in my seat.

Not soon enough.

"So obviously, you and Wes are getting it on."

My cheeks warmed as I laughed at Nina's comment. We were sitting at a booth at a suburban deli, chatting over soup and sandwiches.

"We haven't gotten it all the way on yet," I confessed.

"Really?" She gave me a skeptical look. "I told Drew on the way home last night that with the way I saw you guys looking at each other, there was a one hundred percent chance of sex."

"Well, we had to go home to the kids and Ben's parents, so…no."

"Yeah, I can see how that would be a buzzkill. But I love that you guys are so into each other. And I know Lauren would, too."

I looked down, smiling sadly when I looked back up at Nina. "Lauren and Ben tried to fix Wes and I up a long time ago…like seven years ago, I think. It didn't go well."

"People change. Drew says he got all the partying out of his system quick when he went pro because it was so much more intense than he realized it would be."

"But with Wes and I…I don't know if it's a good idea to go there. I mean, do I *want* to go there? Absolutely. But we still don't know which of us will be raising the kids."

"Oh, I thought you were going to be raising the kids together. Is that not the case?"

I shook my head. "I don't see how it can be. My boss said I can work remotely for now, but she's not happy with how it's going. I'm the first to admit that I can't keep up. Even with the new nanny. I used to work ten to twelve hours a day, and I just can't do that with the kids."

"You know the situation better than I do," Nina said, "but it seems like it makes sense for you and Wes to raise the kids together. If you took them back to New York, you'd have to hire full-time help to continue working that much."

"I know. I worry about all of this stuff all the time. And I feel like Wes and I getting involved romantically will only complicate things more. Especially if it doesn't work out."

Nina nodded. "It's smart to think about that, even though it has to be hard."

"Annalise and Benny have already lost their parents. Ben and Lauren were their world. And I don't want them to lose me or Wes because we started sleeping together and things went bad. It's not right."

"Life is so messy sometimes, isn't it?"

"Amen to that." I finished my sandwich and moved the plate aside, putting my elbows on the table. "On a much easier subject, how do I throw a birthday party for a four-year-old?"

"Depends how elaborate you want it to be."

"I want to do it like Lauren would have. Or as close as I can get to it."

"Perfect. I've always liked the way she did her kids' parties. They were fun, but not over the top."

"I was thinking maybe a *Frozen* theme? Some ice-skating and a cake decorated with snowflakes in different shades of blue?"

"But doesn't Annalise love the Avengers now?"

"She does, but I don't know how to put together an Avengers party. I want to make the cake myself, like Lauren always did, but I'm not a professional cake decorator. Actually, I'm not even close to a professional. I can't do any elaborate decorations."

"I can help you. Oh! And we already know the perfect person to dress up as Thor and make an appearance at the party. It'll be great and he can play with the kids."

"We do?"

Nina grinned. "Lars."

"Will he be willing to do that?"

She laughed. "For Ben's daughter, trust me, we'll probably have the entire Avengers lineup at the party. The team will always love those kids like their own."

I smiled, grateful that Benny and Annalise were surrounded with such a great support system. Inside, though, I was more conflicted than ever. Taking the kids to New York no longer felt like the clear choice.

Nina was right—life *was* messy sometimes. There didn't seem to be a way out of this that didn't involve someone getting hurt. But it couldn't be the kids. Neither Wes nor I would allow that.

CHAPTER ELEVEN

WES

"Wes, are you mad at me?" Gina asked, her full red lips drawing up into a pout.

Or was it Jenna?

Shit, I couldn't remember. It had been pure luck that I'd run into her at the grocery store this morning while picking up a birthday card for Annalise. My girlfriend of six months had dumped me last night, and the last thing I wanted to do was show up at Annalise's first birthday party without a date. Hadley was in town, which meant she would be busting my balls from the minute I got there, and in a moment of temporary insanity, I'd invited Gina or Jenna—Jeannie?—to come with me. We'd hooked up a few times last year, when I'd first moved to St. Louis, but that had been nothing but sex. This was an actual date.

And I couldn't even remember her name.

Dammit.

"Wes?" She looked sad now and I absently shook my head as I opened the passenger side door of my new Mustang for her.

"Sorry, doll. I'm not mad. You look beautiful. It's just, you know, you're dressed for a grown-up party and this is a kid party."

She looked down at her hot pink miniskirt and red, four-inch fuck-me pumps. "But you love this skirt."

"I know. I do. It's just...never mind." It was too late now and it wasn't Gina/Jenna's fault I was an asshole.

"Don't worry, kids love me," she said, sliding into the passenger seat and fluffing up her hair.

She kept up a steady stream of chatter the whole way to Ben and Lauren's suburban McMansion, and I pulled into their wide, circular driveway. I grabbed Annalise's huge, brightly wrapped gift from the back and walked around to the backyard with Gina/Jenna following me.

We followed the sound of laughter since Ben and Lauren were cooking out. Initially, the party was supposed to be indoors but when it turned out to be unseasonably warm, they'd moved it outside. Which made Gina/Jenna's stupidly high heels stand out even more.

"Hey, handsome!" Lauren called out as she swung past me carrying a tray of cupcakes and blowing me a kiss.

"Hey, beautiful."

Lauren put the cupcakes down and came over to us, a

curious smile on her face since no one yet knew Sadie and I had broken up. "Who's this?"

"This is my friend...Ginnie..." I said her name under my breath, so low Lauren couldn't possibly hear it.

"I'm sorry..." Lauren turned to Gina/Jenna holding out her hand. "What was your name?"

"Jeannie." Jeannie smiled and looked around, her eyes wide. "Wow, this place is something. I hope I get to live in a house like this one day."

"Thank you." Lauren gave me a funny look before pointing at Ben. "Ben's started cooking, Annalise is still napping, and a few of the Mavericks are wandering around somewhere."

"Hey, man!" Ben lifted a hand, waving.

"Hey." I started walking in his direction but Jeannie grabbed my arm.

"I didn't know we were going to be outside," she said. "My shoes are getting dirty."

"Then let's go inside," I said. "You can sit in the kitchen for a while."

"By myself?" She looked sad again.

"Er, no. I'll, uh, sit with you after I say hello to everyone."

Christ. What had I done?

Bringing Jeannie with me today had been stupid, but I'd been bummed about the breakup and really didn't want to show up without a date, knowing Hadley would be here. Instead, I'd just made it worse. Sometimes I couldn't get out of my own way, and nothing made me stupider than being around Hadley.

"Yo, Kirbs!" Nash came over and shook my hand.

"Hey, man." I grinned. "How's it hangin'?"

"Oh, you know, a little to the left."

We both chuckled and Jeannie giggled. "That's so hot."

I opted to ignore her and said hello to a few other guys on the team, wondering if I could just take Jeannie home and call it a night. Ben would never forgive me if I left, but I had a bad feeling already and we'd just gotten here.

"Wes, aren't you going to introduce me to your teammates?"

I really didn't want to, but I did the polite thing and made the rounds with her, avoiding where Hadley and Lauren were chatting with a few of the WAGs.

"How about a beer, Jeannie?" Nash asked her.

She blinked. "Ew. Gross. I don't drink beer. Is there any wine? Or better yet, tequila?"

"It's a kid's birthday party," I said gently. "Just beer and wine. Let me get you a glass."

I left her with my teammates and went inside to get a wine glass just as Hadley was going in. Nope, Lady Luck wasn't with me today.

"Hello, Wes." She gave me a perfunctory nod.

"Hi, Hadley."

"I heard you have a new girlfriend," she said, her eyes inscrutable as she looked at me.

"That didn't work out," I replied.

"So the bimbo in the four-inch heels and barely covered ass isn't the new girlfriend?"

"She's just a friend."

She chuckled. "Really? How much do you pay your friend per hour?"

I huffed out a breath. "Could you be any bitchier?"

"Could you be any less classy? You brought a woman who literally looks like a hooker to your goddaughter's first birthday party. In front of friends, family, and teammates. You truly don't have an ounce of decorum in you."

"So good of you to judge a book by its cover," I snapped. "She might not be the sharpest tool in the drawer, but at least she's nice. Something you could try for once in your life. What happened to women sticking together?" I turned and stalked out of the kitchen.

Hadley got under my skin like no one else ever had and the urge to tell her off got stronger every time I saw her.

"I'm afraid to ask where Sadie is," Ben said, looking up from the grill when I approached him.

"She dumped me," I muttered.

"Wow, I'm sorry. I thought things were going well."

"She doesn't like how much I travel."

"That's part of the life. If she can't deal with it, it's better to break things off now."

"Yeah."

"So, uh, you and Hadley already go at it?" I followed his gaze to where Hadley had just slammed the kitchen door behind her as she made her way back over to Lauren.

"I can't win with her, man. I literally said hello and she called Jeannie a hooker."

"Well, you did bring a chick wearing six-inch heels and a skirt that barely covers her ass to a family birthday party."

"I needed a date! And they're not six inches tall!"

"Why?" Ben looked at me like I was crazy. "This is Annalise's birthday. No one's here but the best of friends and family. Who cares if you have a date?"

"I care!" I snapped. "You invite Hadley to everything and she makes it so that I don't even want to come! Every fucking minute of the day, every time we're together, she has something nasty to say."

"Sometimes you bring it on yourself, buddy." Ben gave me the same look he sometimes gave the guys in the locker room when they were being dumbasses. But this was different.

"Like I've said a dozen times, you always take her side."

"If you'd just give her a chance..."

I scratched the side of my face. "You know what? I

think I'm gonna go. It's not like Annalise is going to remember who was here today." I turned and started making my way over to Jeannie.

"Hey." Ben caught up to me and put a hand on my shoulder. "I'm sorry. You're right. I do take her side but it's only because I don't see what you see, and the only thing I can think of is that you two are so perfect for each other, while you're fighting it for all you're worth."

I shook my head. "Me and Hadley? Perfect for each other? That's never gonna happen, buddy. You can take that to the bank."

"Fine. But please don't go. We want you here and I promise to keep you far away from Hadley."

I sighed. "Fine. But you're buying drinks on the next road trip."

"Deal."

THE DAY of Annalise's birthday party was a bright, sunny day. It was still cool, only in the low fifties with a strong wind, but it was perfect for what we'd planned. Well, mostly what Hadley planned since I'd been on two road trips in the last month. Though the original plan had been to keep things relatively simple, the Avengers theme took root and then it was all hands on deck. We had representation for almost all of them—Thor, Iron Man, Captain America, Black Widow, and even the Hulk.

It had taken a little explaining to get Lars on board as Thor, but once he'd said yes, the rest of the team had jumped at the chance to portray Annalise's favorite superheroes. Drew was Captain America, Van was Iron Man, and to our surprise, it was Konstantin who offered to be the Hulk. Nina had volunteered to be the Black Widow and the lineup was complete.

"Everything looks amazing," Greg Brandt said. Greg was Lauren's father. He and her mother, Tasha, had flown in for the weekend to spend Annalise's birthday with her. Though Tasha's MS was in remission, she tired easily and couldn't always do the things she wanted to do. We were glad to have them, though, because they were so loving and easygoing. Unlike Patrick and Susan, who'd left in a snit. We'd let them see how hard it was to take care of the kids and they hadn't been happy about how little we'd done while they were here.

It was all by design, of course, orchestrated by me to give them a taste of what parenting would be like at their age. I didn't know if it had done more harm than good, but I was too busy to care and the lawyer I'd hired said they didn't have a leg to stand on.

"What can we do?" Tasha asked, leaning on her

cane as she looked around at the great room, which had been transformed into a science lab. Hadley had decided if we were going all out, we'd at least make it educational, so there were stations set up with different scientific activities that were loosely related to the Avengers, but more about keeping twenty-three four-year-olds busy. Annalise wanted her entire preschool class to be invited, along with a handful of the kids she knew from my Mavericks teammates, so it was going to be a zoo soon. Thank God we'd be able to put them on the screened-in porch for cake and ice cream.

"I think we're good," Hadley said, putting her hands on her hips as she looked around. "Tori's got her at the nail salon getting birthday nails done and they'll be home in about twenty minutes."

"She's going to love it," Tasha said softly. "You've done a wonderful job, you two."

"Thanks." Hadley smiled. "I know it's probably more than Lauren would have wanted, but we need this year to be special because Annalise has been asking about when Mommy and Daddy are coming back more and more often. I don't think she quite grasps the finality of death."

"Of course not." Tasha swallowed, blinking back tears. "But as she gets a little older, Greg and I will make sure both she and Benny hear all the stories about their mommy."

"Looks like they're back," I said, going to the door to greet Tori and Annalise.

"Is it time for my party yet?" Annalise demanded.

"Almost." I laughed, tweaking her nose.

"Thank you for letting me get a manicure too," Tori told me, blinking bright blue eyes up at me. She held out her hands and wiggled the fingers. "You like?"

"Er, yeah. They look nice." Yikes. Tori was practically right up against me and I took a slow step back. As far as I was concerned, she was nothing but a kid, even though technically she was a legal adult, so I hadn't given her a second thought. But she was definitely flirting with me, her eyes fixed on my face, a cute little smile on her lips.

Shit. I had to nip this in the bud and be super careful. This was just the type of thing that could derail our custody battle, and frankly, even if there was no custody situation, she was way too young for me. I didn't even hook up with women her age anymore. Twenty-four was about as young as I'd go. Not that I had time for that these days. Or the inclination since the only woman I thought about lately was Hadley.

"Why don't you see if there's anything you can

help Hadley with?" I suggested, grabbing Annalise and scooping her up.

We walked into the great room and Annalise squealed with delight, wiggling to get down and run around to check out every station, every decoration, every sweet, detailed touch Hadley had come up with to make this a birthday Annalise would never forget. It was costing a fortune too, even though I'd paid every bill with a smile.

"Gramps, did you see my balloons?" Annalise asked.

"I did!"

Annalise crawled onto his lap, talking animatedly and I leaned in to Hadley, whispering, "Want to blow this popsicle stand and go get a hotel room?"

She snickered. "Honestly? Not today. Maybe tonight, but right now, I want to see her face when the guys arrive."

I grinned. "Yeah, I do too."

Kids and their parents started to arrive, and within thirty minutes, the house was packed to the gills. And it wasn't a small house. Ben and Lauren had been planning on at least one more baby, if not two, so this was six thousand square feet of bells and whistles I'd never even thought of for my high-end two-bedroom condo. We'd arranged for the Avengers to arrive about thirty minutes after the party started, to leave time for any stragglers, and I was glad I'd talked Hadley into a professional photographer because there was barely time to breathe, much less take pictures. Hadley had said she would do it, but that wasn't happening.

My phone buzzed and I read a text from Drew, asking if we were ready for them. I shot him a quick affirmative answer and motioned to Hadley that it was time. She would make sure the kids were all in one place while I went to let in the guys and Nina.

A wave of emotion washed over me when I opened the door. The gang had outdone themselves. They'd rented costumes and really looked the part. Nina was wearing a dark red wig and heavy makeup, Lars wielded his hammer like a pro, and Konstantin had painted most of his body with green body paint.

"Wow, you guys, this is amazing," I said, nodding.

"Let's do this!" Drew moved forward and they essentially marched into the great room.

I was behind them but I heard the kids' screams and squeals of delight. Especially Annalise who launched herself at Lars.

"Thor came to my birthday! Thor came to my birthday!" She said it over and over, grabbing his hand and pulling him around the room.

I held my breath, waiting to see how Lars would react to so much touching, but apparently his dislike of it didn't extend to kids. Or at the very least, he tolerated it from the kids because he was totally in character, rambling on about thunder and hammers and the like. The kids were eating it up, too, and I caught Hadley's eye across the room. This was what we'd been hoping for, the magic of being four coupled with the love that came from our extended Mavericks family. Most of the kids here weren't part of the Mavericks family since there weren't many her age and none in her preschool class, but they didn't care about professional hockey players anyway.

"If I ever have kids," Nash said in my ear, "I'm totally doing this shit for them."

I grinned. "It's epic, right?"

"Who's the blond hottie?" he asked, checking out Tori.

"That's our nineteen-year-old nanny," I said. "So behave yourself."

"Nineteen is legal," he protested.

"If you piss her off and she quits, I'll kill you in your sleep."

"Fine." He headed in the opposite direction. "Maybe there's a single mom in the group over by the fireplace."

———

THE KIDS WERE HAVING a blast and we owed my teammates huge. The Avengers were such a hit, especially Thor and the Hulk. Konstantin spoke halting, heavily accented English so instead of trying to communicate, he grunted and spoke in monosyllabic sentences. Mostly, he growled at them, made them scream, and chased them until they were shrieking with laughter. Annalise now had a new best friend—Thor/Lars—and didn't leave his side for a second. She and two of her little friends followed him like the Pied Piper and he didn't seem at all stressed to be the object of so much attention, which was a relief for me because he could be extremely rigid when it came to his routines and social quirks.

"I think it's time for cake," Hadley whispered to me about two hours later.

"I think it's time for a nap," I chuckled.

"Cake first." She went toward the kitchen and I followed, lighting the candles as she gathered everything she'd need to cut and serve pieces of cake.

"Ready?" I asked her, lifting the massive two-tier Avengers-themed cake. She'd run out of time to make it herself and wound up buying one, but it was absolutely amazing, full of intricate detail, little plastic Avengers in the midst of battle, and "Happy Birthday, Annalise" printed on a banner held up by

Captain America and the Black Panther. It was such a cool cake, I was almost jealous.

Hadley started to sing "Happy Birthday," and everyone joined in, ending with me putting the cake down on a table that had been set up for that very purpose.

"Thor, will you help me blow out the candles?" Annalise asked Lars, who nodded amiably. He got down on one knee, one of his massive arms around her tiny torso, as she squeezed her eyes shut and whispered, "I wish Mommy and Daddy come home soon." Then she blew out the candles.

While the kids ate, drank, and laughed, the adults in the room dealt with myriad emotions, myself included, and I watched Hadley and Nina swipe at their eyes while some of the guys turned away, probably too embarrassed to show any emotion they were feeling since we'd all heard what Annalise wished for.

"Can we play outside?" Annalise asked once everyone had stuffed themselves on cake and ice cream.

Hadley looked at me and I nodded. "Sure. I'll help corral them."

"I'm in," Nash added.

Before we knew it, all the kids were outside along with most of the parents, playing tag and whatever else four-year-olds did. Hadley and I stood off to the side, watching and sipping wine out of plastic cups.

"I think she's had a great day," I told her. "And it's all because of you."

She shook her head. "Don't be ridiculous. You got the guys to do the Avengers thing. If it hadn't been for that, this party would have been a dud."

"I doubt it, but it just goes to show how good of a team we make. We did it together."

Her eyes met mine and she smiled faintly. "You're making it really hard not to like you, Wes."

"Is that the goal?" I laughed. "To *not* like me?"

"We have to put what these kids need before our own needs."

"That's what we've been doing, isn't it?"

"Mostly. But the sexual chemistry going on lately has the potential to blow up in our faces, and the main people who'll get burned are those kids. We have to be friends, and have a good relationship, because if we start something and it doesn't work out, how are we going to co-parent?"

I sighed. Partly because I was frustrated but also because she was right. And I fucking hated it. But there was no time to respond because the photographer we'd hired approached us with a smile.

"I've gotten a ton of candid photos, and some

great shots of both kids with their grandparents, but very few with the two of you. I thought we could do a handful of posed pictures with the four of you, and maybe each of you with both kids? I think it'll be nice to have a variety to choose from."

"Absolutely." I nodded. "I'll round up Annalise." I walked away because it was easier than trying to continue a dead-end conversation in the middle of all this chaos. While I mostly agreed with Hadley, I had a different perspective. We were adults. There was no reason we couldn't follow wherever this thing between us led and still be friends afterward if it either didn't work out or it was nothing more than sex. Why did everything have to be so black and white with her?

———

BY THE TIME the guests had left, and we cleaned up Benny and Annalise and put them to bed, Hadley and I collapsed on the sectional in the living room. It was only eight o'clock, but Annalise had been completely wiped out and fell asleep in the tub. Benny would probably be up again at midnight but at least we had a little quiet time.

"No offense, but those tiny slices of pizza and the world's coolest cake does not fill up a guy my size," I said. "Either we order some food or I might have to start chewing on your arm."

"I can make us something—" she began, starting to get up.

"Oh, shut up and sit down," I said, shaking my head. "You busted your ass today. You're not cooking shit."

She smiled. "Okay. What about ordering Chinese?"

"I could do Chinese." I reached for my phone. "And I have my favorite place on speed dial. What do you like?"

I placed an order and then we just sat there. It had been a great day, if not a little bittersweet, but fuck, I was tired. And I had both a morning skate and a game tomorrow. I needed to get some sleep, but I was starving and sitting here with Hadley was kind of nice. In fact, it was a lot nice. Too bad she'd made it clear things needed to cool down between us. My dick was definitely annoyed about this new development.

"Do you think Ben and Lauren would have liked the party?" she whispered.

"I think Lauren would have complained about how much money we spent, but they would have loved the way the guys dressed up and were here for

Annalise and the other kids. They loved our extended Mavericks family."

"God, when does it stop? I keep thinking it's getting better and then there's a day like today where it hurts so much I almost can't breathe. I still reach for my phone every damn day to call her…"

"I know." I slid an arm around her shoulders and drew her against me. She stiffened for a fraction of a second but then it was like all the fight drained out of her and she collapsed against my shoulder, burying the side of her face in my chest.

"I can never tell if you're hurting," she said after a moment. "I feel so weak because I want to cry every day and you're kicking ass and taking names."

"Believe me, the pain is always just below the surface. I'm not kicking anything and I don't even know what names I'm supposed to take. I just don't have the luxury of grieving too long. I have a job that requires a fucking ton of energy and two kids at home that take up the rest. No matter how much I hurt on the inside, I have to keep going for them, for the team, and for you."

"I'm so glad we've been here for each other. I know it doesn't seem like it, but you've been my rock through all of this."

I wanted to tell her she'd been my rock, too, but another few minutes of cuddling and intimate conversation, and I'd never be able to respect her wishes to keep things platonic.

"I think I just heard Benny," I lied, sliding out from under her embrace. "I better check on him."

I saw the surprise on her face, but what choice did I have? The closer we got, the more I wanted, but if she wasn't there for it, I had to protect myself in addition to the kids. Losing Ben and Lauren had been all the heartbreak I could handle; anything else might break me.

CHAPTER TWELVE

HADLEY

"And…done. Try complaining about that, Liz."

I clicked the *Send* button and officially sent my story for the magazine about planning a child's birthday party on any budget. It had been a week since Annalise's party, and I'd been inspired to write a package, complete with cake recipes, game ideas and a companion story about being inclusive of children of differing abilities at parties.

We'd talked at our last semiannual retreat about catering to the growing demographic of moms who subscribed to *Willow*, but I'd never imagined that just a few months later, I'd be in a position to write stories like the one I'd just turned in.

A confirmation message popped up in my inbox immediately. Liz got the email I just sent her. Scoffing, I looked at the clock on the wall of Ben's study—

it was nine fifteen and the sun had set hours ago. I'd privately joked to other staffers at the magazine that Liz didn't actually have a home; she just coiled up beneath her desk for a few hours each night to digest whomever she'd eaten whole that day and slithered out a few hours later to do it all again.

I'd envied her work ethic. But I now realized it was a hell of a lot easier to put in twelve plus hours a day when you didn't have any other responsibilities.

I quickly closed my computer so I wouldn't see any more messages from my boss until tomorrow. I was exhausted. It had been a long day of laundry, taking care of the kids and working. I'd come into Ben's study around three this afternoon, leaving Wes to take care of the kids.

My plan to close the door and focus entirely on work this evening had mostly worked. I hadn't been able to resist turning on the baby monitors that were connected to the kids' rooms when Wes was putting them to bed.

He'd told them stories about Ben as he fed Benny his bottle, tasking Annalise with organizing Benny's dresser drawers to keep her busy. It was bittersweet, tears forming in my eyes as I smiled at his recollections of Ben's first car, their first NHL game against each other and the time they tried skydiving.

"I was the chicken," Wes had told the kids. "I had

to tell your dad to push me out of the plane. He was smiling and laughing the whole way down and I was screaming my ass off. Sorry, my butt."

"Daddy said ass too, Uncle Wes," Annalise said. "When Mommy wasn't around, he said shit, ass and fuck. Mostly when we were watching hockey."

Wes had laughed at that, and I had, too, wiping tears from my cheeks. Even after nearly two months, the loss of Ben and Lauren still felt so raw. Every time one of the kids did something cute, I longed for Lauren to be here to see it.

There was a picture of Ben and Lauren on Ben's large walnut desk, and I picked it up for a closer look. It was the two of them on their honeymoon in Hawaii, smiling happily as they took a selfie in front of a waterfall.

Little did they know. I was grateful they'd found their great loves in each other and had two children together. But they'd been taken from this world far too soon. Wes had gotten a call from the local state's attorney's office a couple days ago letting us know all the toxicology results were in and the case review was complete. DUI charges were being filed against the driver who'd killed Ben and Lauren.

Wes had been stoic when he'd told me, but I knew it had to be emotional for him, too, even if he wasn't showing it.

It was a gut punch. One person's stupid decision to drive drunk had cost two beautiful young children their parents. Wes and I both supported the state's attorney's decision to charge the driver, but there was no penalty that would come close to comforting me. The world had been a better place with Ben and Lauren in it.

With a deep breath, I picked up my phone and got up from Ben's office chair, opening my personal email. I let out a little squeal of excitement when I saw a message from the photographer I'd hired to shoot Annalise's party. The photos were in.

I went to the kitchen to find something to eat. There was leftover pizza from the place Wes had ordered delivery from for dinner. I put a few pieces on a plate and set it in the microwave, pushing the buttons.

"Hey, there's pizza in the fridge," Wes called from the family room. "And I already poured your wine; it's waiting for you."

I smiled as I took my plate from the microwave, grabbed a napkin and walked into the family room, where Wes was sitting on the couch watching *Sports-Center*, his feet propped on the coffee table.

"I don't know," I said as I sat down beside him. "Do you think maybe when others know you want a glass of wine before you even say anything, it might be one of the Top Ten Signs You Have a Problem?"

Wes shrugged. "I say wine's not your problem, but your solution."

I snorted out a laugh. "Also a contender for that Top Ten list."

"Did you get your work done?"

"Yeah. But the viper will have a whole new list for me tomorrow."

"She seems like a real bitch of a boss."

I scoffed and took a sip of the red wine Wes had poured me. "You know, it's ironic. I always wanted to be just like her. I saw Liz as someone who took no shit, outworked everyone and made hard decisions. Do you know that when she's interviewing a woman for a job, she pries for information about whether she has kids or wants them, and she's less likely to hire them if she thinks someone will need maternity leave or use all their vacation days?"

"That's fucked."

"It really is. But I was so stupid. I thought it made sense. Now that I'm on the other side of it, I get it. Women shouldn't have to choose between their career and their family."

I took another drink of my wine as Wes said, "Totally agree."

"You know you're missing the hockey highlights, right?" I said, my gaze on the TV screen.

"I do, and it's killing me. I'm trying to be all sensitive and shit, and listen to you."

Rolling my eyes, I said, "Watch your highlights and I'll eat. We can talk after."

Five minutes later, when I was no longer ravenous, I poured a second glass of wine, and Wes's attention was focused on me again.

"Did your mom work?" I asked him. "You never mention your family."

"Yeah, she did. My parents were both attorneys, and they mostly did medical malpractice. They busted ass, made a shit ton of money and retired when my dad was fifty-five and my mom was fifty-three. They go back and forth between London and Miami now."

"Really? Do you ever visit?"

He shrugged. "About once a year I go see them and once a year they come here."

"It doesn't sound like you guys are close."

"Nah, we're not. But they'd be there for me if I needed anything. They're proud of me and all, just doing their own thing." He looked at me intently, a charged silence surrounding us, making me wonder if he was going to kiss me or keep talking. "What about you? You've never mentioned your family, either."

I sighed softly. "There's not much to mention. My dad left my mom when I was two and we never saw him again. My mom wasn't the best mom, but she wasn't the worst, either. My brother and I kept our heads down and got good grades, because we wanted to get out of the little town where we were born in Iowa. Our mom died of cancer when he was twenty and I was eighteen."

"I'm sorry, Hadley."

"Thanks. It was a long time ago."

"Do you still keep in touch with your brother?"

"Yes, when I can. He's a Navy SEAL, so he has to go off-grid a lot, and I never really know where he is. But I'm crazy proud of him."

"What's his name?"

"Griff. Short for Griffin."

"Does he know about Ben and Lauren? And about us getting the kids?"

I nodded. "We email pretty often. It works better since he's in other countries and his hours are different than mine."

"Hope I can meet him sometime."

"I'm sure you will. I told him I'll send him pictures from the party." I picked up my phone from the couch. "Which reminds me, the photographer sent the pictures."

I opened the email and scooted closer to Wes so we could look at them together. He put an arm around me and I snuggled in, my heart pounding from the intimacy. It had been a long time since I'd snuggled with a man. Like years. The men I'd slept with in the past were just hit-it-and-quit-it types, and honestly, I'd been ready to quit them before the hitting was even over.

"That's awesome," Wes said when I opened the first photo.

It was Annalise posing with all the Mavericks players who'd dressed up as Avengers for her party. She was beaming, and so were they.

I scrolled through the pictures, Wes and I oohing, aahing and laughing at most of them. Then I got to the first one of the two of us with Benny and Annalise. I was holding Benny and Wes had his arm around Annalise as she smiled, her cake off to the side.

We were both silent as we took in the picture. I was bombarded with emotions. It was supposed to be Ben and Lauren in that picture with their babies. The four of us looked like a family, and even though we lived as a family every day, it was another thing to see us posed like one in a photo.

"Damn," Wes whispered.

I blew out a breath and set my phone aside. "I didn't expect to feel so…I don't know, sad, I guess."

"It's hard. Ben was such a great dad. I already feel like a piss-poor imposter. And then to see that picture, it just…"

"I know." I hugged his chest. "We just have to take this one day at a time."

"You want to watch a show or something? Get things feeling a little lighter?"

"Yeah, that sounds good."

"Or we could continue our last kiss," he said, holding me close. "I think about doing that about a dozen times a day."

I was exhausted, had pepperoni breath and hadn't showered today, but I still considered it. We both wanted more than a kiss, and somehow I knew if Wes and I slept together, all my other emotions and worries would be swept away for however blissfully long it lasted. Kind of like when we kissed, but magnified many times over.

The baby monitor crackled, and it wasn't Benny making the noise as usual, but Annalise.

"Aunt Hadley?" she said in a sleepy tone.

She was used to lying down with me at night. If she fell asleep in the family room, Wes would carry her to bed, but we never made her go to bed alone. It was probably a bad habit, but we wanted to give her every comfort we could.

Instinctively, I jumped up from the couch. Wes sighed deeply and picked up the remote.

"Let me know if you need any help," he said.

"Thanks."

I actually welcomed the distraction, because I'd been close to telling Wes yes. I wanted to forget all the feelings that had hit when we saw that picture of us and the kids. And as much as I would've liked it, it wouldn't have fixed anything. The feelings weren't going away, and if I slept with Wes, I was pretty sure I'd have even more feelings to contend with.

I just didn't have emotional bandwidth left for anything else. Parenting, working and mourning already took everything I had and more each day. The last thing Wes and I needed was to complicate things even further.

"I'M REGRETTING THE GLITTER GUNS," I said to Lauren, turning my face from side to side to see my reflection in the mirror of the nightclub's bathroom.

I was covered in gold sparkles; it would take forever to scrub each speck off.

"We're still drunk, which means you're not allowed to

kill my buzz yet." She grinned at me from the sink next to the one I stood in front of.

"It takes nothing to get you wasted these days," I said, laughing. "You're a lot drunker than I am."

"I hardly ever go out! It's New Year's Eve and I'm in New York City! The big fucking apple."

"No one calls it that," I said, snorting loudly.

"Can you guys hurry up?" an annoyed female voice said from behind us.

I turned and glared. "You look fine. Use some sanitizer on your hands and get back to the party."

"Come on," Lauren said, grabbing my arm and taking off. "I want to find my sexy husband so I can kiss him when the ball drops." She laughed loudly. "I said ball."

Ben and Lauren had come to the city to celebrate New Year's Eve at a trendy new club I'd gotten us into. Annalise was at a hotel with a babysitter Ben and Lauren had flown in with them. They were paying her a fortune so they could go out but not be far from their daughter. And of course, they'd asked Wes to come out with us, too. He was getting Ben shit-faced on whiskey, the two of them laughing obliviously as two women approached them.

"Oh, hell no," Lauren muttered as we walked closer.

The women had just gotten Ben and Wes to turn and look at them when we reached them.

"He's taken," Lauren said sharply, sliding onto her husband's lap.

"Oh, sorry," the blond said, turning to Wes. "What about you?"

Her friend looked at me, likely waiting to see if I was about to show my claws like Lauren just had.

"He's all yours," I said, putting my palms up.

"Can we share you?" the dark-haired woman asked, giving Wes a coy look.

"Uh, I wish." He grinned. "I'm really flattered, ladies, but I'm here with my friends and I just want to spend time with them."

"Aw, but who are you gonna kiss when the ball drops?" the blond asked with a fake pout.

"Uh..." Wes looked at me.

"No," I said firmly.

"Relax, I wasn't even thinking it."

"It's happening in ten minutes!" the blond said, putting a hand on Wes's thigh. "Let's get drinks so we're ready to toast!"

"You two need to fuck off," Lauren said, waving a hand. "I'll kiss him if I have to, but you're not staying."

"You're not kissing him," Ben said, lowering his brows as the two women rolled their eyes and left.

"I didn't mean like with tongue," Lauren said.

"You want me to kiss Hadley, then?" Ben asked.

Lauren's expression morphed from annoyed to disbelieving.

"Guys, no one's kissing but you two, okay? We're gonna toast with shots."

A waitress arrived then with a tray of shots and Wes passed them out. We gathered around our table and watched the large screen at the bar where the Times Square ball drop was being broadcasted. It was a fifteen-minute walk from where we were, but it was freezing and none of us had wanted to spend the evening outside.

"To great friends," Ben said as people in the bar counted down to the big moment.

"To friends!" Wes echoed, and we all clinked glasses.

Music played and confetti flew as we threw back the shots, my throat burning as the alcohol hit. When I set my glass down, Lauren had her palms on Ben's cheeks and they were kissing. Wes moved closer to me, his steps uneven and his eyes bloodshot. He was wasted.

"Don't even think about kissing me," I cautioned, light-headed from the shot but still very aware of not letting my guard down.

I'd experienced a painful breakup a few weeks ago, and I was feeling vulnerable. I couldn't let too much alcohol and a broken heart allow me to make an awful decision about Wes.

Wes leaned in and I turned my face away to make sure he couldn't kiss me.

"Trust me, I'm not thinking about it," he said in my ear. "I was just gonna say I hope this is your year, Hadley.

I hope the massive icicle wedged in your ass gets a chance to defrost this year and maybe you can finally get laid."

I scoffed, but my pulse pounded anxiously as his words hit home.

"I get laid plenty, thanks," I said crisply.

"Sure you do. I'm sure there are lots of guys looking for a woman to criticize their every move." Wes laughed, and I hated him just a little more than before.

Maybe this would be the year he stopped being such a dick. I seriously doubted it, though. Wes Kirby would never change.

CHAPTER THIRTEEN

WES

Losing three out of six games on the road was brutal. I'd tried every trick in the book to motivate and encourage my teammates, but we were in a death spiral of losses and I was frustrated as fuck. We'd dropped to fourth place overall and third in our division, so even though we were still on target for the playoffs, there would be no way to save this season if we didn't start winning. Ten days felt like ten years and when I walked into the house at ten thirty at night, I was in a piss-poor mood.

Hadley was in the kitchen scrubbing the food processor and ridding it of what appeared to be another baby food disaster, and I wished I had it in me to smile. She wore calf-length yoga pants that fit her ass like a glove, an oversized T-shirt, and sweet baby Jesus, no bra. Her hair was up in a messy half-ponytail thing, with tendrils that had escaped and now framed her face, and she was covered in something purplish-blue.

"Blueberry baby food?" I asked, setting down my bag.

"Yes." She turned with a smile. "How are you?"

"How do you think? It was the road trip from hell." I rummaged in the fridge for something to eat but all I saw was string cheese, fruit, and baby food. "Jesus fucking Christ, is there ever anything to eat in this house that isn't for kids?"

Hadley paused what she was doing and narrowed her eyes. "Yes, but only if you ask nicely."

"Sorry." It wasn't her fault we were sucking ass on the ice, but I didn't have anyone else to take it out on.

"There are cold cuts if you'd like me to make you a sandwich or—"

"Never mind. I'm not hungry." I slammed the refrigerator door shut and reached for my bag.

"Wes." She put a gentle hand on my arm. "What's wrong?"

"You wouldn't understand."

"Try me." Her eyes were soft and understanding, as if she actually did understand even though I hadn't told her anything.

"It's hard to explain. It's hockey stuff, and while I

appreciate you trying to help, you wouldn't get how off the dynamic is in the locker room right now. We're just not gelling the way we used to, the way we should be and I don't know how to fix it."

"What can I do to make you feel better?"

I grunted. "I can think of at least one thing."

It wasn't the way I'd been planning to seduce her if and when the opportunity presented itself, but instead of telling me I was pig, she surprised me by merely cocking her head.

"Would that truly help?"

"How long has it been since you've had sex, Hadley?"

She grimaced. "Er, a long time. Almost, um, I guess almost a year."

Jesus, that *was* a long time.

"And you're okay with that?"

"I'm…well, no, I guess not, but I can take care of my needs myself." Her cheeks burned pink.

"You'd rather masturbate than let me fuck you?" I had her up against the island, looming over her even though she didn't seem the least bit intimidated.

"Of course not, but I'd rather not do something that's going to get emotional or messy because of the kids. We've talked about this."

"Honey, no one said anything about emotions. This is just sex. We're consenting adults who've both been without for far too long. I can do you so dirty you won't be thinking about anything except how many times I can make you come." I cupped the back of her neck and felt the gooseflesh break out on her skin.

Her breath hitched a little as she looked up at me. "Wes…"

"Say yes, Hadley." I was so fucking hard.

"But what if—"

"Jesus, woman, yes or no." I was already pushing her back onto the island and instead of answering, she reached up, grabbed my head, and brought it down to hers. She kissed me this time and holy fucking hotness. She held nothing back, moaning softly as our tongues tangled, her breath hot and her chest pressed against mine. The woman scrubbing dishes a few seconds ago was nowhere to be seen. This wasn't just about her taking my mind off my professional death spiral. She needed it, too.

I lifted her onto the counter, and she wrapped her legs around my waist, our mouths still fused together. Her tongue was dueling with mine, swirling and twirling, our lips a tangled mass of desire. I slid my hands beneath her ass, kneading and squeezing the firm globes, pulling her against my groin. She whimpered when I moved my hands to pull the hair band the rest of the way out of her ponytail, but I needed raw, horny Hadley, not buttoned-up executive Hadley. And fuck, she was gorgeous with her lips swollen from kissing, her hair falling wildly around her face, and her eyes glassy with need.

There was a touch of indecision there, though, so before she could change her mind, I lifted her shirt over her head and damn, what awaited me there was beyond every fantasy I'd had about her. Her tits were about as perfect as they could be. Firm and round, sitting high on her chest, with the palest pink nipples that were already hard for me.

"34D, right?" I murmured, dipping my head to get my first taste.

"Are you an expert on more than just size?" Her quip quickly turned into a moan, her fingers digging into my hair, pulling me closer.

I just laughed, licking and teasing her nipple until her nails were pinpricks of pain against my scalp.

"Lean back," I said, dropping to my knees.

"What?" She looked startled as I tugged at her yoga pants.

"Off."

"Wes, the kids—"

"Annalise will call out to us first, so we're safe." I made short work of her pants and underwear and seeing Hadley naked on the kitchen island, legs open, her pussy wet with arousal, made my cock strain painfully. But the first orgasm would go to her. Then I was going to fuck her into the middle of next week.

I used my fingers to spread her delicate lips and my tongue to get my first taste. Damn, she was musky woman and delicious dessert all rolled into one. Her clit was already a hard little nub against my lips and I sucked on it playfully, getting a feel for what she liked. Gentle didn't do it for her and I increased the pressure until she cried out. I fit my shoulders beneath her thighs so I had easy access to her pussy, and she gasped a little, arms flailing as she tried to get her balance. I heard something skid across the counter but didn't give a shit because I was tongue fucking her now, and she was riding my face like a bronco.

"Wes! Oh my god, Wes!"

She was so damn wet, my face was soaked, but I loved it. Having the prim and proper woman I'd fought with so many times coming undone for me was beyond my wildest dreams. I pushed a finger inside of her and she started to pant, whispering my name over and over. When I added a second finger, simultaneously sucking on her clit, her whispers turned to groans.

"Ready to come for me?" I asked, lightly scissoring my fingers inside of her.

"Yes, god, yes!"

Two fingers and the grazing of my teeth on her clit was all it took. She shrieked out my name as she convulsed around my fingers and face, bucking wildly and sending a big bowl of something flying across the room as she fell back on the counter. We were both oblivious to the mess. Watching her come was glorious and hearing my name on her lips was heady.

She'd barely finished coming before I scooped her up and headed up the stairs.

"Where are we going?" she whispered, collapsing into my arms.

"Into that big king-size bed where I can fuck you like you want me to."

"But Annalise is there."

"I'm putting her little behind in her own room tonight."

I put Hadley down gently so as not to wake Annalise, and then hurried to wash my hands before picking her up and carrying her to her own bed. She didn't stir, thankfully, and I tucked her in, kissing her forehead. I made sure to turn on the baby monitor and quietly shut the door behind me. Then

I was stripping off my clothes as I walked back to the master bedroom.

Hadley was just where I'd left her, a naked goddess bathed in the faint light from the single lamp in the room, and I was so glad I still kept a condom in my wallet. I pulled it out, tossed it on the bed and then crawled over her. "How do you want it, Had?"

"I don't know," she said softly. "I get the feeling you're way more experienced than I am. So you do what you like."

"Oh, baby, that's not how this works." I took a moment to stare into her pretty face. "Don't your lovers take the time to find out what makes you tick in bed?"

"Mm, not so far."

"Well, that ends now." I paused. "Can you come with straight missionary?"

She shook her head. "I don't think so. Well, I never have. Usually only when I'm on top. But it takes me a long time."

"That's okay. I have all the staying power you need. What else do you like?"

"I like what you just did."

"And we'll do that again but I desperately need to be inside of you."

"I want that too."

"How about reverse cowgirl? Ever tried that?"

She shook her head.

"Come here." I tugged her off the bed and onto the settee by the window. I rolled on the condom and sat down with my feet on the floor, knees bent. Then I pulled her onto my lap facing away from me, moving her legs so her thighs were mostly on the outside of mine, her legs spread wide. "Lean back and let me do all the work," I whispered.

She rested the back of her head against my chest and I reached around, using one hand to fondle her breast and the other to go back to teasing her clit. She was so damn responsive, her body instantly reacting when I touched her. Her nipple hardened against my fingers and she was wet again. Fuck, was she made for me or what?

Now it was just a matter of getting her to relax. Though her body was primed and ready to go again, I sensed a touch of insecurity. Hadley definitely wasn't as experienced as I was. In fact, I was willing to bet she wasn't experienced at all. Not with a real man who knew how to make it good and take care of her needs before his own.

"Sit up a little, baby." I nudged her forward and positioned myself at her entrance. "Now slide down right on my cock…oh, yeah, just like that."

Fuck.

She was tighter and wetter than anyone I'd ever been with, closing around me and taking every inch until I bottomed out. The urge to let go came out of nowhere and I had to hold her in place to keep her from moving until I could get control again. Jesus. That never happened to me, almost losing control so quickly, but Hadley was spectacular and being inside of her was indescribable.

I closed my eyes and kissed her shoulder gently, taking in the sweet scent of her hair. In this moment, she belonged to me in every possible way, and I never wanted it to end.

"Wes, please…" She was straining against my hands, anxious to get more of me but I needed to make sure she was ready.

"I'm going to fuck you hard and dirty, just like you asked me to, so I want you to relax and let me do the work."

"Please, just do it already."

I rumbled out a laugh. "Feet on the floor, beautiful. And hold on tight." I slammed up into her hard enough to make her cry out. Then I pulled out to the tip and just sat there, waiting for her to react. She was truly the one who would guide our pace but she wasn't sure of herself yet, so I'd let her think I was in control. I had no doubt, though, that once she got going this was going to be intense.

I thrust up, paused, and pulled out again. I did it over and over until she started to move with me, her body finding the rhythm that would get her where she needed to go.

"Touch yourself, Hadley. Play with your clit while I fuck you."

She made a strangled little sound, but reached down and though I couldn't see it, I knew she was doing it because of the way she started to clench around me.

"Just like that." I started to move faster and so did she, her sweet little ass bouncing on my lap until she lost control. I let her ride out the wave of her orgasm before shooting off inside of her, my fingers digging into her hips as I held on for dear life.

"Fuck…that was amazing." I wrapped my arms around her waist as she collapsed back against my chest.

She was quiet for a long time and I momentarily worried that I'd hurt her, but I knew better. She'd come hard and fast, the way we'd both needed, and now that enterprising brain of hers was probably going a mile a minute.

"Let's go clean up," I said softly, gently nudging her onto her feet.

Her legs were a little shaky and I reached for her,

pulling her against me as we walked into the bathroom.

Damn, she was beautiful when she was thoroughly fucked. Her hair was wild, her eyes at half-mast, her skin flushed.

"You're fucking gorgeous," I told her as I disposed of the condom. "And that was incredible."

"Um, yes. It was."

"You okay?"

"Fine. Yes." She was just standing there looking at me, as if confused. "Wes, I—" she began.

I put a finger over her lips, hoping this wasn't going where I thought it was. "Unless the next words out of your mouth are 'fuck me again, Wes,' I don't want to hear it."

She licked her lips, her eyes burning into mine. "Fuck me again, Wes."

CHAPTER FOURTEEN

HADLEY

"Aunt Hadley, let's have a tea party."

Annalise sat down at the little play table and chairs in the corner of the family room, picking up her plastic teapot and looking at me hopefully.

Yikes. I couldn't tell her that Aunt Hadley's entire pelvic region was so sore it hurt to move, let alone sit on a tiny wooden chair.

What had felt like heaven on earth last night felt like I needed some Advil, ice and a nap this morning. Wes had fucked me like we were starring in a porno last night, showing me positions I wouldn't have even imagined. I'd had more orgasms with him than I'd had in monthslong relationships with other men.

I knew I should probably regret it and fret about how much it could complicate everything, but just couldn't bring myself to do it. It had felt too amazing. I was more relaxed right now than I'd been in a very long time. Wes had woken up the woman in me, and made me feel sexier than I ever had.

He was in the kitchen right now, feeding Benny his morning oatmeal and talking to him about the Mavericks' next game.

"Lars has been watching film and calculating odds, and he thinks McCoy is their best puck handler," he said. "He's not as showy as the rest, but he has a higher scoring percentage. So Uncle Wes has to keep the puck away from him, buddy. And he's a fast little fucker. I mean…I don't know, I can't even think of an appropriate word for you. The guy's a fast fucker and that's all there is to it. We'll have to explain that to Aunt Hadley. Here, let's wipe your chin off, my man."

I smiled, took a sip of my coffee and looked at Annalise.

"I have a great idea," I said. "Let's have a *big* tea party. At the big kitchen table. I'll make a fancy tea party dessert called crepes."

Her eyes widened and she jumped up from the play table. "Can I help?"

"Absolutely. And Uncle Wes is off today, so he can come to our tea party, too."

"And Benny!" she cried, running into the kitchen.

"Uncle Wes and Benny, would you like to come to our big tea party?"

I walked into the kitchen and set my coffee mug on the island, briefly meeting Wes's gaze. There was something new in his expression—straight-up lust. I'd known he was attracted to me before, but now that we'd actually done the deed, several times, he looked like he wanted me more than ever.

I wanted him, too. I didn't think I could actually, physically do it again tonight because I was so sore, but I wanted it.

I bent over to pick up the Goldfish crackers I'd accidentally sent flying last night when Wes had blown my mind on the kitchen island, groaning from the pain in my hips and thighs.

"Are you okay, Aunt Hadley?" Annalise asked, coming over to me.

"I'm okay, baby. Just a little sore from some new exercises I did."

I couldn't help it—I snuck a glance at Wes. He was smirking at me.

"Aunt Hadley needs to do more of those exercises and then they won't make her sore anymore," he said.

I smiled to myself as I gathered ingredients for crepes. Wes finished feeding Benny and then finished washing the dishes I'd been in the middle of last night when he got home.

"Your mommy and I used to make crepes all the time when we were in college," I told Annalise.

"I want her to come back," she said, her eyes wide and her lips turned down.

My heart hurt as I stopped what I was doing and pulled her into my arms. "I know, baby. And if there was any way for her to come back, she would."

"Doesn't she miss me and Benny?"

"I know your parents miss you with all their hearts. You and Benny were everything to them."

"But they can't come here ever again," she said sadly.

"No, they can't."

"Can we go to heaven and visit them?"

"I wish we could, but we can't."

I locked eyes with Wes, and he looked as gutted as I felt. I would have done anything to comfort Annalise, but I didn't know what would help. She pulled away from the hug.

"Do you want to pour and stir things for our crepes?"

She didn't respond, and when I brushed the dark curls back from her face I saw that she was crying. Her heartbreak made my throat tighten as tears filled my eyes.

"It's okay to cry," I told her, my voice breaking.

"Crying is for babies," she said, wiping her cheeks dry.

"Who told you that?"

She shrugged. "My dad used to say baseball guys were crybabies."

Wes came over and sat down next to Annalise.

"Those guys cry over pulled hamstrings, and that's totally different than this. When you have big feelings about your mom and dad, it's okay to cry."

"I cry, and I'm not a baby," I said.

"Me too," Wes added.

"I want my mommy and daddy," Annalise said, unshed tears pooling in her eyes. "I want them to come back home."

My tears spilled over as I said, "I wish they could, baby."

"Can we still have a tea party?" she asked.

"Absolutely."

Wes moved a kitchen chair over to the counter and Annalise stood on it to help me make crepes. I didn't bring up Lauren again, because I felt like I'd brought on her sadness before by mentioning her mother. I wanted to keep Ben and Lauren's memories alive for Annalise, but I didn't want to remind her of her loss. It was so hard to know what to say, and to find the perfect balance.

Wes approached to watch us work, running his palm over my back in soothing circles. I felt his unspoken message that we were doing our best and that was all we could do.

"Annalise, after our tea party I have something to show you," I said. "Something you're going to love."

"What?"

"Pictures from your birthday party. There's one of you and all the Avengers who came."

"Is Thor in it?"

"He is, and I have some of just you and Thor, too."

She grinned. "He's my best friend. I asked him if we could be best friends and he said yes."

"Wow," Wes said, brows arched. "You're the coolest four-year-old I know. I wish Thor would be my best friend."

We finished the crepes, complete with strawberries and whipped cream, and sat around the table eating them. I got out a few pieces of Lauren's wedding china, which made Annalise happy because it was a "real" tea party then. Wes and I drank coffee —lots of coffee to compensate for only getting a couple hours of sleep—and Annalise drank juice. Benny tried to eat his hands.

I couldn't take away Annalise's sadness, no matter how badly I wanted to. It was hard explaining to her that her parents were gone forever when it was a difficult concept for her young mind to understand. All I could do was the same thing Lauren and I had done for each other when one of us had a broken heart. Be there.

As the four of us sat at the table that morning, I thought about the polished, professional photo from the party that made us look like a family. A photo truly showing us as a family, though, would be of a moment like this—where we were laughing, crying and just *living*, together.

———

THAT NIGHT, I sat up in bed, woken from a deep sleep by Annalise sliding out of bed and running out of the bedroom.

Dazed, I slipped out of bed to follow her. Ben and Lauren's room had a bathroom in it, so I knew that wasn't where she was going.

I was so damn tired. Wes and I had chosen sex over sleep last night and then the day had been filled with laundry, grocery shopping and playing with the kids. By the time I'd fallen face-first into bed, I could hardly keep my eyes open. Wes was on Benny duty tonight and I'd been planning on nine blissful, uninterrupted hours of sleep.

When I found Annalise in the darkened family room, she was shaking her arms and wiggling around in a circle. I squinted, trying to get a better look at her.

Was she sleep walking? Sleep rain dancing?

"Hey, what's going on?" Wes whispered, walking into the room. "I heard you go downstairs and thought something might be wrong."

"I don't know. I followed her down here."

Wes flipped a light switch and Annalise grinned at us, still wiggling her booty and waving her arms. She was very much awake.

"What are you doing?" I asked her, yawning.

"You said Mommy and Daddy can get out of bed whenever they want and dance in heaven. I think they're dancing right now, and I wanted to dance with them."

My heart filled with emotion and I looked at Wes. I was so freaking tired, and I wanted to go back to bed so badly. But I couldn't make Annalise stop dancing. I was about to tell Wes he could go back to bed and I'd dance with Annalise when he spoke instead.

"If we're gonna have a dance party, we need some music."

He walked over to the digital control panel for Ben and Lauren's sound system, pushing a few buttons. I was expecting rock or alternative, but he surprised me.

"Build Me Up Buttercup" by The Foundations started and Wes danced over to Annalise.

"May I have this dance?"

She laughed and nodded, and he took both her hands in his and they swayed together. Then he spun her around, and I knew Ben had danced with his daughter when he was alive. She knew exactly what to do.

I joined them, though I wasn't much of a dancer. Wes, on the other hand, had *moves*. His rhythm was perfect and he was having fun with it. He gyrated his hips and kept his steps in time with the music as he danced over to me, and I laughed. In his white T-shirt and boxer briefs, with Annalise gazing at him adoringly, he was irresistible.

"The Way You Look Tonight" by Frank Sinatra came on next, and Wes put one arm around my waist and clasped our hands together with his other one, pulling our interlocked fingers up to his chest. His eyes locked on mine as we danced past the couch. Something about this moment was more inti-mate than the sex had been last night. It was exhila-rating and terrifying at the same time.

"Uncle Wes, dance me like that!" Annalise cried.

He winked at me before bending down to show

Annalise how to waltz. Her eyes shone with happiness as she danced and called out, "Look at us, Mommy and Daddy! We're dancing, too!"

I wiped my tears away quickly, not wanting her to think I was sad. Because while this moment was bittersweet, there was a lot more sweetness than bitterness.

The song ended, and "Let Love In" by the Goo Goo Dolls—Lauren's favorite—started up. We did a dance circle, Annalise's smile never fading. She was having the time of her life.

Song after song, we danced for nearly an hour before Annalise announced she was tired and wanted to go back to bed. We all got some water and headed back upstairs, Wes taking my hand outside the doorway of Ben and Lauren's room after Annalise had walked in.

He gave me a quick, chaste kiss and squeezed my hand, not saying a word.

I ignored the feelings building inside my chest as I crawled back into bed. I wasn't going to waste this precious chance to sleep by spending it overanalyzing. Sleep was too precious a commodity in this house.

CHAPTER FIFTEEN

WES

The end of the regular season was just a couple of weeks away as we hit the road at the end of March and the mood in the locker room was dismal. We were losing fifty percent of our games, both at home and away, and nothing anyone did seemed to work. I was trying my best but I was tired. I had to help out at home no matter how much I wanted and needed to rest, and though Tori was a big help, she was in school and couldn't work as many hours as we wanted her to. The solution would be to go through an agency and find someone who could work a full-time schedule, but a college student was more along the lines of what we wanted, instead of someone who would come in with agency rules and regulations.

Benny was sleeping better, thank God, but still

only about seven or eight hours at a stretch, which meant we were always up late and awake early. We tried to alternate nights so we each got a little sleep, but it didn't always work because Annalise refused to sleep in her own bed, which was also cutting into our sex life. We'd only had sex a couple of times since that first night and now I was gone again.

We'd lost again tonight, so we were a somber group as we filed off the bus back at the hotel. Tonight had been Detroit, tomorrow was Chicago, and then we had a day off to fly to Minnesota. We'd play Minnesota, Winnipeg, and Calgary before heading home for our final games of the season. The season that had started out so strong and had crashed and burned with Ben's death.

It pissed me off and broke my heart at the same time. We were a strong, solid team with tons of talent and the potential to go all the way but our hearts just weren't in it. I could accomplish many things both on the ice and in the locker room, but speeding up the grieving process wasn't one of them.

I was almost to the elevator when I heard raised voices behind me and I turned, frowning at Konstantin and one of the vets on the team, Keegan Miller. Keegan was a hothead who'd only been on the team a year, traded to us from Philly. He was kind of a dick, though he did his job on the ice, which was all I cared about. However, he'd just shoved Konstantin and though Konstantin wasn't a fighter or a tough guy, he looked pissed.

"*Yop tvayu mhat!*" Konstantin yelled, shoving Keegan back. *Fuck you.*

Shit. I didn't speak Russian but had been around enough players to know what that meant and I hurried in their direction just as Keegan caught Konstantin around the waist and slammed him against the wall.

"Hey!" I grabbed Keegan around the middle and Nash pulled Konstantin back.

"Fuck you, you fucking Commie!" Keegan was yelling, jerking out of my grasp. "You and your skanky whore should go back to Russia."

This time it was Konstantin who lunged and Lars grabbed him just before his fist could connect with Keegan's jaw.

"Watch your fucking mouth!" I snapped at Keegan. Then I turned to Konstantin. "Come on, man, this isn't you."

He pointed at Keegan and said something in Russian that none of us understood, his eyes burning into Keegan's.

"What's going on?" I demanded.

"None of your fucking business," Keegan said, picking up his bag.

"You made it my business when you started something here in the public lobby of our hotel." I had my hands on my hips.

"You know what?" Keegan gave me a disparaging look. "You're not the boss. I know you think you can replace Ben, but you can't. You don't have his class or presence in the locker room. Ask around—you don't have the respect and you're definitely not getting it from me. So instead of trying to play captain, why don't you focus on playing hockey and leave us the fuck alone the rest of the time?" He stalked off in the other direction.

"Keegan, what the fuck, man?" I called after him but he didn't turn around.

I looked around at the group of guys that had gathered and narrowed my eyes. "That true? You guys want me out as captain? Because I didn't ask for this."

A few guys looked away and my heart sank.

"I think this is not best time to discuss this," Lars said quietly, which surprised me since he rarely spoke up like that.

"You okay?" I looked to Konstantin but his face was red and he looked furious.

"This is not okay!" He pointed in the direction Keegan had gone. Then he went off in Russian again.

I waited for him to finish before saying, "I need you to tell me what happened."

"He and Svetlana..." His voice trailed off. "I cannot stay here. I must go." The elevator doors opened and he got inside, putting up a hand to stop one of the other guys from joining him. Then the doors closed and everyone looked at each other uncomfortably.

What the fuck had just happened?

I got up to the room and threw my bag down before ripping off my suit and stomping into the bathroom. I was equal parts furious and embarrassed, my heart thudding painfully against my chest. Did the guys resent me? Was it somehow my fault that we couldn't win to save our lives lately?

The letter Ben had left me addressed the important things, but it hadn't even touched upon hockey because that wasn't an area of my life where I struggled. He'd had advice about the kids, life, even Hadley, but nowhere did he have any words of wisdom about how to replicate his presence with the Mavericks.

With no answers readily available, I stretched out on the bed and dug my phone out of my pants pocket. I longed to hear Hadley's voice, to talk about the kids or her new baby food recipe, or anything but hockey. Because hockey sucked right now.

"Hey." She answered on the first ring.

"Hey." I sighed. "Kids asleep?"

"Yes. And, Annalise is in her own bed."

"Really?"

"I'm bribing her with a trip to the Disney store, but she needs to start transitioning back to her own room and I need a little privacy."

"Oh, really?" My voice got deep. "Why do you need privacy?"

"Don't tell anyone, but there's this really hot hockey player who sneaks into my room at night. I keep having to turn him away because of Annalise. But now, I might let him stay."

"Wow. Lucky guy."

We chuckled.

"So, another rough night," she said after a moment.

"Yeah. Even worse than you know."

"What do you mean?"

I told her what had happened in the lobby and she listened quietly.

"Do you think they resent me?" I asked when I was done.

"No. I don't know them the way you do, of course, but we spend time with a lot of them and I don't sense that at all. They all admire you and look up to you. Maybe there's one or two who don't, but that's to be expected, and I don't think I've ever seen Keegan at any of the events we've been to with the team."

"He's definitely a loner and I don't know what's going on with Svetlana."

"Oh." Hadley coughed. "I, uh, might be able to help with that. I'm not supposed to say anything because it's just gossip, but rumor has it that Svetlana is cheating on Konstantin with Keegan. Apparently, Keegan played in the KHL for a season after knee surgery and he and Svetlana were a thing. They broke up when he came back to the U.S. and she started dating Konstantin. Now something is happening."

"How do you know this?" I demanded.

"WAGs gossip mill."

The wives and girlfriends gossip mill was notorious for knowing everything, but this was bad. This was the last fucking thing we needed.

"In the future, telling me stuff like this could help me," I said quietly. "If I'd known, I might have been able to prevent tonight's altercation."

"Nina said gossip that isn't corroborated, especially when it's personal stuff, shouldn't be shared with you guys because distractions aren't good for the game. Especially with the season you're having."

"That might be true for other guys, but right now

I'm the captain, and as captain, I need to know that kind of thing."

"I'm sorry."

"Not your fault. You've only been in this world a few months. It's hard to navigate all the different channels of information."

"I'll be more aware and definitely won't keep any big secrets like that from you again."

"Thank you."

"I'm sorry this happened. I wish there was something I could do."

"Last time you asked what you could do, I wound up going down on you on the counter."

She chuckled. "Sadly, that's not an option tonight."

"No, but phone sex is."

"Is it?"

"Uh-huh. Take your clothes off, babe."

———

THE NEXT MORNING at breakfast I sat with Nash, Lars, and Drew. Keegan was with a couple of guys at another table and Konstantin hadn't yet come down, which worried me. Breakfast wasn't optional. We did meals as a team on the road, especially breakfast and dinner, and not showing up usually earned you some laps at the next practice.

"I knocked on his door before I came down," Drew said, "but he didn't answer."

"Listen, I heard some gossip," I said, repeating what Hadley had told me, though I didn't say it came from her.

"Christ." Nash shook his head. "That's not cool at all. You think it's true?"

"It would make sense." I looked at them. "Listen, I need to get a feel for what's going on. Do you guys agree that I'm not the right guy to be captain?"

Drew shook his head. "Fuck that. He was talking out his ass."

"No one contradicted him," I pointed out. "I mean, I'm not talking about you guys, but Ayres and Sully wouldn't even look me in the eye."

"Ayres is in the middle of a messy-as-fuck divorce," Nash said. "He hates everyone right now. Sully's a rookie and if I didn't know better, I'd think he has a crush on Keegan. He follows him around like a lost puppy. You can't look at them."

"But they're exactly who I have to look at," I said. "They're the ones I have to reach. If I can't, then I don't deserve to wear the C."

"Not everyone can be reached," Lars said,

speaking for the first time. "Sometimes, they must find their own way. This is not your job."

"Thanks." I smiled at him. "By the way, I understand you're taking my goddaughter out on a date."

Lars's ears turned red but he smiled. "Yes. We are going for the ice cream and…" He made a face. "Building of Bears?"

There was a moment of confusion and then Drew burst out laughing. "She's got you taking her to the Build-A-Bear store? Oh, man, you have a few credit cards, right?"

Lars looked completely blank. "Credit cards? Yes. I have many. Why?"

We cracked up as Drew tried to explain what kind of store it was and the mood lightened up considerably. I still felt like shit but at least there was a core group of guys who had my back. And not just mine, but Hadley's and the kids' too.

Konstantin wandered into the dining room about ten minutes before we were supposed to leave, grabbing a cup of coffee and a bagel off the buffet, but sitting by himself in the corner of the room. Keegan shot a few looks in his direction but seemed content to stay on his side of the restaurant.

This was my chance to talk with Konstantin. I didn't know what was going on and if the rumors about Svetlana were true, but I needed to try.

"Hey, man." I sank into the seat across from him.

He looked up, his face devoid of any emotion. "Good morning."

"Listen, I'm sorry about last night. It was hard to help with you talking in Russian…" I let my voice trail off, hoping he'd say something.

He nodded but was quiet for a bit. "Is okay. I was angry."

"If you need to talk, if something's going on, you can come to me."

"I ask for trade," he said abruptly. "I cannot stay."

"So it's true." I cleared my throat and met his gaze directly. "About Keegan and Svetlana?"

His mouth tightened with irritation as he nodded. "Yes. She say she cannot choose. She love both us."

I grimaced. "I'm sorry, man."

He mumbled in Russian under his breath.

"Have you talked to Coach about this?"

He shook his head. "Later. For now, I must control temper. Stay cool."

"I'll do my best to keep the two of you apart."

"I am sorry for being difficult. What he says about you, this is not true. You have much respect. Only Keegan does not."

"I appreciate you saying that. And hold off before

you talk to any other teams, okay? I'd rather we traded him, instead of you."

"Nothing will happen until summer, but my agent knows I wish to leave."

"Fuck, man, give me a little time to sort things out, okay? Like you said, nothing can happen until the season's over anyway."

He hesitated but then nodded. "My agent will look, but I will not sign anything until we talk."

Sonofabitch. That was the last thing I wanted. I had to talk to Coach sooner rather than later. Losing Konstantin would be devastating to the team. We needed his goaltending talent and his laid-back attitude in the locker room. I had to do something before things went from bad to worse.

CHAPTER SIXTEEN

HADLEY

My pulse pounded at the sound of the front door being closed, followed by the beeps of the home security system as Wes reset the alarm. He went to the kitchen, probably for a drink of water, and then I heard his feet on the stairs.

Soft thudding noises sounded on Benny's baby monitor as Wes went into the room to check on him, and then I heard the same in Annalise's room.

As he made his way into the master bedroom, I regretted my decision to wear nothing but a lacy red bra and panty set to bed. I was exposed, not just physically, but emotionally. If Wes was in a bad mood, which was likely after the way the team had played on the road trip and the tension he'd been dealing with between the players, I couldn't pretend I'd been sleeping.

This lingerie sent a clear message—I wanted sex. And if he didn't, I was going to feel rejected.

Wes walked into the bedroom and set his bags down, then walked over to the bed.

"Hey, you awake?" he whispered, sitting down on the edge of the bed and leaning close to get a look at my face.

I had the covers pulled up to my chin, so he wouldn't be able to see the sex trap I'd tried to set for him just yet.

"Yeah, I'm up. You can turn on the light."

He switched on the bedside lamp, and I could tell by his expression that he wasn't in a good mood.

Fuck. Why had I waxed, shaved, moisturized and put on brand-new lingerie? It was possible I could turn his mood from bad to good, but knowing he was cranky made me feel vulnerable, and I didn't like it.

Wes sighed heavily and said, "I need to be honest with you about something."

Oh shit. Shit, shit, shit. He was about to tell me that he'd slept with another woman on his road trip. I felt it in my bones. And here I was in lingerie. I was mortified.

"Okay," I said, steeling myself.

"Don't take this the wrong way, but…"

"Wes, it's fine," I said crisply. "You don't owe me anything."

He furrowed his brow. "I wanted to tell you that living in Ben and Lauren's house is hard for me."

Oh. That wasn't *at all* what I was expecting.

"It is?"

He nodded, looking both weary and guilty. "I'm trying so fucking hard to hold the team together and deal with all the bad press we're getting. I'm no Ben, though, and I never will be. I feel the weight of trying to take his place even though it's impossible. And then I have to come cook on his grill, walk past his study every day…sleep in his bed. I loved Ben, but living here, raising his kids and taking over as captain…it's making me feel like I'm trying to *be* Ben. And all I feel is inadequate. I miss my bed. I miss my goddamn couch. And I feel like an asshole for it."

I sat up, the covers forgotten. "You are *not* an asshole. But what are you saying? Is this only about the house, or is it about the kids, too?"

"It's the house. I love the kids. It was the right choice to move in here right after they died, and maybe the time isn't right yet, but…"

"You want to sell the house," I finished.

"Yeah. We're using their dishes and bath towels, and…I think a new house might be the best thing for all of us. We can stay in the school district Ben and Lauren wanted the kids in, but buy something that's ours instead of theirs."

His gaze wandered to my breasts as I said, "You mean, you'd buy it? Because I'm in no position to pay for half."

He waved a hand. "Money isn't an issue for us. I've got plenty, and we'll also have what we make from selling this house. But I wanted to ask you if you think it's the right move for the kids."

I considered the pros and cons, as well as the permanency of buying a house. "It's hard to say. I think there are going to be things that are tough for all of us, no matter when we do them. But I hear you on how you feel about living here."

"Does it feel that way for you at all?"

I shook my head. "It's kind of the opposite for me. When I'm using Lauren's hand mixer and writing things on her calendar, it reminds me of her. But I get you, Wes. It's a little morbid that we live here with all their stuff. I'd much rather have my own office than work in Ben's study forever."

His gaze was back on my breasts. "You look fucking spectacular in that bra, babe."

"Thanks."

He reached up and brushed his thumb over the

soft satin covering one of my nipples, sending a shiver from the tip of my spine to the base.

"We don't need to do anything right away on the house," he said. "But this boner you gave me by wearing that bra is fucking urgent."

My body heated in response to his hungry look as he stood and stripped off his dress shirt and the plain T-shirt beneath it. I hadn't just been angling for sex with Wes when he got home tonight, I'd been *dying* for it. It had taken more than an hour of bedtime stories to get Annalise to fall asleep in her bed tonight. I could now recite each word of the *Chicka Chicka Boom Boom* book verbatim.

Worth it, I thought as Wes dropped his pants and boxer briefs, his erection jutting out in front of him. He truly had a flawless body, all long lines and defined muscles.

He pulled the covers away from my body and took in the lingerie in its entirety. He laughed softly, raking his gaze up and down my body.

"Damn, baby. Ready to spread those legs?"

I smiled. "I am if you got your STD results back. Mine came in and I'm clean as a whistle."

"Yeah, I got mine, too—all good. I had the team doctor give me a note to prove it."

Laughing, I said, "You don't need to do that, Wes. I trust you."

Since I was on the pill, this meant no more condoms for us. I'd never say it out loud, but god was I looking forward to Wes coming inside me.

As he stroked himself, Wes looked at me and said, "I've been fantasizing about you constantly, babe."

"Really? Tell me more."

"I think about the way you look and sound when you come." He put a knee on the bed and moved closer, his hand sliding from my calf up to my thigh. "The way you look in a T-shirt that doesn't cover your whole ass—I fucking love seeing those curved ass cheeks. And I've been imagining what you'd look like on your knees with my cock in your gorgeous mouth."

The arousal swirling in my belly became mixed with worry and it must have shown on my face.

"What?" Wes asked.

"What?" I echoed.

"You just got a look on your face. If you don't like giving oral, it's okay. There are plenty of other things I like."

I licked my lips, nervous as I tried to decide how to respond.

"It's not that I don't like it...it's that I'm not good at it."

Wes arched his brows. "Not good at it?"

"So I've been told."

My cheeks burned with embarrassment. I'd been hoping he'd be balls deep in me by now, not asking for more details on my inadequate oral skills.

"Sounds like you've been with some whiny bitches, then," he said.

"I mean, I have, but…"

"Come here," he said, getting up from the bed.

I followed him, and when we were both standing, he put his hands on my waist and kissed me. It was soft and sensual, pulling me into the moment and taking me out of my head.

Pulling back slightly, he asked, "You want me to show you?"

"Show me? Are you going to suck a dick for me, Wes?"

He laughed and kissed me again. "Come here, smart-ass."

When he took my hand and led me over to the chair, upholstered in a dark green velvet material, in the corner, I smiled.

"Are you planning on sitting there?" I asked.

"Yep."

"I'm going to grab a towel. I helped Lauren pick out that chair and it took months. It was stupid expensive and I don't want ass stains on it."

"Jesus Christ, Hadley, my ass is clean."

"Yeah, but when you sit and things spread out… just let me get a towel."

He smiled and looked up at the ceiling, hands on his hips. "You better at least jog so I can see your tits and ass jiggling."

I complied with his request and grabbed a bath towel from the linen closet in the bathroom, unfolding it and placing it over the chair. Wes sat down, a smile playing on his lips and his eyes dark with desire as he said, "Get on your knees."

This was starting out hotter than my past oral experiences. Instead of forcing my head down to his crotch, Wes was telling me what he wanted, and it was surprisingly sexy.

When I was on my knees in front of him, he put a hand in my hair, his fingertips massaging my scalp.

"Play with me," he said in a low tone. "Tease me."

I hesitated a moment before leaning forward and licking the head of his cock, swirling my tongue around it gently. He groaned in response, his fingertips still rubbing my head.

"That's good, babe. Keep your lips over your teeth and keep things wet. If you do that, it's hard for anything to—oh, fuck yeah."

I'd gotten him wet with my mouth and then run my hand up and down his shaft. I tried it again, using both my mouth and my hand. From the sound of his labored breathing, I could tell he liked it.

"A little slower," he said in a coaxing tone. "Ah, that's perfect. Keep doing that."

It wasn't so much his words, but his groans and the way his hand would tighten in my hair that told me when I was doing something he liked. And once I was able to take nearly all of him in my mouth, and I picked up the pace, he started thrusting his hips slightly and groaning louder.

"Don't fucking stop...oh fuck...use your hand if you don't want me to come in your mouth, babe."

There was nothing I wanted more than for him to come in my mouth. He'd made me feel powerful and sexy, and I had a feeling I was enjoying this almost as much as he was. I continued, and soon I was rewarded with the taste of his release flooding my mouth.

He exhaled hard and his body went slack.

"Those other guys were fucking liars," he said, grinning. "That was incredible."

"You helped me make it good," I said, still feeling a surge of pride.

"Nah. Everyone should tell their partner what they like. It's what grown adults do. And I fucking loved that."

He took my face in his hands and kissed me.

Maybe he was right, and I just hadn't been with a real man before. I'd definitely never been with anyone who made me feel like he did.

"Now lie down and get ready to take it like a good girl," he said, standing up.

Holy shit. I considered myself a strong, independent woman, but when he commanded me in the bedroom, I always wanted to comply. It was nice to not have to be in control all the time.

He slid my panties down my legs and over my feet, tossing them on the floor before kissing his way up my thighs.

Good god, the man knew his way around a woman's body. He licked and sucked and stroked until I was on the edge, but stopped short of letting me come. Instead, he parted my legs and pushed his way inside me, both of us groaning with pleasure.

I bucked my hips beneath him, my body desperate for the release it knew was coming. I'd been thinking about this moment every night he was on the road.

I came quickly, burying my face in his shoulder to muffle my moans so as not to wake the kids. He was right behind me, his face freezing in an expression of complete ecstasy as he held himself inside me while he came.

"Is it me, or does it just keep getting better?" he asked, exhaling hard and lying down on his side.

"No, you're right."

"Think about all the great sex you missed out on by turning me down all those years ago," he said with a wink.

"But then I wouldn't have had the benefit of your extensive experience," I said, grinning.

"Uh-huh." He said, a small smirk on his face. "Want to take a shower?"

"Sure."

He got out of bed and went over to the chair in the corner, picking up the towel. "I'll just use my filthy ass towel to save on laundry," he said as he walked into the bathroom.

Practical *and* sexy. Wes was really starting to grow on me.

CHAPTER SEVENTEEN

WES

Despite how great things were going at home, things with the team were an absolute shit show. Keegan and Konstantin were constantly at each other's throats, we lost more often than not, and though I'd asked Coach if I could meet with him, he'd been putting me off. He surprised me after practice today, though, saying he wanted to see me in his office.

He sat down as soon as I closed the door and said, "What the fuck is happening in the locker room, Kirby?"

"There's a lot, Coach."

"As acting captain, it's your job to make it stop."

"I can't force them to grieve any faster, and this shit between Miller and Kon is heating up. Which is what I needed to talk to you about."

Coach narrowed his eyes. "Are you telling me you can't handle a little bickering between a couple of the boys?"

"It's more than bickering. Apparently, Keegan is sleeping with Kon's girlfriend."

Coach looked less than impressed. "This is what you were coming to me with? Jesus Christ, Kirby, what do you want me to do with that? When Ben came to me, it was all about the hockey."

"This *is* about hockey," I said calmly. "Kon is looking to get traded this summer, and frankly, I don't see how that's in the best interest of the team. We need Kon a hell of a lot more than we need Miller. If we lose him, the first line loses all its momentum."

"Let's be clear about something, Wes—right now, this team has no momentum. Not the first line, not the tenth line. And to be honest with you, I don't see you stepping up to change things."

"I'm trying, Coach. We're just way off-kilter and running out of time."

"Ben wouldn't have let this happen. Ben was able to motivate these guys to do better, and he would've handled this situation between Kon and Miller."

"I'm not Ben," I said quietly. "If I'm going to be captain, I have to do things my way, and my way was to come to you, tell you the situation, and let you know that we're going to lose Kon if we don't do something about Keegan. They're not going to just make nice and get past this. Svetlana is currently living with Kon and sleeping with Keegan. I don't have the power to change that; you and Levoie do." Mitch Levoie was our GM.

Coach looked up at the ceiling for a few seconds before fixing me with one of his steely gazes. "I need you to find a way to get through to them, son. Otherwise, we're going to lose more than Kon this summer."

Christ, was he threatening my place on the team?

"There's only a week left in the season. I don't know what I can do between now and then."

"I know." Coach suddenly seemed a little defeated. "We were having such a goddamn good season. I've never lost a player before. I've seen career-ending injuries, but not death, not like this. I don't know how the fuck we move forward."

"Maybe it's because we never said goodbye," I said slowly. "I mean, we talked about him in the locker room and had a moment of silence before that first game after the funeral, but we never said goodbye. The funeral was short and afterward, it was just family. Maybe we need to do something meaningful. A dinner, just the guys, a tribute to Ben. Tell our favorite stories, talk about who he was to us, give the guys a chance to say goodbye. I know I'm fucking haunted living in his house, using his stuff, sitting on his couch…" I cleared my throat. "I could set it up."

"The day before the last game of the season," Coach said quietly. "Instead of a morning skate the day of, we'll have a team dinner the night before. Maybe Giovanna's?"

"And let's invite support staff, you know? Trainers, all the coaches, equipment managers. We need something like this."

"It certainly can't hurt. Make the arrangements, and I'll get the staff on board."

"I'll text you the details once Vicenzo tells me if the back room is available."

Coach nodded and I was dismissed.

Now I just had to figure out how to get the guys to bond, while keeping Keegan and Konstantin apart, and maybe end the season on a high note.

I was so lost in thought I almost missed the snickering in the dressing room, where most of the guys were changing into street clothes. I glanced around and saw Lars leaning against his locker, a look of annoyance on his face.

"Was I supposed to say no?" he demanded. "She's just four."

Keegan was laughing so hard he was holding his stomach and there was a faint smile playing on Drew's lips. Everyone seemed to be focused on something on the floor and when I looked down, I almost laughed too. Lars's toenails were painted a bright, fire engine red. And it was absolutely ridiculous. Except Annalise had talked about nothing but her "date" with Thor for two days. She'd been happier than I'd seen her since her birthday, her eyes shining every time she picked up her hockey playing teddy bear that Lars had bought her at Build-A-Bear Workshop. I'd offered to pay him for what he'd spent, but he'd refused money from me, saying it was his pleasure to spend time with Annalise.

Apparently, despite the constant need to hold his hand, she didn't annoy him.

"You absolutely could have said no," I said out loud, almost daring anyone to contradict me. "But you didn't and you're a fucking rock star of an honorary uncle." I clapped him on the shoulder. "Thank you for being so good to Ben's daughter."

"She is my friend."

"You look like a fucking pansy-ass!" Keegan was still laughing, and Drew smacked him on the back of the head.

"Shut the fuck up. If my daughter asked me to paint my toenails, I wouldn't even hesitate."

"Yeah, well, not me. That's what her mom will be for."

"I like it." Lars shrugged and turned to pull on his jeans. At six foot six, and shoulders as wide as most doorways, no one would ever confuse him for a pansy, not even figuratively, and though I couldn't know for certain since he was a pretty private guy, my gut told me he had no issues with his masculinity.

"So do I," I told him. "And yeah, if she asked me to, I'd do it too."

"I bet it was an epic date," Nash said to Lars. "How much did you drop at that bear place?"

Lars didn't even turn around. "Two hundred fifty-seven dollars and thirty-eight cents."

I grimaced, wishing I could pay him back, but even if he'd take it, I'd never offer here in front of the guys. And they were all gaping at him.

"For a *teddy bear*?" Nash demanded, wide-eyed with surprise.

"You customize them," Drew said. "And you can buy accessories, like hats and stuff."

"I'm *never* having kids," Van said, shaking his head.

"And definitely not girls," Keegan muttered.

"I'm pretty sure you don't have much of a choice," Drew laughed.

"Isn't it true that if you do it doggy style, it's always a boy?"

"I think that's an old wives' tale," Drew said, "but I don't know for sure. Nina and I didn't care if we had boys or girls."

Luckily, conversation turned from Lars's toenails to sex positions and other things that had nothing to do with what was going on with the team. Though Lars either wasn't aware or simply didn't care when the guys picked on him, it bothered me. It was one of many things I wanted to find a way to address if I was captain next year. And now that was a big fucking if.

———

MY PHONE RANG when I was driving home from practice and I was surprised to see "Dad" on the screen. I only heard from my parents a few times a year, usually around the holidays, my birthday, or if they were somewhere close to where I was playing and they wanted to see me. Otherwise, I usually kept up with what they were doing and where they were via social media.

"Hey, Dad." I accepted the call through the hands-free Bluetooth speaker in the car.

"How's it going, son?"

"It's been a rough few months, as you can imagine."

"Are you still playing surrogate dad to Ben's kids?"

"Well, yeah. I'm not playing, though. He left custody of them to me."

"I thought he left custody to you and that friend of Lauren's, and the two of you needed to decide who would get final custody?"

"I'm not letting them go, Dad. They're part of me now. I don't know how else to explain it."

"Ben was your best friend. He would understand that you need to move on with your own life. How are you going to meet someone and have a family of your own with his brats tying you down?"

"They're not brats and they're not tying me down."

"What woman is going to want to marry you when she finds out you come with two kids that you're going to need her to take care of because you're always gone with hockey?"

"I don't know, Dad, but lots of people marry someone who already has kids from previous relationships."

"They're not even yours."

"Dad, come on, knock it off. I love Annalise and Benny. And they need me."

"Let Lauren's friend have them. Women are more cut out for that kind of thing anyway."

"Could you be any more sexist?"

"I'm a realist and sexism is reality."

"Can we not have this conversation? Things are going well, except for the damn team not playing for shit and Ben's parents suing us for custody."

"Jesus, that's your way out and you act like it's a nuisance."

"I don't want or need a way out. I'm happy."

There was a moment of silence before my father said, "Oh, for fuck's sake, are you sleeping with her? Please tell me you're being careful."

"Her name is Hadley," I said through gritted teeth, hands tightening on the steering wheel.

"Whatever. Does she know who your family is and how much money you're worth?"

"We've never talked about it, but I'm sure she does since she and Lauren were best friends. She's not after my money, Dad."

"How do you know?"

"I just do. Ben and Lauren wouldn't leave custody of their kids to someone like that."

"She might be a great surrogate mom, but that

doesn't mean she's not a gold digger. You used to be more careful than this, son."

"Dad, everything is fine. Hadley's a great woman. You'd like her."

"Liking her isn't the issue—your future is. It's time for you to think about settling down and it's not going to be with some wannabe journalist from New York."

"Dad, she's an editor for one of the biggest lifestyle magazines in the country. She's not a wannabe anything."

"Wannabe wife of a Kirby."

"You don't know that and, frankly, it's a little insulting, both to me and to her. I'm not an idiot and I've managed to avoid marrying a gold digger these past twenty-nine years, so I think I've got it under control."

My father snorted. "Just the fact that you're entertaining the thought of raising these kids makes me doubt everything you're doing. Why would you do this to yourself? Seriously, having a convenient piece in your bed isn't—"

"Okay, stop. That's not what this is and I never said I was sleeping with her."

"But you are, and we both know it. I'm trying to look out for you, son, since you obviously aren't thinking straight."

"I'm fine, Dad."

"Somehow, I doubt that. Anyway, your mother wants to say hello. Don't mention any of this to her, okay? It upsets her."

I resisted the urge to roll my eyes since no one would see it anyway.

CHAPTER EIGHTEEN

HADLEY

"That one is Mommy's favorite," Annalise said as I picked up a bottle of perfume from Lauren's bathroom vanity.

Miss Dior. She'd sent me a bottle of this perfume a few years ago, and I'd thought of her whenever I saw it sitting on my bathroom counter, or when I'd spritzed it on.

"Squirt it on you," Annalise said.

As I put Lauren's perfume on, I realized Wes was right. Living here and leaving everything as it was had been the best move for Annalise right after Ben and Lauren died. But we couldn't do it forever.

A couple weeks ago, Nina had told me she and Drew would come over and pack up Lauren and Ben's clothes and personal things whenever we were ready, and I'd thought I could never be ready. The things Lauren had left behind comforted me. I couldn't ever be her, or raise her children as well as she would have, but I could use her handwritten blueberry muffin recipe. I could bake those muffins in her muffin pans, and arrange them on her favorite stoneware platter.

But would I still be doing that six months from now? A year from now? Wes and I still hadn't had a decisive conversation about the future. In their will, Ben and Lauren had asked us to decide who would raise the kids, but that was an impossible decision. Wes and I both loved them dearly.

What had started out as scratching an itch—sleeping with Wes—was becoming something more for me. We were going out on a date tonight. Nash and Lars were coming over to babysit.

There were difficult decisions that had to be made—eventually. For now, I was getting ready for my date and spending time with Annalise.

"I look pretty," she said, admiring herself in the mirror.

I glanced at her and laughed. While I'd been concentrating on applying my fake eyelashes, she'd opened one of my eye shadow palettes and rubbed a dark green shade on her eyelids.

"You always look pretty," I said. "Makeup or not."

"Will Thor like it?"

I shook my head and laughed again. Annalise was developing a serious crush on Lars. She'd gotten her nails painted turquoise on their "date" and slept with her new stuffed bear every night.

"I think Thor prefers your natural look, baby," I said, putting makeup remover on a cotton pad and removing the eye shadow.

"You should wear a dress," she said as I finished putting on the rest of my makeup. "Mommy wore dresses when she went on dates with Daddy."

"I might. I have three outfits to try on, and one of them is a dress. I'm going to wear whichever one you like best."

"I love you, Aunt Hadley."

My heart melted. It was the first time she'd said that, and it moved me so much tears welled in my eyes.

"I love you, too, baby."

Her lips turned down in a frown.

"What's wrong?" I asked.

She looked away, not saying anything. I got down on my knees so I was at her level and asked again.

"What if you and Uncle Wes don't come back? Will Thor take care of me and Benny?"

It hit me all at once. Date night. Ben and Lauren had been on a date when a drunk driver hit their car. I closed my eyes, feeling like an asshole.

"We'll be back, Annalise," I said, holding her gaze. "We will. We'll just go out for dinner and then we'll come right back home."

"Mommy and Daddy didn't come back," she said softly.

"That was a terrible accident, and—" My voice caught, and I cleared my throat. "And it makes sense that you'd worry about the same thing happening to me and Uncle Wes. But you can call us while we're gone, as many times as you want, to make sure we're still okay."

She nodded, and I hugged her. My first instinct was to call off the date. To curl up in bed with Annalise and watch the Disney Channel where she could see me and know everything was okay.

I couldn't be with her all the time, though. It was brutally unfair for a four-year-old to worry about losing the people she loves, but it was Annalise's reality.

"Why don't you let me do your hair before it's time to leave? We'll do something really fancy." I said. "I can put some sparkly pins in it."

"Yes!"

She was excited as she sat on the stool in front of Lauren's vanity and watched me work. I pinned her curls up loosely and finished the updo with a bit of hairspray. After that, I tried on each outfit I'd considered for tonight, and she tried on three of her own dresses for me.

We went downstairs hand in hand. She was wearing a replica of the dress Anna wore in *Frozen* and I was wearing a little black dress that Annalise chose for me. I was a half hour late meeting Wes in the family room for the start of our date, but when I met his gaze, I saw he was smiling.

"My girls look spectacular," he murmured, kissing my cheek.

"Sorry I'm so late," I said in his ear. "She needed some girl time with me."

"It's all good," he said. "Nash is having a crawling race with Benny and Lars is picking up pizza."

I arched my brows in question. "A crawling race?"

"Yeah, and knowing him, he'll pull ahead at the finish line and trash talk Benny for being so slow."

Benny crawled everywhere these days. We had to keep him in his baby jumper or the playpen anytime we turned our backs for even a minute. Every day, he grew a little bigger and a little cuter, displaying his two bottom teeth when he smiled. When I combed his dark hair over to the side, he looked like a little man and all I wanted to do was snuggle with him. Now that he was crawling, though, he didn't like to be held long.

"There's your giraffe!" I heard Nash say from the dining room. "I'm gonna get it, Benny! That giraffe's gonna be mine if you don't pick it up, my dude."

I cringed, laughing, just as I heard Annalise chiming in from the other room.

"It's not fair to race him, Uncle Nash. He's a baby!"

Wes kissed my forehead. "Let's get out of here while we still can. We might want to leave Annalise in charge, though."

———

"I DIDN'T EVEN THINK about that," Wes said an hour later over drinks at a downtown St. Louis steak house. "Poor kid, worried she's going to lose us just like she lost her parents."

"It broke my heart. I did my best to reassure her."

He reached across the small table and took my hand. "I'm sure you did great. You're good at that stuff."

Wes was wearing dark gray dress pants and a light blue dress shirt, the shirt making his eyes look even bluer than usual. I remembered the first time we'd sat together at a nice restaurant—dinner with Ben and Lauren in New York five years ago. I'd considered him an irredeemable playboy back then, a guy who just wasn't that deep and never would be.

Everything was different now. I'd been forced to see the real Wes—the man beneath the facade. He was everything Lauren had always told me he was—hardworking, generous, and loyal.

"Have we changed?" I asked him.

"What do you mean?"

"We used to be like oil and water. I thought you were…well, you know what I thought."

He grins. "Yeah, you were never shy about making sure I knew."

"Was I…wrong?"

He laughed and squeezed my hand. "It was hard for you to even say those words, wasn't it?"

I smiled. "A little."

"You were both right and wrong. I was an asshole to you the first time we met—like I told you, I'd had too much to drink and I was used to hearing *yes* from women. I was a young professional athlete, and I enjoyed the hell out of all the perks. But I've never been a bad guy. I had some maturing to do—hell, I probably still do. I'm not letting you and the kids down, though. I'll never do that."

I tucked my hair behind my ear and took a sip of my wine.

He gave me a sheepish look. "No idea."

"You were right about me, too," I admitted. "About me being too uptight and not having a life. And about me being nothing like Lauren."

Wes's face turned down, his expression going from lighthearted to serious. "No, I was wrong about that, Hadley. You're a lot like Lauren."

"I'm not, though. Lauren was sweet and funny, and she made everything look effortless. She always made people feel good when she was with them."

"You make me feel really good," Wes said, his gaze loaded with meaning.

"I think most women have that effect on you in bed," I quipped.

"No, that's not what I mean. I'm talking about when you fold my laundry and don't say anything about me not doing it. When I get home from a road trip and see you left me a plate of dinner in the fridge. When everything with the team feels like shit and you're the only one I want to talk to about it. When I overhear you telling the kids stories about when they were born, and when you take such great care of them even though you're tired and stressed from your own job. You're a lot like Lauren."

My heart pounded and my eyes stayed locked with Wes's. I knew we were compatible in bed and we'd learned to get along, but what he'd just said to me felt like…more. And it felt good. It felt damn good. Other men had told me I was too harsh, too honest, too independent. Wes had been the first man to see the caring, nurturing woman I was deep down.

"Thank you," I said, looking away so he wouldn't see the tears threatening to spill over.

Wes smiled at his phone screen and turned it to face me. There was a picture Nash had sent of him, Lars, Benny and Annalise in the playroom. Nash was wearing a dark red wig and Lars, with a stone-faced expression, was getting his hair brushed by Annalise. She looked like she was having the time of her life.

"Oh." I smiled and put a palm on my chest. "I needed this night out so much, but I still miss them."

"Let's get dinner and then we can pick up stuff for ice cream sundaes and take it home."

"Really?"

Wes nodded. "I'd love to spend the entire night with you at the nearest hotel, but with Annalise worried we might not make it home, I think we need to keep our time out short."

My shoulders relaxed with relief, because I felt the same way.

"Excuse me, Wes Kirby?" a man said from beside our table. Wes looked over and the man continued. "I'm sorry to bother you, but my dad's a huge Mavericks fan. He's eighty-three years old and about to go into hospice. Could I get you to maybe write a short note to him?"

Wes smiled and said, "Sure, no problem. I wish I had a puck I could sign for him, but I don't have anything, even in the car."

"That's okay. Just a quick note signed by you will mean a lot to him."

Wes took the pen and paper the man held out and started writing. It hit me once again how very wrong I'd been about this man. And then I felt a pang, because I knew this was the moment when Lauren would say that she told me so.

CHAPTER NINETEEN
WES

The final game of the season was at home against Detroit. We'd wiped the floor with them earlier in the season, but tonight we were like a Little League baseball team playing their very first hockey game. That might have been a slight exaggeration, but damn, we looked awful out there.

Last night's bonding dinner had been a fucking disaster. It started out okay but halfway through dinner Svetlana showed up. She'd been drunk, crying, and out of control. Konstantin tried to calm her down and get her to take a cab home, but she'd resisted, making a huge scene. Then Keegan got involved. And things devolved faster than any of us could have predicted. Even Coach had tried to defuse the situation to no avail. Keegan threw a punch, Kon hit back, and Svetlana jumped in the middle. If we'd been anywhere but Giovanna's, the cops probably would have been called.

Thankfully, Vicenzo let us handle it, and between a handful of us, we'd separated Kon and Keegan, put Svetlana in a cab, and calmed everyone down. Keegan stormed off after Svetlana, though. We kept Kon at the restaurant, worried about what might happen if he and Keegan ran into each other again so soon.

The only good thing about the incident was that Coach finally understood how serious the situation was between Kon and Keegan, and had pulled me aside to tell me he would be talking to management about trading Keegan this summer. There was no way we could keep them both after what had happened, and at this point, Coach was over it. If we were honest, the whole team was, but everyone had tried to intervene without taking sides.

The end result was a horrible end to a tragic season, trades on the horizon for the off-season, and my own status on the team up in the air as well. Coach hadn't been happy with how I'd done as acting captain, and I couldn't blame him. It scared me, though. I didn't know what I'd do if I got traded. We were already talking about putting the house up for sale and buying something new, where we could all get a fresh start, but I wasn't planning on doing it in another city. Or god forbid, another country.

I brought it up that night in bed with Hadley. We'd made love a couple of times and she was soft and warm and sated, cuddled against me as we talked.

"You think you could get traded?" she asked in surprise.

"Coach is pissed about everything. The season, the vibe in the locker room, my captain skills, and of course, Kon and Keegan."

"Keegan's an asshole," she said. "Even if he's totally in love with Svetlana, they should have handled it better. He could have asked for a trade, or they could have kept it under wraps until the season was over. And why doesn't Kon just kick her out?"

I shrugged in the darkness. "I honestly don't know. I think he promised her father he'd take care of her or something like that, before he brought her to the U.S. with him."

"I think that promise should have been nullified once she cheated on him."

"Agreed."

"So…what would it mean if you got traded?" she asked after a moment.

I tightened my arms around her. "I don't know, babe. I mean, we're already talking about selling the house, so it would be a clean break for all of us, but if that happened, I don't know where we'd wind up." I paused. "Which includes Canada."

"Canada?" She stiffened a little. "I can't move to Canada, Wes. I mean…my boss is already freaking out about me being in St. Louis. She'll lose her mind if I move to another country."

"We have to talk about it, though. We can't just bury our heads in the sand because it'll happen this summer if it happens."

"Summer's a long way away."

"Six weeks, babe."

"Ugh." She nestled deeper into my chest. "I don't want to talk about that. We've had a stressful enough year and we're just settling into a routine."

"Yeah, but the season's over for us, which means we have to start talking about all the stressful stuff."

"Tonight?" she asked, tipping up her head and giving me a mischievous smile as she reached between my legs and wrapped her hand around my cock. It instantly sprang to attention and I kissed her, taking her mouth with deep, sensual pulls on her tongue until she climbed on top of me.

"We definitely don't have to talk anymore tonight," I whispered against her mouth, palming her ass.

"What should we do instead?" she teased,

running her hands over her breasts as she watched my face.

"You should let me fuck you until you can't walk and your pussy screams for mercy."

She licked her lips. "Now that sounds like something I'd want to talk about." She dipped her head to kiss me again. "If I wanted to talk."

"Mmhm." I lifted her by the hips and lowered her down on my cock, pushing deep inside of her. "What were you saying?"

"Fuuuuck."

———

THE NEXT COUPLE of days were nice. Cleaning out my locker and saying goodbye to the guys kind of sucked, but I knew I'd see most of them during the off-season, so it was kind of a relief not to have to worry about the Mavericks for a while. The kids kept us busy, Hadley and I were all over each other at night and a well-oiled machine during the day, and it felt like this was the first time I'd been able to breathe since that horrible night in January when we'd lost Ben and Lauren.

Hadley and I had agreed to table any serious conversations about the future until I'd had a chance to chat with my agent and find out what kind of interest there was for me in the hockey world. I was sure lots of teams would love to have me, but it had to be the right fit, both for my skills and personality, and my personal life. With Hadley and the kids in the mix, I couldn't just go anywhere. Sometimes it happened that way, but I had enough pull in the industry to have at least a little say in where I went unless the team planned to unload me to the first taker. I didn't think that would be the case, though. If anything, they were looking to dump Keegan as quickly and quietly as possible. My biggest hope was that when it all shook out, the core of the team would remain intact. Including me.

"Uncle Wes, Aunt Hadley's on the phone with the boss bitch and Benny's crying." Annalise marched into the kitchen with her hands on her hips.

"You know better than to use that word," I told her, mentally grimacing as I dried my hands. Hadley's boss had been on a tear lately, and we'd probably used the B-word a few too many times, but I had to nip it in the bud no matter how funny it was to hear that word coming out of Annalise's mouth.

"Sorry." She dipped her head and I reached down to tweak her nose.

"It's okay, Anna Peas. But don't let Aunt Hadley hear you use that word—she'll probably put you in the corner."

Her lips turned down. "I don't like the corner."

"I know you don't, so don't use that word."

"Okay."

I took the stairs two at a time to grab Benny, who'd been napping. I'd just finished putting the lunch dishes in the dishwasher while Hadley got on a conference call with the editorial team of the magazine, and I didn't want Benny's crying to reach her down in Ben's study.

"Hey, big guy." I lifted him and held him against my chest until he settled down. "Did you have a good nap?"

He nestled into the hollow of my shoulder and I put him on the changing table, grabbing a diaper so I could put a fresh one on him. I'd done this a lot the last few months, so it was second nature now, and it occurred to me that I'd fallen into the role of father to these kids a lot more easily than I'd thought I would. I didn't think about what I had to do anymore; I just did it. It was a hell of a lot simpler now that I didn't have to rush off to work every day, though, and I hoped Hadley didn't have to work until midnight again, like she had last night.

Her boss had been giving her shit about everything lately, and though she tried to hide it from me, I could tell it upset her. That was why I'd told her to do her thing this afternoon and I'd take over with the kids. Tori was off today so it was just me, Annalise, and Benny.

"When is Thor coming over?" Annalise asked me as we headed downstairs.

"I don't know," I said. "Maybe we can call him later."

"He said we could go to the park."

I smiled to myself, wondering if Lars really enjoyed her company or if he was just going along with it because he didn't know how to say no. At some point, I'd have to ask him because I didn't want him to resent me for getting him into this situation where a four-year-old demanded a lot of his time. He was young and single, so being at Annalise's beck and call probably cramped his style big-time. Although, it was hard to tell with Lars, since he kept his private life pretty private.

"Can I watch *Doc McStuffins*?" Annalise asked.

"Sure." I reached for the remote and turned on her favorite show just as my phone started to ring. I had Benny bouncing on my hip and I pulled it out of my pocket to see who it was.

Crap.

The lawyer.

I answered and then walked into the kitchen so Annalise wouldn't hear my conversation since she was nosy as hell and didn't miss a trick. "Hello?"

"Hey, Wes, it's Timothy Sutton."

"Hey, Tim. What's going on?"

"Ben's parents have filed an emergency motion to get temporary custody and the judge has agreed to hear it. The hearing is on Monday."

"Jesus Christ. What do you think? Are we in trouble?"

"I think you need to sit down."

"I thought you said the will as ironclad?" My heart sank.

"It is, but the problem is that you and Hadley have had three months to decide which of you is raising the kids, and so far you haven't, leaving the kids' future in limbo. The grandparents have made a case for them to move into the house to give the kids some stability while the two of you work it out. I don't know this judge, but I hear she's a huge kids' advocate, so it could go either way." He paused. "*Have* you decided which of you is going to raise the kids?"

I swallowed. "No. We...well, we've got a really great routine going and decided not to mess with it for now. I didn't think Patrick and Susan would do something like this. They're really starting to piss me off."

"Agreed, and with that in mind, I think we should meet. Are you and Hadley available tomorrow?"

"I am, and I'll see what Hadley can do with her schedule. Our nanny comes tomorrow so it should be okay."

"We could do it on the phone if need be, just let me know."

"I will. Thanks."

I disconnected and leaned against the island, nuzzling Benny's neck until he giggled.

There was no way in hell I was letting these kids go after the last three months, but my gut told me it wouldn't be easy to raise them without Hadley. The problem was that I didn't want to let *her* go either, and I had no idea how she would feel about that. Hell, I didn't even know how I felt about it.

We definitely had to find some time to talk.

CHAPTER TWENTY

HADLEY

"Sorry I'm late," I said, glancing at the clock as I sat down behind Ben's desk in his office and joined a Zoom meeting with Liz. "Benny spit up all over his clothes right as our nanny was getting here."

It was exactly four minutes after nine in the morning, and our one-on-one meeting had been scheduled for nine sharp. It shouldn't have been a big deal, but with Liz, there were no small deals.

"Jesus, Hadley, you look like shit."

She cringed at my appearance, and I unconsciously reached up to smooth out my hair. I'd had just enough time to wash my face, moisturize while brushing my teeth, run a brush through my hair and pull it back in a ponytail. The days of blowing out my hair, putting on a full face of makeup and thinking about what I wore to the office were in the past. Yoga pants and a T-shirt were my work uniform these days.

"Yeah, the only video meeting I have today is this one," I said to Liz, "so the natural look it is."

She sighed softly and said, "Is beauty even part of your life anymore?"

My lips parted with surprise. "What do you mean?"

"*Willow* is a lifestyle magazine, Hadley. A huge part of our focus is beauty. You used to come in bright and early every Monday morning raving about the new facial mask or flat iron you'd tried over the weekend."

I wanted to laugh, though I wasn't the least bit amused. When I worked in the office, I'd sat across from my boss's desk as she complained about women "letting themselves go" after they'd had children. I'd even agreed with her at times, and now, fate was showing me what it felt like to be on the receiving end of her vapid bullshit.

"Liz, you wore a baseball cap to our Zoom meeting a couple Friday mornings ago. Why does it matter if I have my hair done when it's just you and me?"

"I was going to a Mets game that afternoon, and I still had on makeup."

"Okay," I said, taking a deep breath. "Did you get

the pitch list I emailed you? I think there are several strong contenders for cover stories."

Liz lowered her brows. "I'm not ready to start the meeting yet. We also need to discuss the fact that you were *late*."

I wanted to slam my laptop screen down and take an extended break from Liz, but I'd worked hard over the past seven years at *Willow*, earning promotions in record time. I was the youngest associate editor the magazine had ever had and I wasn't going to let Liz's lack of interpersonal skills ruin everything for me.

"I was four minutes late, yes," I said. "And I'm sorry about that."

"Don't get snarky with me. I've bent over backward to help you since your friend died, but this isn't working, Hadley. You asked me if you could work remotely while you figured things out to move your friend's kids to New York. It's been three months. You're barely managing your workload. You're one of our best, and I don't want to let you go, but something has to give here. So when can I expect you back in the office?"

I fell against the back of Ben's cushy desk chair, so shocked I couldn't even breathe. "Let me go? Are you firing me?"

"I don't want it to come to that. But I do need you back in the office full time."

Full time. I wanted to laugh but this really wasn't funny. Before Lauren died, I was in the office by seven every morning, and I never left before six. Many nights I just ate dinner at my desk and stayed until I needed to go home, take a shower and get some sleep. Then I did it all again the next day. My weekends were always mine, but I worked a minimum of sixty hours a week Monday through Friday. How could I do that now? I'd never see Annalise and Benny.

There was also the issue of moving to New York. I didn't want to take the kids away from Wes. That had been my original plan, but the three months we'd been together had shown me how wrong I was. The kids adored Wes, and he loved them more than anything.

I needed Wes to get traded to New York. That was the only way I could keep my job and we could raise the kids together. We weren't ever going to be an official, mad-about-each-other couple or anything, but what we had going now was enough for me.

Probably. But that was the least of my worries right now.

"I have a court hearing this afternoon about the

kids," I told Liz. "I'll know more about my situation tomorrow. Can we talk about this then?"

"Sure." Her expression softened. "I want this to work out, Hadley. You're a real asset, but I just need a lot more of you than I'm getting right now."

I'd seen Liz use this approach with other women at *Willow*. She was both the good cop and the bad cop, depending on her mood and what suited her. I'd watched her drive women out of their jobs because they needed time to process the death of a parent or they were struggling with depression after a divorce.

If they can't keep up, no one can blame her for getting rid of them, I'd thought at the time.

But now it was me. I wanted to go back and apologize to all the women I hadn't stood up for and been more supportive of, but I couldn't do that right now, though. I was drowning in my own situation.

Wes and I were in danger of losing custody of the kids today. It was all I'd been able to think about since our meeting with the attorney. And while I'd been overwhelmed and completely out of my element when I'd started taking care of them, everything was different now.

I loved them. Not like before, as an auntie or a godmother who sent great gifts and played with them while visiting, but in a deeper, more authentic way I hadn't known possible. I knew which of

Benny's cries meant whether he was tired, hungry or having teething pain. I knew Annalise's favorite bedtime stories by heart. I'd always miss Lauren, but her children had filled the hole her loss left in my heart.

I couldn't lose them.

———

"It's chaos in that house," Susan said sadly from the witness stand. "Always so loud, and no home-cooked meals. Wes and Hadley work all the time. My husband and I have time to take care of our grand-children. And we're their family."

I tightened my death grip on Wes's hand, not letting my feelings show on my face. Inside, though, I was raging. Susan Whitmer was shameless, putting on a pathetic performance in an effort to overturn her own son and daughter-in-law's will.

"So it's a lack of stability you're concerned about?" Patrick and Susan's lawyer was asking all the right questions to paint Wes and I in a negative light. I wanted to punch him in the face.

"Yes, exactly. Wes and Hadley are just living in Ben and Lauren's house, with no plan for which of them is going to raise the children. Patrick and I don't know which of them will be taking the kids, or where they'll be taking them, or when they'll be doing it. We think the children need to be settled into their new normal as soon as possible."

I wanted to throw something at her, and from the tight set of Wes's jaw, I was pretty sure he felt the same way. She was being completely unfair. Three months isn't that much time when you're grieving and working and caring for children.

"And should you be granted temporary custody today, will you be taking the children back to your home in California?" Susan's attorney asked her.

"No, we'll stay in St. Louis for now, preferably at Ben and Lauren's home. We want to keep Annalise at her current preschool."

The whole hearing was an absolute nightmare. The effort Wes and I had made to create stability for the kids had been painted as self-serving by the Whitmers' attorney, suggesting that the reason we hadn't decided who would raise the kids was that neither of us wanted the responsibility. He'd shown the judge Wes's travel schedule, saying he could never be a full-time parent. Our attorney was flat-footed and unprepared, not countering any of the arguments made about me and Wes. He just kept saying Ben and Lauren's will should be upheld.

"This is a tough situation," the judge said after the closing arguments. "My heart goes out to all of you, due to the loss of your loved ones and your mutual concern for these children. And while this isn't an easy decision, I'm going to grant the petitioners' request for temporary custody. Mr. Kirby and Miss Ellis, your friends left you with a very difficult choice. You're going to have to make it, though. I want to reconvene in two weeks and see where we are then. Both of you, please take this time away from the children and each other to reflect on what would truly be best for them."

I turned to Wes, tears streaming down my cheeks. I was devastated and shocked. The smug expression on Susan Whitmer's face made my insides boil on Ben and Lauren's behalf.

Wes kept ahold of my hand as we walked out of the courtroom with our attorney.

"We'll be ready in two weeks," our attorney said, seeming to take the ruling in stride. "You guys make a decision about which of you will be the kids' guardian, and you'll get them back."

"But...two weeks," I managed to get out. "The kids haven't been away from us for more than a few hours at a time since their parents died."

"The grandparents have spent time with them, though. Listen, just take your two weeks and get this decision made. Everything will work out."

Wes spoke up, his eyes dark and his tone firm.

"Yeah, we'll be bringing in at least one more attorney on this case, and I expect your full cooperation with anyone else I hire."

"Mr. Kirby, I have extensive experience in these—"

"Your extensive experience didn't do shit for us back there, did it? I'm not taking any chances with the next hearing. I'll hire a dozen attorneys if I have to, and you'd better make helping them your full-time job."

Wes rubbed a hand over his jaw and tugged gently on my hand. "Let's get out of here; I can't lay eyes on Patrick and Susan right now."

We walked out of the courthouse in silence, and I was numb to everything around me. I didn't even remember where Wes had parked. I just let him lead me as I thought about the judge's words. Two weeks away from the kids. And Wes and I had to choose which of us would get them.

"What are we going to do?" I asked him, my heart hammering wildly.

He just exhaled deeply, shook his head and said nothing. It looked like he was feeling the same way I was—backed against a wall with a clock ticking, facing the most gut-wrenching situation life had ever handed me.

CHAPTER TWENTY-ONE
WES

I'd taken a load of our stuff over to my condo, but now that there wasn't much left to move out of Ben and Lauren's house, reality was hitting me hard. Hadley looked completely wrecked, her eyes puffy from crying, and every time I caught a glimpse of Susan, I reached a new level of disgust. I'd known the woman more than half my life but in this moment, I fucking hated her. And I knew with every fiber of my being that Ben would be furious with his mother right now. Hadley and I had been trying to give Ben's parents the benefit of the doubt because they had to be grieving, but this was a dick move, and the fact that the judge had fallen for it pissed me right the fuck off.

We hadn't had time to do anything but pack and

try to keep Annalise calm, so I had no idea what we were going to do, but the one thing I knew for sure was that I was going to use every goddamn resource at my disposal to beat them when we went back to court. I rarely called on my father for help in anything because I was a grown man with plenty of money and success, but this was different. My father was one of those men who often played dirty in business, one of the many reasons I'd distanced myself from him professionally, but this? This was right up his alley, and I didn't care what I had to do to make sure Annalise and Benny stayed with me. And Hadley.

"I don't want you to go!" Annalise stomped her foot for what had to be the dozenth time today since we'd told her we were moving out for two weeks. We'd said it was so she could spend time with her grandma and grandpa, but she wasn't buying it and wasn't happy at all.

"Grandma and Gramps have lots of fun things planned with you," I told her, squatting down so we were eye level.

"I don't like them." She stuck out her lower lip and tears filled her eyes.

Christ. I didn't know what to say or do.

"Don't be silly, sweetheart." Susan swooped in,

reaching for her, but Annalise shook her head vehemently as she moved closer to me and away from her grandmother.

"You're not nice," she said, scowling. "You always yell. I want Uncle Wes and Aunt Hadley."

"I'm sorry I've yelled at you," Susan said slowly, blowing out a breath. "But you have to learn to behave like a little lady. We'll work on it now that you'll be with us."

"No!" Annalise threw her sippy cup across the room and ran out of the kitchen.

"This is what you've taught her to do?" Susan asked, folding her arms. "Behavior like this is exactly the reason why we need custody of the kids."

"We're not the ones who yell all the time," I said, grabbing my protein powder out of the pantry.

"Of course not. You probably don't know the first thing about discipline."

I opened my mouth to respond but Hadley beat me to it.

"There are more ways to discipline a child than to yell," she said, eyeing the other woman. "Annalise knows if she behaves that way with us, she'll go right to the corner for a time-out."

"Time-out." Susan scoffed. "That's newfangled parenting, resulting in a generation of spoiled brats."

"They're not—" Hadley began.

"Forget it." I squeezed Hadley's arm as I interrupted her because this would escalate quickly if we let it, and we didn't want to do that in front of Annalise. "Let's just get out of here, okay?"

Hadley picked up the shopping bag she'd filled with a few of her own kitchen essentials, since she didn't want to leave them with Patrick and Susan, and grabbed her purse.

"It's better this way," Susan called after us. "You'll see that we're doing you a favor."

"Go to hell," I muttered under my breath as I shut the front door behind me.

We drove to my condo in two cars—me in my SUV and Hadley in Ben's Escalade—and I barely remembered getting there. My mind was a blur of images, switching back and forth from the judge's order to Susan's smug face to Annalise's crying fit this morning when we told her we had to leave for a while. God, I'd never yearned for Ben's counsel more than right now. What would he advise me to do if he were still here?

I had no fucking idea, and of course, none of this would be happening if he were still here.

"Hey, I'll come down and get the rest of your stuff," I called to Hadley as she pulled into my second parking spot. "Let's just get everything upstairs for now."

She hesitated but then nodded. She seemed as numb as I felt, but there hadn't been any time to talk. Annalise had clung to her leg most of the morning, and though Benny obviously had no idea what was going on, his little arms had been outstretched, his face screwed up in a scream as I kissed the top of his head before he'd gone down for his nap.

It fucking killed me just thinking about it.

"You want to just order in?" I asked Hadley when I got the last of her things inside.

"Sure. Okay." She nodded, looking around for a moment and then sinking into the couch.

"It's going to be okay," I told her. "I'm going to figure this out."

"Wes, I don't know what to do."

"I know." I sat beside her and pulled her into my chest. She resisted for a second but then relaxed into me, her body going limp, though the fingers of one hand had a death grip on my shirt. I stroked her hair and we just sat there, as if we suddenly had no purpose. No kids, no hockey, no nothing but the silence of my very quiet and sterile condo.

Had it always felt this way?

No. I'd loved my condo until all of this happened.

Hell, I hadn't even put it on the market because I wasn't sure what we were doing and I didn't want to live anywhere else if I wasn't going to be with Hadley and the kids. Except now everything had changed. I wanted to live in a big house with Hadley and the kids. I wanted to buy something new that she and I could make into a home, both for us and for them.

Fuck.

When had I started thinking this way?

"I'm kinda hungry," I said after a while. "Let me order something and I'll come right back."

"Okay." She looked so lost; I would have done anything to fix it. To make her smile again.

Instead, I ordered Chinese food from our favorite place and then sank back down next to her. I reached out my hand and she slowly placed hers in it.

"You okay?" I asked.

"No." She shook her head. "I still see Annalise's face, crying and calling for me. I feel like the worst human being on the planet right now."

"I'm so fucking pissed right now."

She didn't respond at first and when she finally turned her head, tears were puddled in her eyes, threatening to spill over any minute.

I reached out to brush them away with my thumbs. "What's wrong, baby?"

"Everything."

"We'll figure it out. I'm going to call my dad and if I get him involved with this custody battle, the Whitmers aren't going to know what hit them. I didn't want to bring in the big guns because they're mourning the loss of their son, but now that they're playing hardball, I'm going to double up our efforts too."

"You don't understand." She rubbed her eyes and sniffled.

"Talk to me."

"There's no we. It's all you now. Don't you see? I have to go back to New York or I'm going to lose my job. And once I'm back, I'll be working sixteen-hour days again, with no support system for the kids. The smarter choice—for the kids—is for you to take custody. You have the money to make sure they're okay, and you have your Mavericks family to help you. I have no one but a handful of worka-holic, single girlfriends who know less about kids than I do, and probably have even less free time than I do."

"But—" I started to protest but she put a gentle finger on my lips.

"This is about the kids. I want them, I love them, and I'll spend every moment of vacation I have being Aunt Hadley, coming to see them, talking to them on the phone…but on a day-to-day basis, you're the better choice, Wes. The writing's on the wall."

I stared at her, trying to understand what she was saying even as my gut churned with disbelief and frustration. Part of me agreed, because I did have more time than she did, even with as much as I traveled. But we were a team, dammit, and this thing between us was more than sex, no matter what it had started out as.

"Hadley." I put one of my hands on the side of her face, forcing her to look at me. "What about us?"

She blinked, and this time a single tear ran down the other side of her face. "I don't have time for an us. Not with the way my job is. Unless you got traded to New York…" Her voice trailed off.

The chances of that happening were slim to none and we both knew it.

"You don't have to work," I said after a moment. "I make millions of dollars a year and we also have everything Ben and Lauren left for the kids. We could make it work, and it would be—"

"You want me to quit?" she demanded, her eyes narrowing slightly.

"I don't *want* you to quit. I'm just saying you have the option."

"And I'd do what? Stay home and be the kids' full-time nanny?"

She looked pissed and I didn't understand what she was mad about.

"You could find a job that's less demanding, with a more understanding boss, someone who'd—"

"I've helped build *Willow* into what it is!" she snapped. "I own stock in the company. That's like me telling you it makes no difference what team you play for as long as you're playing hockey."

"It was just a suggestion, Hadley. I thought you and I—hold that thought." I cut myself off and shook my head because the buzzer sounded, indicating our dinner had arrived. I got up, signed the check, and grabbed the bag of food. I put it on the counter before going back into the living room.

Hadley got up and walked toward me, a look on her face I'd never seen before. "I think it's best if I head back to New York in the morning."

"You're going to just cut and run?" I demanded, staring at her.

"I'm not running. I'm just doing what's best for everyone. The deal was that we'd figure out who was better suited to have custody and that's obviously you. You have the money and the extended family to help, and I don't. Even if I had Ben and Lauren's money, I'd burn through all of it buying a compara- ble house in New York, private schools, full-time nannies, and so on. And I'd barely see them to boot.

At least you're around when you're not on the road, and you're off anywhere from three to five months in the summer, depending on whether you make the playoffs. So this is the mature, responsible thing to do. For the kids."

"And what about the *right* thing to do for us?" I asked.

She shook her head. "There isn't an us. *Us* was just a convenient fantasy while we were playing house. We bonded because of the kids, but we've never even liked each other. Nothing has really changed."

That one cut deep and I couldn't believe she'd said it. "How can you say that?"

"Even after all we've been through, you have no respect for who I am professionally and as an independent woman. The first words out of your mouth were for me to quit, as if I somehow need a man to ride in and take care of me, and that right there shows me that this thing between us would never work."

Ah, there she was. The Hadley of the past. The one who busted my balls about every damn thing even though she was full of shit. Because this thing between us wasn't just good, it was damn good, and she was throwing it—and me—away like I'd meant nothing to her.

I'm sorry, Ben, I thought to myself as I watched her turn her back and walk toward the kitchen. *I tried to make it work. I really did, buddy.*

This time, I wasn't taking any of the blame for what happened between us. This time, it was all on her. And it fucking gutted me.

CHAPTER TWENTY-TWO

HADLEY

I was finally back in the office at *Willow*, which was located in a suite of offices on the fourth floor of a downtown high-rise. My lips turned up in a small smile as I walked down the hallway to the break room and saw my reflection in a mirror hanging on the wall.

No makeup. Messy bun. Fuck you, Liz.

It was my first day back at work, and this was the last place I wanted to be. Since leaving St. Louis to come home, everything felt heavy and quiet. Since I had to end my lease on my studio apartment when I moved to St. Louis, I was staying in a hotel for now, and there was silence all the time. No baby coos or toddler belly laughs. No goofy questions from Annalise and no middle of the night wake-up cries from Benny.

And no Wes to hold me when I cried about all of it. Of all the days I should have chosen to put on some makeup, today called for it. There were dark circles lining my puffy eyes and I looked pale. I was emotionally spent, though, and I wasn't going to put on lipstick or mascara and doll myself up to give Liz the impression she'd won.

"Hadley!" my colleague Rona West said as I walked into the employee break room. "It's so good to see you."

I hugged her, squeezing my eyes closed and trying to imagine it was Wes. She was much smaller than him, though, and he didn't wear perfume laced with lemon notes.

"How are the kids?" she asked me.

"They're good."

I used my tone, and my lack of eye contact, to send her the message that I wasn't in a good place to talk about the kids. I was pretty sure I'd lose my shit and burst into tears if I did.

"Well, if there's anything I can do to help out, just let me know," she said softly. "Really, Hadley. My wife is traveling for work this week and the house is too quiet, so I'll be working a lot. If you need to get anything off your plate, just slide it onto mine."

"Thanks, I appreciate it."

"Hadley!"

Two more coworkers entered the room, one of them bearing two boxes filled with my favorite donuts to celebrate my return. When I opened it and the sweet, sugary scent wafted out, I smiled fully for the first time since leaving the kids.

"Ugh, those things are loaded with sugar," Liz said as she walked into the break room.

I grabbed a donut and took a huge bite out of it.

"Delicious," I said, looking right at my boss.

She held my gaze for a few seconds before saying, "Welcome back, Hadley. You're in the office across from mine now. And you can hit up the swag room for makeup if you want to make yourself look a little more presentable."

The office across from hers was smaller than the one I'd earned my way into two years ago, but that wasn't the reason it was the least favorite office of all the editors. Being across from Liz put you in her direct line of sight, and every time she was pissed off, which was often, whoever was in that office would take the brunt of her ire.

"Guess I'd better get started moving my stuff," I said.

"Oh, it's already done. Sierra moved into your old office last month."

I pursed my lips as I imagined the maintenance guy dumping the drawers filled with my personal items into boxes. And Liz hadn't even mentioned it until now.

Before, I would have been angry about something like this for weeks. I'd have gone straight into my office to line up drinks with coworkers tonight so I could vent about our reptilian boss.

But I didn't have it in me to care much anymore, though. My worries about Annalise and Benny were more important. Wes and I had told her we'd only be gone for two weeks. She didn't know that when I came back for the next hearing, I'd have to leave again soon after. Permanently.

At least they'd be with Wes instead of Susan and Patrick, but even that wasn't much of a consolation. The kids had started to feel like part of me, and Wes and I had become a team. I'd spent so many years hating him without really knowing him, and I wanted to make up for my mistakes.

I was facing the age-old dilemma of so many other women—not enough of me to go around. I wanted to be in St. Louis with Wes and the kids, but I also wanted to be here in New York hanging on to the job I'd worked so hard to get. Liz wouldn't be the executive editor here forever. I'd planned on getting her job when she left, and I'd be a very different kind of boss.

For now, though, I just had to survive. I went into

my new, windowless office and sat down behind the desk.

Forcing thoughts of the kids from my mind, I got my laptop out and opened my email, hoping to bury myself in work. The first day would be the hardest.

It turned out to be harder than I thought. I couldn't stop thinking about how I'd get to see the kids when I went back to St. Louis for the hearing, but not for long enough. I couldn't bear the thought of saying goodbye to them over and over, every time I visited and had to return to New York.

I wanted Wes. No one else could understand how I felt. I'd left him, though. I'd left him at a time when it wasn't just me hurting, but him, too.

The judge was right, though. What we were doing wouldn't have worked forever.

This whole thing was just fucked. Horrible. My chest ached and tears welled in my eyes as I wished I could talk things through with Lauren. I couldn't, though. I had a matter of days to make the biggest decision of my life—whether to quit my job and go back to St. Louis to be with the kids, and take a leap of faith that Wes wouldn't eventually crush my heart —and I was entirely alone in making it.

———

LATER THAT NIGHT, I walked into my vacant hotel room, a paper bag in hand with my dinner. I looked at photos on my phone as I ate the pastrami on rye.

There were photos of Annalise and me at a St. Louis museum, of Benny grinning at Wes while he made a funny face, of the four of us clowning around, and of the kids in their jammies right after bath time. If only I could reach into the photos and hug them.

For the first time since Ben and Lauren died, I kept scrolling until I found some pictures that included them. Tears pooled in my eyes as I saw a picture of all of us from this past Christmas, one of me, Lauren, Ben and Wes all wearing ugly sweaters. We were all so carefree that day, none of us having any idea what was about to happen. There was a photo of Annalise opening the Barbie Jeep Uncle Wes had gotten her, her eyes sparkling and her mouth wide with surprise.

I kept scrolling, letting the tears fall. There was a photo of Lauren holding Benny right after he was born, her smiling joyfully and him bundled up in a blanket with only his tiny face visible. I let out a small sob when I saw one she'd texted me one day of Ben sitting with Annalise at her play table for a tea party. She'd written that seeing her big husband sitting like that, his knees higher than the top of the table, made her want to jump him and make more babies immediately.

I wanted to talk to her so badly, even for a couple minutes. To hug her and ask her what I should do. I'd never be able to get advice from my best friend again, though. All I had were memories.

Memories, and also the letter the attorney had given me at the reading of the will, which I still hadn't been able to bring myself to open.

My heart pounded hard as I stood up and went over to one of my suitcases, where the letter was tucked safely into a side pocket. As much as it hurt to know the last words Lauren would ever say to me were inside the white envelope I held in my shaking hands, I needed Lauren more right now than ever before.

I took a deep breath, let it out slowly, and opened the sealed envelope, taking out the letter and sitting on the edge of the bed to read it.

DEAR HADLEY,

I HOPE you never have to read this. I hope someday, when we're both in our nineties and living our best lives as roommates in a nursing home, I can tell you about this letter and we can laugh about it together. Over margaritas, of course, because we'll still be living it up then.

This is so hard. I've been putting off writing this for so long because just thinking about it makes me cry. But I have to do it, so don't mind the tear stains on the pages.

If you're reading this, Ben and I are both dead. I usually cope with difficult conversations by using sarcasm, but this time, I've got nothing. Before Annalise was born, I would have had all the jokes. But now, the thought of her being alone in this world without her parents is too painful. It's unimaginable.

Ben and I want you and Wes to raise our baby girl, and any other kids we might have. I know it's a shock, and I'm sorry. We went back and forth a lot over whether we should ask you guys if you even want to do it, but we come back to the same decision every time—it has to be you guys. We can't risk you guys trying to talk us out of it, because the next option is Ben's parents, and we don't want that.

If our babies can't have me and Ben, we want them to have you guys. I know you and Wes don't get along and you're probably reeling as you read this, wondering how this could ever work. But it will, Hadley. It will. Ben and I know the two of you better than anyone.

You're a lot like Ben. Practical and organized. Devoted, caring and hardworking. You're also a nurturer, even though you probably don't think so. You're like me in that way, but mostly, I'm like Wes. I let the little stuff go. I love to laugh and I don't take things too seriously unless I have to. I take chances. Like Ben and I, you and Wes balance each other out.

Maybe one of you is married by now. Maybe both of you are. Maybe you have kids of your own. I would actually love for my kids to have other kids to grow up with. Ben and I wanted to give you and Wes room to decide which of you would be best for the kids, if it comes to that. But as crazy as it sounds, my gut tells me you guys can find a way to do it together. It's such a huge thing to ask of you both. But I'd do it for you, in a heartbeat, and Ben would do it for Wes. We love the two of you and you're our family.

Don't feel like you have to try to replace me. I want you to raise my kids because you're you, not me. Love them your way. Don't quit your job and take up organic gardening unless you truly want to. You are a wonderful role model exactly as you are. Don't be too hard on Wes. He's a great guy, and I hope you get a chance to see why Ben and I love him so much.

Read to my kids. There's a box in the basement of all my favorite childhood books. Please read all of them with my babies and tell them how much those books meant to their mommy. Snuggle them often. Cheer them on and remind them that everyone makes mistakes. Just love them and try to help them know who their parents were and how much we love them.

I can't keep writing, I'm crying so hard I've given myself a headache. Just know that I love you and Wes so dearly, and I know our daughter and any other children we might have are in the best hands.

Lauren

I READ the letter three times before folding it up and placing it back in the envelope. I walked into the bathroom to wash the tears from my cheeks and as I looked at my reflection in the mirror, eyes puffy and hair escaping from my ponytail, I felt more lost than ever. I'd let Lauren down. Her babies needed me, and when things had gotten hard, I'd run back to New York, convincing myself there was no other way.

I couldn't have it all. I had to make a choice—my career at *Willow*, or the kids and the possibility of a relationship with Wes. And I had to make that choice now.

CHAPTER TWENTY-THREE

WES

South Beach was a fucking shit show. Even on a Monday night in early May, the streets, restaurants, and hotels were packed. My parents had flown in to spend a few weeks at their condo there and with nothing to do in St. Louis, I'd flown down to join them. I hadn't seen them in over a year since they'd spent the holidays in Europe last year, and it had been nice catching up for a couple of days.

I was over it now, though. My mother was pulling out all the stops to find me a wife, calling pretty much everyone she knew with an eligible daughter that might pique my interest. It was like a revolving door of debutantes, parading past my lounger at the pool, stopping by our dinner table at restaurants, and even dropping by unannounced at my parents' condo. At first, I hadn't realized what was going on since my parents had a lot of friends here, but I'd finally caught on and now I was just annoyed and resigned.

"Seriously, Mom, enough," I told her, after yet another potential future Mrs. Kirby stopped by our table at lunch.

"Really? Not even Rosalie?" she asked in disappointment, daintily dabbing her lips with her napkin. "She graduated from Yale, has a degree in engineering, and is going to be on three European magazine covers next month. What more could you possibly want? Brains, money, and beauty?"

I sighed. "The last thing I want right now is a woman."

Dad arched his brows. "Is there something you need to tell us?"

It took me a second, but then I realized what he meant and chuckled. "No, Dad. I'm still straight. What I meant was, I have feelings for someone else and another woman isn't going to make those feelings go away. Not this soon anyway."

"Hadley." Mom fixed me with a look. "All right, it appears we've missed quite a bit over the last several months. Why don't you catch us up on exactly what's been happening since losing Ben and Lauren." My parents had known Ben almost as well as his parents knew me.

"It started out sad and overwhelming and hard as fuck," I said, staring out at the busy street. "It turned into a family, with two people who adore those babies and potentially each other. Then fucking Patrick and Susan stepped in trying to make us look bad, got temporary custody of the kids, and ruined fucking everything."

"That's a lot of fucking for so few sentences," Mom said, chuckling. "So you're upset about losing the kids. Do you really want to go back to that kind of responsibility? Seems to me this was your out."

"I don't want or need an out," I growled. "I love those kids and I'm falling hard for Hadley too. I need them and they need me."

"You're sure?" Dad gave me a stern look.

"Yes!" I threw up my hands. "What do you want me to do to prove it, sacrifice a virgin to the gods?"

Dad smiled. "Not necessary. But if this is what you want, I don't understand what you're doing in Florida then."

"What do you mean? The judge gave them temporary custody and—"

"What I mean is, you're a Kirby. *My* son. You have both your own wealth as well as money in a trust from us. Why aren't you using your resources to put those people in their place?"

"I hired an attorney with a fantastic reputation

for family law and he didn't do shit," I protested. "I don't know how this happened."

"Technically, you and Hadley were supposed to decide which of you was getting the kids," Mom reminded me. "I'm guessing the judge wanted to light a fire under the two of you to make that decision."

"She's decided to go back to New York," I admitted quietly. "And I let her go because her career is important to her."

"What does she do?" Mom asked.

"She's an editor at *Willow*—"

"*Willow?!*" Mom exclaimed. "That's one of my favorite magazines! I didn't realize she was part of it."

"Yeah, and she's busted her ass to get where she is, but she couldn't keep working remotely from St. Louis. She had to make a choice and I guess the judge made it for her."

"I thought you were a couple now?" Dad asked in confusion. "Or was that just convenience?"

I scratched my chin. "It's a gray area. I thought we were getting somewhere with it, too. We'd just gotten to a point where things felt...serious. Then shit hit the fan. I don't know what to do at this point."

"Have you told her how you feel?" Dad asked pointedly.

"Well, no, but—"

"Did you really expect a successful young woman like that to give up everything without some kind of promise? A proclamation of love, a ring, *something* to let her know you're serious?" My father looked equal parts amused and annoyed.

I gave him a dirty look. "Last time we talked, you were telling me to forget the gold-digging wannabe journalist and walk away."

"Well, I hadn't checked her out yet then."

I stared at him, dumbfounded. "You did a background check on Hadley?"

"Of course. Once I realized you were serious about this whole situation, I needed to make sure she was what you thought she was."

"And?" I asked dryly. There was no point being pissed; what was done was done.

"There were no red flags. She has no criminal record, no bankruptcies, no messy or public entanglements or affairs, her bank account is modest but respectable and—"

"Ugh. Stop." I held up a hand. "Thanks. I know why you did it, but I don't want to know anything else. It feels dirty."

"That's your problem, son. You don't know the

difference between dirty and important. I didn't hurt her. I merely made sure she wasn't hiding anything that could hurt *you*. And now you need to grow a pair and take on the Whitmers the way Ben and I would want you to—you're not out to hurt them, but you're going to get those kids. Do you want me to get the ball rolling?"

I looked him right in the eyes without an ounce of hesitation. "Yes."

He smiled. "Watch and learn, son. Watch and learn." He picked up his phone and sent someone a text. "We'll have a handle on this by supper."

It was almost comical to see my dad at work. It wasn't that I couldn't handle what was going on with the custody battle, but simply that I didn't operate in the world of cutthroat business like he did. He chewed entire corporations up and spit them out before breakfast most days, and that just wasn't me, so I tended to do things my way. However, for Annalise and Benny, I was more than willing to let him do some of the heavy lifting.

"And while your dad is handling the custody situation," Mom said to me, "you're going to have to figure out what you want with Hadley."

"I want custody of the kids," I responded automatically. "Once I've taken care of that, I'll work on getting Hadley back."

"Multitasking, son," Dad chuckled. "It's a skill you need in business and in life."

"Wesley!" A tall, stacked brunette with dark red lips and long red fingernails came running in my direction.

Fuuuuuck. I'd hooked up with her a couple of years ago when I was visiting my folks, but now I didn't even remember her name.

"Heyyyy..." I held out a hand to her to try and head her off but she wasn't having it, throwing her arms around my neck and kissing the side of my face.

"Dolores." Mom gave her a cold smile. "It's good to see you, dear, but we're in the middle of lunch."

"Wesley, you're here and you *didn't call*." She was still clinging to my neck.

"It's Weston," I said, giving my mother a pleading look.

"Dolores, I think you're choking him," Mom said. "Now go on back to your table so we can eat, and you and Wes can talk later."

"I'll call you in an hour!" Dolores said, pressing her lips to mine, though I turned my head at the last minute, so she caught the corner of my mouth instead.

"That girl." Mom shook her head. "I'm going to

have a word with her mother. Dolores is a grown woman, but she acts like a teenager."

"This is your fault," I grumbled. "You had to put the word out that I was in the market."

"Well, how was I to know you'd fallen for this friend of Lauren's? You have to tell me these things, Weston."

Technically, I didn't, but I wasn't going to point that out.

———

I SPOKE to two different lawyers the next day. One was my father's personal attorney who handled everything my father dealt with outside his business dealings, and then a woman he handpicked to handle this for me. Her name was Regina Rittenhouse and when I looked her up online, she was badass. We spent several hours on the phone getting her up to speed on the case and then I had Tim email her copies of everything from the will to the temporary custody agreement.

"This shouldn't be a big problem," Regina said after she'd reviewed everything. "I don't see any reason for the judge to go against the parents' wishes, but you do need to be clear that you're taking custody and that Hadley is on board."

"I'll call her today," I said, though the thought made me cringe a little. We hadn't spoken since she'd been back in New York beyond a text telling me she'd arrived okay and then a subsequent one with a funny and insulting meme directed at Liz. That had been the last time, though, and then I'd traveled to Miami so I hadn't had anything to text her about anyway.

"I think it's important that Hadley come to the next hearing, so the judge understands that this is all on the up-and-up and not you pulling a fast one to get custody back."

"That's Monday, right?" I asked, opening the calendar program on my phone since she was on speaker.

"Yes. I'll fly in from Chicago that morning and we can meet at Mr. Sutton's office since we're working together on this."

"Technically, you're in charge."

"He understands that," she said. "Don't worry, just leave it all to me."

"No offense, Ms. Rittenhouse, but I left it all to Tim Sutton and this is where it got me."

"Yes, but Mr. Sutton is not me, and believe me, when you get my bill, you'll understand why it's so high."

I chuckled. "I'm kind of looking forward to it."

"Excellent. See you Monday. If there's any issue with Hadley being there, let me know immediately, because that changes my strategy."

"I'll call her now." I disconnected and had just switched to the screen with my "favorites," where the people I called most often were listed, when my phone alerted me I had another call coming in.

Susan Whitmer.

Fuck me.

I took a deep breath before answering, hoping my voice didn't reflect my irritation. "Hello, Susan."

"Wes!" She sounded frantic. "Where's Annalise? Do you have her?!"

"What are you talking about?" I demanded. "Of course, I don't have her. I'm on vacation in Miami."

"Do you swear?" She sounded like she was about to cry. "If you have her, just say so because I'm on the verge of a heart attack."

"Susan, I'm in Miami with my parents. Annalise is supposed to be in St. Louis with you. What the fuck is going on?!"

"She's gone, Wes! We thought she was playing hide and seek or something, and now it's been hours and we've looked everywhere and all I could hope was that you took her…"

"No, I didn't fucking take her." My own heart rate

had just kicked up to full speed. "Tell me exactly what happened."

"She's been…difficult." Susan took a breath. "Asking for you and Hadley constantly, all day, every day. She doesn't do anything I say, won't eat what I prepare, and it's been a challenge. This morning she threw her bowl of oatmeal across the room so I…put her in the corner." She took a shaky breath. "I told her it would be fifteen minutes. That's what it said online for her age. I looked it up after you and Hadley—"

"Susan!" I took a breath. "Focus."

"I, I'm sorry. So Patrick went to the store for me and I went upstairs to get Benny and when I came down she was gone. I thought she was just being naughty, so I didn't chase her right away. I figured she was in her room playing and maybe it would give us both time to calm down. It was probably half an hour before I went looking for her. Patrick and I were going to sit her down, talk to her, and then we couldn't find her."

"How long has she been gone?" I demanded.

"Four hours."

"Have you called the police?!"

"N-no…I truly thought she'd called you and you had come and picked her up, just to frighten us or make us angry or something. You really don't have her?"

"You want to talk to my mother?" I yelled. "Jesus fucking Christ, no, I don't have her!" I was so loud my mother came running into the room, looking at me worriedly.

Susan burst into tears.

The next few minutes were chaotic as I disconnected with her and immediately called Nash to get the local guys on the job of scouring the neighborhood for her, as well as Britney since it was likely Annalise would go to her if she was lost or scared.

I called Hadley on the way to the airport.

"Wes." She sounded surprised and exhausted.

"Annalise is missing," I said abruptly.

"What?"

I told her what had happened.

"Are you kidding me? They fucking lost her?" Hadley sounded about as furious as I was.

"I'm on my way to the airport. I got a last-minute seat on a flight, but it'll still be hours before I get home."

"I'll meet you there."

"I'll be at the airport in a couple of minutes," I said, "so it might be easier for me to book it for you in person with a ticket agent since they'll see openings right away."

"I'm going to leave for the airport now."

"I'll call you back."

I disconnected and stared out at the city, but I didn't see anything. All I heard was Ben's voice in my head.

"Find her, Wes. Find my baby girl."

CHAPTER TWENTY-FOUR

HADLEY

I sighed with relief as the plane touched the runway, jolting slightly. Finally, I'd made it to St. Louis.

"Good luck, Hadley," the woman sitting next to me said, squeezing my hand.

Her name was Netta and she was a very kind mother of five and grandmother of twelve. When she'd noticed I was crying as the flight took off, she'd asked me what was wrong.

I'd spent the next hour telling her everything, starting with meeting Wes seven years ago at Ben and Lauren's engagement party and ending with returning to New York just over a week ago. Netta had listened to every word, peering at me intently over the rims of her glasses.

"Wait, hold up, Susan said *what?*" she'd cried

when I'd told her about the court hearing. "Aw, hell no. That's not okay."

Waiting for the pilot to taxi all the way down to our gate and come to a complete stop was painful. I wanted to jump out of my seat and run for the door. All I could think about was Annalise. Was she safe? Had someone hurt her? Just the thought made my chest tighten and my stomach clench.

I was never leaving the kids again. I'd move to St. Louis to be with them. Maybe I'd end up hurt and whatever Wes and I had been building before I left for New York wouldn't work out, but I'd risk it. I knew before getting Wes's frantic phone call that I'd never be happy in New York again. He and the kids were my world now.

What I hadn't been able to work out, though, was whether I could sacrifice the career I'd worked so hard for. But the moment I found out Annalise was missing my decision had been made. I wanted to be with the kids and Wes, no matter the cost, because no job was worth losing time with them.

"Excuse me!" Netta called to a flight attendant as everyone started unbuckling their seat belts. "We have an emergency here. This young woman needs to be the first person off this plane; she has a missing child."

The flight attendant looked at me and frowned

sympathetically, then gestured for me to get up from my seat.

"Thank you so much," I said to the flight attendant before looking back at Netta over my shoulder.

"You message me on Facebook and tell me when you've got your little girl back," she said. "I'll be praying for her."

I nodded and said, "Thanks, Netta, for everything."

The flight attendant led me to the airplane door, and as soon as she could open it, I sprinted down the jet bridge and exited into the airport. I had nothing but my purse—I'd gone straight to the airport after getting Wes's call.

Wes had been able to get the ticket agent to book me on a flight from JKF to O'Hare, and then a connecting flight nearly two hours later from O'Hare to St. Louis. Wes had texted me that his parents got him a direct flight on a private plane some friends of theirs owned; he was already at Ben and Lauren's house talking to the police.

As I walked to the airport exit, I opened my phone and ordered an Uber. The driver arrived quickly and we got to the house in less than twenty minutes. I yelled out my thanks as I bolted from the car.

I walked through the front door and immediately

scanned the entryway and sitting room in search of Wes. A couple of his teammates were there, and several people I didn't recognize. Nina was holding Benny.

The moment my eyes found Wes's, I flew across the room and into his arms. His embrace was exactly what I needed. He held me tightly as he spoke in my ear.

"We've got lots of people out searching for her. Patrick and Susan are out looking, and a bunch of the guys. Lots of neighbors, too."

Tears pooled in my eyes as I pulled back and looked at him, holding on to his wrists. "It's been so long. She's so little. I can't stop thinking about—"

"I know." Wes kissed my forehead. "But we have to focus on searching. Keep your mind on that."

"I want to go look for her."

He nodded. "We'll go together. Just let me finish up with the police officer I was talking to."

I hesitated for a second before saying, "I shouldn't have left, Wes."

His expression softened. "This didn't happen because you weren't here. This is all on Susan and Patrick; they were supposed to be keeping the kids safe."

"No, I know. What I mean is…not because of what's going on, but…I wish I hadn't left."

He held my gaze, searching out if I meant it or not, and said, "It's okay, Hadley. We're gonna be okay."

I nodded, unable to talk past the lump in my throat. I wanted us to be okay so badly, but it couldn't happen until Annalise was safely home with us again. How had I ever thought any job was more important than being with her and Benny?

"Let's go," Wes said, taking my hand and leading me across the room.

He led the way out of the house to the rental car he'd gotten at the airport—a minivan, which was parked on the curb. I gave him a confused look.

"It was all they had so I took it," he said.

We got in and drove to a neighborhood a few miles away that other searchers hadn't gotten to yet, my hands clutched together in my lap the whole way.

"I need her to be okay," I said softly. "She has to be okay."

Wes parked the car and we split up, him on one side of the street and me on the other. I tried not to think about how close we were getting to sunset as I called out Annalise's name and walked up random driveways to look in people's backyards.

I said a silent prayer that Annalise was safe. Everything I'd ever considered a problem paled in comparison to this. Why had I been so stupid about things with me and Wes? We were happy. We were doing well with the kids. Whether we told the judge it was me or him raising the kids, we could still do it our way. We just needed a chance.

"Hadley!"

I turned at the sound of Wes calling my name, my heart pounding in hopeful anticipation. He wouldn't yell for me so urgently unless…

"You found her?" I cried as I ran toward him.

He moved his phone away from his mouth. "Not me. Nash did, though." I dropped to my knees on the sidewalk, sobbing with relief as Wes went back to the phone call. "Yeah, text me the address and call that police officer. Stay with her. Thank you so much, man."

Wes helped me up and we both ran to the minivan.

"She's okay?" I asked him as he started the car and pulled away from the curb.

"Yeah, she's good. Nash found her at a park about three miles from the house. She was sitting on a bench with an older guy, petting his dog."

"Oh my god." I shook my head. "Three miles? How did she even make it that far? I'm never leaving the kids with Patrick and Susan, Wes. Never again. They can have me arrested if they want."

He patted my knee. "Let's get to Annalise. We'll deal with them later."

We got to the park and Wes dropped me off by the playground, where Nash said he and Annalise would be waiting. I spotted them sitting at a picnic table, eating snow cones, and I rushed toward them.

"Aunt Hadley!" Annalise cried as I got close.

She passed her snow cone to Nash and got up from the table, running to greet me. I swept her into my arms and held her tightly, crying with relief.

"I got lost," she said in a tiny voice. "Am I in trouble?"

"No, baby." I pulled back and cupped her face in my hands. "You're not in any trouble. I'm just so glad you're safe. That's all that matters."

"Uncle Wes!" she cried, looking behind me.

Wes came up and hugged her, her feet leaving the ground as he picked her up and held her close.

"Thank God," he said.

The police officer that had been at the house pulled up in a police cruiser and got out of the driver's seat. Patrick and Susan exited the back seat of the car and ran over to us.

I glared at them, silently daring Susan to say a single word to Annalise about this being her fault. I was done being nice to Susan. When I thought about the horrible things that could have happened to

Annalise because of their negligence, I wanted to rage.

"Wes and I will be staying at the house until the next hearing," I said coldly.

Susan narrowed her eyes at me. "I never meant for this to happen. We love our grandchildren."

Wes approached and put an arm around my shoulders, addressing Patrick and Susan.

"We aren't leaving until the case is settled."

Patrick nodded, silencing his wife with a look. "You're both welcome at the house, of course."

"Aunt Hadley, I'm hungry," Annalise said from a few feet away. "Can we go to the place with the chickens?"

"Chick-fil-A?" I asked her.

She grinned. "Yeah, I like those chickens."

"Of course we can, baby." I looked at Susan. "Why don't we take her to get some food and then we'll meet you guys back at the house?"

"Okay, we'll see you there. I'll feed Benny if he's hungry."

She wasn't snarly and combative now, but I knew she wasn't giving up on getting custody of the kids. Losing Annalise was going to hurt their case considerably, though. I was sorry it had happened, but hoping that it would lead to the judge doing the right thing and returning custody of the kids to Wes and me.

Annalise asked to ride on Wes's shoulders, and as he swung her up there, she said, "That was two weeks, right? You guys are coming back home now?"

I smiled up at her. "That's right."

"Yay!" She threw her arms in the air and cheered.

Wes put her down when we got to the minivan and he fished the keys from his pocket.

"Uncle Wes has a new car," Annalise said, clapping. "It's beautiful!"

Wes gave me a look, shaking his head.

"I'm never buying a minivan," he said under his breath.

"You so are," I told him, laughing. "Might as well get some white knee socks and white sneakers, too."

"Shit," he said softly, looking at me. "There's no car seat in the rental."

"Can we have one of the guys at the house bring us Ben's car?" I asked.

"Yeah, I'll ask Lars," he said, taking out his phone.

"His name is Thor," Annalise said, giving Wes an admonishing look.

I bent down and hugged her again, then kissed each of her cheeks several times. Lauren had told me so many times that she loved her kids so much she sometimes thought she'd burst—that it was a love like no other.

And now, I knew what she meant. I felt it, too. And I was never, ever going back to a life without this love.

CHAPTER TWENTY-FIVE

WES

Chaos. The next few hours were absolute fucking chaos. The women, from Hadley to Susan to Tori, started to cry as soon as we walked into the house with Annalise. Once they started to cry, Benny seemed to think it was his job in life to join them, and he did it louder and more vigorously than anyone else. By the time we got him settled down, everyone heard the story about how Nash found Annalise, and the police finally left. I was wiped out. I did order pizza for everyone, though, to thank my teammates and several neighbors that had all joined in the search.

Annalise fell asleep with a slice of pizza in her hand and Hadley got up to carry her upstairs before Susan could move. I wasn't sure if she was going to force the issue of a bath or just put her to bed, but

Hadley and I had no plans to go anywhere tonight. Once we'd told Patrick and Susan we were sleeping in the guest room until the hearing next week, they'd quietly excused themselves and gone to bed. It was probably better that way, since I had a lot I wanted to say to them, but I wouldn't do it in front of our friends and neighbors. I wouldn't say anything in front of Annalise either.

I needed to know what had happened, though. How, why, what, all the details. Not just because they fucked up, but also because I'd need the information so I could make sure it didn't happen again. Annalise was smart and headstrong, so this type of behavior didn't necessarily surprise me, but it wasn't a risk we could take in the future. She couldn't just leave the house when she was being punished for something, and the more I understood about why it happened the better I would be at preventing it. At least that's what I told myself. Maybe I really just wanted to make Patrick and Susan admit they were dumbasses who couldn't take care of our kids.

Our kids.

Mine and Hadley's.

Ours.

Us.

"We're going to take off," Drew said, startling me back to the present as he and Nina got up.

I shook his hand. "Thanks again," I told him. "We really appreciate you rallying the troops to help out."

"That's what friends do." He nodded and took Nina's hand as they headed out.

The other guys followed suit and within fifteen minutes, the house was quiet except for Benny cooing from his high chair. I'd put him there as I'd cleaned up the kitchen and I scooped him up before heading upstairs. I heard Hadley reading to Annalise in her room and opted not to interrupt because if I brought Benny in there, it would take forever to get them to settle down again. Annalise had probably woken up in the tub and now was having trouble settling down. Benny was probably overtired and overexcited too, but after a week away from him, I brought him into the guest room with me so I could spend a little time with him.

I stretched out on the bed and plopped Benny on his stomach on my chest. He pretended to crawl, sticking his butt up in the air and wiggling it. Then he gave me a toothless grin and I laughed. He had Ben's dark hair and Lauren's light eyes, which made me equal parts nostalgic and sad. I'd see Ben and Lauren in their children's faces forever, and while I was happy for their memory to live on, it was heartbreaking to think they wouldn't remember their parents at all.

"You tired yet, buddy?" I asked him, pulling him up into a sitting position on my stomach since I was mostly sprawled out.

"Da da." He said the word haltingly and then blew a raspberry.

Oh, holy shit. He'd just called me Dada. He would never know Ben. And as the man raising him, it was inevitable he would call me Dad. *Daddy*. I closed my eyes and breathed in and out a few times. Sometimes the grief washed over me with such ferocity it was like being in that hospital room all over again. That scratchiness behind my eyes was all too familiar now, but this time it was mixed with joy.

Da da.

"Da da da da da!" Benny was on a roll and I opened my eyes again, refusing to miss out on such an important moment, no matter how hard it was. I wouldn't replace Ben, but I'd step in and fill his shoes, even though they were huge.

"What about Mama?" I asked him.

He frowned at me. "Da da da!"

"Well, we'll work on mama tomorrow, okay?" I kissed the top of his head, his silky hair tickling my skin. I hadn't realized how much I loved these kids until I'd been away from them for a week.

"Hey." Hadley came into the room, smiling down at Benny.

"Annalise finally settle down?"

"She fell asleep at dinner, but she was filthy so I put her in the bath anyway, and that woke her right up. She had to tell me every detail of her adventure today, twice, and then said I had to read all her favorite stories to her because Grandma doesn't read them."

I scowled. "I can't wait to get them back in court. I was going to call you to tell you about our new attorney, but then this happened and I kind of forgot about it."

"Oh?" She sat on the bed cross-legged, one hand resting on Benny's back as he cuddled into my shoulder.

I told her about Regina Rittenhouse and how I'd gotten my father involved.

"He's a powerhouse," I told her. "I don't usually go to him for stuff like this because he's way over the top, but it was time to get custody finalized. One way or another."

She was gently tickling Benny's toes and he giggled, his foot moving out of the way and then going back for more.

"I want you to know," she said after a moment. "I'm not giving up these kids. Regardless of what we have to do to get custody at the hearing, I'm going to be in their lives."

"I never suggested otherwise," I said slowly, watching her. She wouldn't look at me, so I wasn't sure what was going on, but I knew her well enough to sense she needed a little time to formulate her thoughts.

"What I mean is…" She cleared her throat and picked up Benny, pulling him against her. "I love these kids and the life we started to build here. So even if we put your name on some document that gives you custody, don't think that when you're tired of me—*of us*—that I'm just going to go away quietly. I will sell everything I own to fight for shared custody if you try to cut me out of their lives."

"That's what you think of me?" I asked in surprise, sitting up a little as I met her gaze. "That I would do something like that?"

"I know what this is and I'm okay with it. What we have right now is good. It's fun and passionate and we've actually become friends through all of this, but I know I'm not the love of your life or anything so—"

"Okay, wait, I feel like I've missed something." I cocked my head. "Last time we talked, you were worried about your job, your career, your life back in New York…and that's why you went back. Has something changed?" I knew what I wanted her to say, but somehow, I had a feeling it wouldn't be that easy. Nothing with us was ever easy.

"I told you—I love the kids and the life we built here." She bounced Benny as he started to squirm to get free. "And after what happened with Annalise, it's pretty obvious that we're the right people to raise the kids. Not Patrick and Susan."

"So you're leaving New York?" Excitement coursed through me at the prospect of having her back here with me. With us.

She nodded. "I haven't worked out exactly what I'm going to do yet, but the kids need me."

I breathed in slowly, trying to read between the lines. She thought the kids needed her but hadn't said anything about me. Didn't she know how much I needed her too? Did she have feelings for me or was this all about the custody battle?

I'd never been unsure of myself when it came to women, but there had never been a woman in my life like Hadley. Hell, there had never been *anyone* in my life that impacted me like Hadley.

"Promise me, Wes."

"What?" I looked up in confusion. "Promise you what?"

"That no matter what the custody agreement says on paper, you won't send me packing once this thing between us burns itself out or you fall in love with someone or whatever." She lifted her chin a notch, as if daring me to disappoint her.

"Babe, that should go without saying." I ran a hand through my hair and resisted a yawn. "But I think—" I had to stop talking as the yawn won out, the day's stressors apparently catching up to me.

"Wes?" She leaned over and lightly pressed her lips to mine.

"Yeah?" God, I fucking needed to touch her, and I slid a hand around her waist, pulling both her and Benny against my chest.

"I'm physically exhausted and mentally drained too. Can we just get Benny settled and go to sleep? I can't think anymore. I can barely keep my eyes open. To be honest, I'd love to just curl up in your arms and go to sleep."

"That sounds like the best thing I've heard in a week," I said. "Let me run down and warm up a bottle for him, and once he's in bed, we can do just that."

She smiled. "Thank you."

I padded down the stairs to the kitchen, my thoughts whirling as I hunted for a clean bottle and Benny's formula. It seemed like Susan had moved everything in the kitchen and it took a minute to find what I needed, but I mixed formula in with the bottled spring water we used and then put it in the microwave. As the seconds ticked by my thoughts drifted back to Hadley.

I was probably as exhausted as she was, but I wasn't too tired to realize she didn't have a clue that I was in love with her. I didn't know for sure whether or not she felt the same, but I was counting on it because we'd been through too much together over the last few months to give up on this little family we were building. It hadn't started out that way, and even though I would have given everything I owned to have Ben and Lauren back, that wasn't going to happen. Instead, I had their beautiful babies. All I wanted in life was to raise them with the infuriatingly intense, passionate, smart, sexy woman who loved them as much as I did.

Raising them might be the easy part, though.

The hard part would be convincing Hadley not just that I loved her, but how right we were for each other. How good we would be together.

That was definitely going to be a challenge because I'd obviously dropped the ball so far. I was up to the task, though. One way or another.

CHAPTER TWENTY-SIX

HADLEY

I relished the pause on the other end of the phone, smiling as Liz processed the two-week notice I'd just given her.

"I'm willing to keep you on," she finally said. "At a lower salary of course, but we can negotiate something where you can work remotely all the time."

"I appreciate it, but my heart's just not there anymore. I want to pursue something new."

"Something new?"

"Yeah, I've been feeling like I had no professional options for so long, but I was just seeing things the wrong way. I have unlimited options and I'm excited about my future."

Was I rubbing it in her face at this point? A little. But if anyone deserved it, it was Liz.

"I'll just remind you about the noncompete clause in your contract," she said sharply.

"Oh, I know. But it's only a year, and it would take me that long to get all the groundwork laid if I decide to launch something new."

A pause. "Launch? Are you going to start your own magazine?"

Probably. But I wasn't telling Liz that. I wanted her to spend time trolling the staff listings for other magazines for the next year, wondering what I was doing but not knowing.

"I don't know," I said, a smile in my tone. "Maybe? Anyway, with my smaller office, I hardly have anything there anymore, so if you guys could just box up my personal items, I'll have someone come by and pick them up."

"Sure. And don't worry about working the next two weeks. I'll have payroll cut your last check."

This bitch. If I wanted to steal any future story ideas from *Willow*, I would have done it before putting in my notice. And it's not like I could overhear anything while working from home. But as soon as she hung up, Liz would send out a company-wide email telling everyone I'm no longer employed by *Willow* and anyone who speaks to me about any ongoing things there risks termination. She liked making it sound like she fired people even when she didn't.

Joke's on her, though. I told all my friends at *Willow* I was quitting yesterday.

"That's so nice of you, thanks," I said. "Best of luck, Liz."

"Same to you."

Liz hung up the phone on me for the last time and I let out a little cheer. I immediately felt lighter. Why had I thought staying at *Willow* was my only professional option?

I planned to take a break from work for the next couple of months. I was going to start boxing up some of Ben and Lauren's things to give to their children one day, and selling some pieces of furniture.

It didn't feel sad anymore. I was going to let Annalise help me pack up some of her mother's beloved baking pans and cooking appliances, knowing that one day she'd have a kitchen of her own to use them in. Wes and I were going to work on Ben's study together, carefully packing up hockey memorabilia for both kids. We had already rented a fireproof, climate-controlled storage unit for most of the stuff we were saving as well as a safety deposit box at a local bank to store some important paper-work for the kids.

It was time. Wes and I had won the court case and Patrick and Susan had left town immediately after. Wes was the kids' permanent legal guardian, and we'd also had wills created for both of us that left full custody to me in the event he died. I hated the thought, but we knew all too well that life could change in the blink of an eye. Ben and Lauren's deaths had left us stunned, but the clouds were lifting and we were finding a way forward together.

And like I had told Wes, it was okay that I wasn't the love of his life. We would always mean a lot to each other because of what we'd been through together, and I hoped our unconventional little family would work for a long time.

The only promise we had made to each other was that we'd always do our best by the kids. It wasn't the promise I'd expected to get from a man I'd fallen hard for, but it was something.

"Aunt Hadley, I need your help!" Annalise cried, running into the master bathroom as I was drying my hair after a shower.

"What's up?" I asked her.

"It's, uh…there's a big, huge animal in our backyard! It's so huge! Come help!"

I furrowed my brow, sensing a tall tale. "What? How can there be a huge animal in the yard when there's a fence?"

Her eyes widened and she spoke solemnly. "It crushed right through the fence. It's so mean and huge, I think it might eat Benny! Come quick, Aunt Hadley!"

I hurried into the closet and closed the door, hanging up my towel and talking to Annalise as I got dressed.

"Where's Wes? Is Benny seriously alone in the backyard right now? I told Wes I was taking a shower and he said he'd take care of both of you."

"Uncle Wes needs your help with the big huge animal!" Annalise cried. "It's true! This is all true!"

She was the worst liar ever, just like her mother. I smiled.

"I'm kind of scared, though," I said. "What does the animal look like?"

"It's big! With brown hair and fur and sharp teeth and claws. You better hurry. It's going to eat Benny!"

"Okay, I'm on my way."

I went into the bathroom and ran a brush through my wet hair and then followed Annalise downstairs.

"Hurry!" She ran to the kitchen and slipped out the back door.

I glanced out the French doors she'd gone through and saw pops of color. Spring had sprouted tulips, hyacinths and other perennial bulbs Lauren had planted in the yard. Knowing her hands had touched those bulbs reminded me that parts of Lauren were still here with me. I planned to dig up the bulbs after they'd finished their blooming cycles and take them with us when we moved. We'd plant them in our new yard and have a small piece of Lauren there.

When I put my hand on the door handle to open it, I frowned as I saw Drew and Nina. Something was definitely up, and it had nothing to do with a big, hairy monster. Glancing down at my cutoff sweats and gray UCLA T-shirt, I shrugged and decided I knew Drew and Nina well enough to wear my comfy clothes in front of them.

But as I walked outside, I saw that it wasn't just Drew and Nina. I rounded a corner and saw several more Mavericks players. Annalise was on Lars's shoulders, beaming.

"There's no monster," she said gleefully.

"I see that," I said, arching a brow at her.

I turned, looking for Wes so I could ask what was going on. I found him behind me, down on one knee. My breath left my lungs in a whoosh as I took him in, grinning nervously.

"Come a little closer, babe," he said, holding a hand out to me.

My heart and mind couldn't seem to catch up

with what I was seeing. Was this what I thought it was?

When I reached him, Wes took one of my hands in both of his. I still hadn't managed to close my mouth, still shocked at the site of him on one knee. On. One. Knee.

"Hadley Ellis, I've never known anyone like you," Wes said, his eyes shining with affection. "You make me want to be better in every way. You're smart and tough, but you also have a huge heart. You don't take any of my bullshit. You pick me up when I need it most. You and me and Annalise and Benny have become a family, and our family means—" He stopped to clear his throat, tears welling in his eyes. "Our family means everything to me. *You* mean everything to me. I should have told you sooner. If you'll let me, I'll tell you every day for the rest of our lives. I love you, Hadley. Will you be my wife?"

A single note of stunned laughter escaped my throat, and tears blurred my vision. I couldn't believe this was real. Wes loved me. He was looking up at me with hopeful eyes as he reached into his pocket and took out a small blue box, popping open the lid.

"Hadley?" he asked softly.

A smile spread across my face as I cried, "Yes! Yes, of course I will!"

He jumped up and swept me into his arms, spinning me in a circle as everyone cheered.

"There was no big animal, Aunt Hadley!" Annalise said from on top of Lars's shoulders. "I made that up to get you out here!"

"You had me scared there for a minute," I said, playing along.

"Let me put this on you," Wes said, taking the ring from the box.

It was a simple, round platinum solitaire, and it was enormous. I smiled, tearing up again as Wes slid it onto my ring finger.

"I measured your finger while you were sleeping the other night," he said. "That was fucking nerve-racking. I was so worried you'd wake up."

"We're getting married?" It came out as a question, because I still couldn't believe it was real.

"We are. I was thinking this summer."

"*This* summer?"

"I'm not waiting 'til *next* summer," he said, frowning.

"But there's so much to do. What if we can't get a venue booked? And I have to find a dress."

"I kind of thought we'd do it right here, in Ben and Lauren's backyard. It's as close as we can get to having them here. One last great memory here before we buy a new home of our own."

I absolutely adored he'd thought of that.

"I love that idea," I said, wiping the tears that had fallen down my cheeks. "And I can find a vintage dress if I can't get a new one fitted in time."

"The saleswoman at Tiffany said we can get a vintage wedding band for your ring, too. I thought you'd want to pick it out yourself."

I put my palms on his cheeks and leaned up to kiss him. "Look at you, being all thoughtful."

He kissed me back, a laugh rumbling in his chest. "If Ben and Lauren could see us right now."

It was definitely not a turn of events I had seen coming. I'd been so wrong about Weston Kirby. He was actually an incredible catch. And he was all mine.

Annalise tugged at Wes's legs, asking him for a piggyback ride. Our moment alone was over, but we'd make up for it tonight.

"Welcome to the family, Hadley," Nina said, hugging me.

"Thank you."

All the other Mavericks players there hugged me, too—except Lars. He gave me a warm congratulations, though.

Wes leaned down and whispered in my ear. "You're gonna be my old lady. Can you believe it?"

I gave him a look and said, "Call me your old lady

again and you'll have to find someone else to wear this ring."

He laughed and kissed me lightly. "There's that fire I love so much. Don't ever change."

As I looked around the yard, and thought about this place, this new life I'd found myself in, I felt Ben and Lauren here with us. Life had taken all of us in directions we never saw coming. The two of them were gone now, but still with us in so many ways. I'd lost my best friend in Lauren and found another one in Wes.

She would have laughed so hard if she could see us now. Until tears were running down her cheeks. Lauren would have loved every single thing about seeing me and Wes together. And thinking about it made me just the tiniest bit happier than I already was.

EPILOGUE
WES

I wore a suit every single time I played a hockey game, but something about wearing one in the backyard of our house as I waited for Hadley to walk down the aisle to become my wife was different. My collar itched; it felt like the buttons of my double-breasted jacket were too tight, and my feet felt sweaty in my leather dress shoes.

I shifted from one foot to the other, trying to breathe through the hot, muggy air. We had fans going and the dais where the ceremony would take place had been set up with a canopy of sorts to protect us from the late July sun, but I was sweating bullets. I didn't think it had much to do with the weather, though.

"Relax," Nash said under his breath. "You look like you're ready to bolt."

"Nah." I grinned over at him. I was battling a lot of emotions, but none of them included wanting to run. The backyard of our house—Ben and Lauren's house—was filled with the people we loved and cared about most in the world. My teammates, coaches and their significant others, my parents, Lauren's parents, and a handful of friends and neighbors. It was only about seventy-five people, so it felt incredibly intimate.

Exactly how we'd envisioned it.

We hadn't wanted it to be a big ordeal. It was a final hurrah before we moved to the new house we'd bought and started the next chapter of our lives together. As husband and wife. Mommy and Daddy to Benny and Annalise. Benny had already made the transition, babbling all kinds of words these days, but Dada and Mama were reserved specifically for me and Hadley. Annalise was still on the fence, but we'd explained as best we could that she could call us whatever she wanted. We'd noticed in private it had become more Mommy and Daddy, while in front of others she stuck to Aunt Hadley and Uncle Wes.

Whatever she wanted was fine with us; we just wanted the kids to be happy.

They were so excited about the wedding. Well, Annalise was excited and Benny was just excited because the rest of us were. Marrying Hadley was the icing on the cake of my life. I hated that we'd had to lose Ben and Lauren to find each other, but we had and making her my wife was all I'd thought about since that last trip to Miami.

"Here we go. You ready?" Nash grinned over at me and I turned.

The light jazz that had been playing stopped and the "Wedding March" began. I might have replied to Nash, but I wasn't sure because the moment I caught sight of Hadley, I couldn't think straight. I was completely mesmerized.

Since her parents were gone, and she'd been extremely close to both Lauren and her parents, Lauren's father, Greg, was walking her down the aisle.

Hadley was a vision in white. Though her dress wasn't a traditional wedding gown, it was pure Hadley. It was white and lacy, with what looked like silky material, but I didn't know what all that stuff was called. All I knew was how gorgeous she was. The dress was calf-length, appropriate for an outdoor, backyard wedding, and both summery and classy. It hugged her curves in all the right places but was strapless so it showed off her shapely shoulders and the elegant line of her neck.

God, she was beautiful.

How had I never thought so until recently?

Then her eyes met mine and she smiled.

Suddenly my suit fit perfectly, I wasn't sweaty, and the funny feeling in the pit of my stomach disappeared. She was walking down the aisle. Toward *me*. Toward our new life together. I took a second to look down at Annalise, who was throwing rose petals on the path ahead of Hadley, and she grinned up at me happily.

"Hi, Daddy!" she called out, oblivious to the rules and traditions of wedding ceremonies.

I noted that Hadley's step faltered for a second, her eyes meeting mine, but I winked at Annalise before mouthing, "don't cry," to Hadley.

Her lips turned up into a tremulous smile and then she was standing next to me.

"Dear friends," the nondenominational pastor we'd hired spoke up. "We are gathered here today…"

———

"WELL, MRS. KIRBY," I said, holding my new wife in my arms as we danced our first dance. "How does it feel?"

"Amazing," she whispered. "We did it."

"We did." She gazed up at me. "Ben and Lauren are *totally* laughing at us right now."

"Totally." I shook my head. "I can literally hear his

voice in my head, telling me what a dumbass I was and how much time I wasted."

"Same. Except in Lauren's voice."

We laughed together as I pulled her against me. "I love you, Hadley."

"I love you too. Much as it pains me to say it." She was teasing. We joked a lot about how we'd felt about each other until recently, and it always made us smile.

"Ready for a week alone in St. Lucia?"

"God, yes." She frowned for a moment. "Though I hate leaving the kids."

"We need us time. They'll be fine. Tasha and Greg are going to take good care of them. Plus they need special time with their grandchildren." Despite Tasha's MS, she and Greg had offered to take the kids while Hadley and I went on a honeymoon. We had Tori staying with them so she could help out overnight, though Benny didn't really wake up much anymore, and Drew and Nina were on call for any emergencies that might come up. Tasha was okay most days, and Greg would be with them, so we weren't worried. It actually made us feel good to know the kids would get to spend quality time with Lauren's parents since we felt like they might be their only present biological grandparents. We hadn't heard from Patrick and Susan since the judge awarded us custody, and while we wouldn't keep them from the kids, we also weren't going to seek them out. If they wanted to see the kids, they had to come to us for now. That might change when they got older, but I wasn't playing games with Ben's kids.

My kids.

Our kids.

Damn, it felt so natural to say that.

"I want more babies," Hadley whispered as we moved.

"What?" I snapped back to the present and dropped my gaze down to her pretty face.

"Not now," she said quickly. "But I'd like one or two more."

"I'm glad you said that because I was thinking the same thing." I glanced over to where Annalise was talking Lars's ear off. "Although we probably need to wait until Annalise gets to kindergarten and we only have one kid at home."

Hadley chuckled. "Agreed."

"Excuse me, Mr. Kirby." A big, burly man approached us as our dance came to an end.

"What's going on, Cal?" We'd had to hire security for the wedding, simply because I was a local celebrity—as were my teammates—and the public could sometimes be thoughtless and overzealous.

"Someone here to see you named Len Harris; says he's an attorney but he's not on the list."

"Oh god." Hadley paled a little. "You think Patrick and Susan…" Her voice trailed off.

"Let me go find out."

"I'll come too." She slid her fingers through mine and we hurried into the house.

"Wes. Hadley." Len was standing by the front door. "I'm so sorry to intrude but I had strict instructions from Ben and Lauren."

Hadley's fingers squeezed mine tightly. "B-ben and Lauren?" she whispered, clearly startled.

He smiled. "Apparently, those two were mind readers or something, because they left a letter that was to be given to you on your wedding day or as soon thereafter as I was able."

"Oh my god." Hadley sagged a little, but I slid my arm around her waist and pulled her into my side.

"Anyway, I didn't mean to cause a fuss. I just wanted to abide by their wishes." He handed me an envelope. "Congratulations. And I'm sorry again for intruding."

"Thank you so much for bringing this," I said, shaking his hand. "You're welcome to stay."

"No, thank you. My grandson has a T-ball game in an hour and if I miss it, my wife and my daughter will both have my head."

I chuckled. "All right. Thank you."

Len headed out and I looked at Hadley. "What do you think the letter says?"

She shook her head. "I can't imagine."

I grinned and handed it to her. "You want to do the honors?"

"We'll read it together." She slowly lifted the seal and pulled out a sheet of paper.

"You read it," I said gently.

Mr. and Mrs. Kirby,

WE KNEW IT!! When we decided to leave custody of our children to the two of you, we knew that if something ever happened to us and you guys were forced to truly get to know each other, you'd fall in love and get married.

Damn, you guys have smart friends. All these years you thought you hated each other, but really it was just sexual tension. We laughed about it afterward every time the two of you were together. Never lose the passion you bring out in each other. See each other's strengths instead of weaknesses. Be each other's best friend. Show our children what true love looks like. It's selfless. Joyful. Messy. Hard. Beautiful.

If only we could be there with you on your wedding day. The two of you are so dear to us. We wanted to spend forever together raising our family, but if we can't be there, it's comforting to know you will be. We wish you a lifetime of love, more babies to love, and beautiful friends to celebrate with.

Writing "in the event of our death" letters is brutal. This is the only one we are smiling while writing. Thanks, you guys. For every moment. Every laugh. Every memory. Make more every day, and never give up on each other.

WITH ALL OUR LOVE,

Ben and Lauren

I USED my thumb to wipe a stray tear from Hadley's cheek but she was smiling. "I really fucking miss them."

"They're right here, though," I said, tapping my fist over my chest. "And apparently here…" I waved the piece of paper.

"They knew us so well."

"Yup."

"Mommy! Daddy! What are you doing?" Annalise came running in indignantly, hands on her hips. "Come watch me and Thor dance."

Hadley turned to her with a smile. "You got Thor to dance?"

"Not yet." Annalise gave us a sheepish smile. "I'm gonna go ask him now."

"Okay, we're coming." Hadley threaded her fingers through mine again, leaning over to whisper, "we're definitely waiting until she's in kindergarten to have more."

We headed back to the reception and I paused to look up at the sky as we got outside. The sky was blue and cloudless, an absolutely perfect day for a wedding.

"Thank you," I whispered silently. "For your friendship, for Hadley, and for trusting me to raise your family. I miss you guys."

A gentle breeze wafted over my skin in response.

"You okay?" Hadley asked, meeting my gaze.

"I'm perfect." I leaned over to kiss the tip of her nose. "Do we rescue Lars or let Annalise have her way with him?"

We burst out laughing.

"I think it's time to get this party started," I told her.

"The party started the first time I met you," she said, her eyes twinkling. "I was just a little late getting there."

"Then we have lots of time to make up for." I tugged her hand and pulled her back out onto the dance floor, twirling her around. "Ready, Mrs. Kirby?"

"Oh, yeah."

I dipped her low, almost to the ground, before hauling her back up and pressing my lips to hers.

Read on for the first chapter of Hard Limit, the second book in the St. Louis Mavericks series, releasing 2.15.2022.

Preorder Hard Limit HERE.

HARD LIMIT

CHAPTER ONE - SHERIDAN

"This was a bad idea," I muttered, staring out the window of the limousine as it inched through St. Louis traffic. "Maybe we should turn around and go home." I turned to my best friend, Vanessa, and she quirked a brow at me.

"We're not going home," she said quietly, folding her arms across her chest. "I did not get all dressed up to sit at your place eating cheesecake. It's going to be fun, Sheridan. You haven't been out in over a year. It's time and we both know it."

"I don't know if I'm ready to be in the spotlight… you know how mean the press can be and I'm not… the same."

"Of course you're the same!" Vanessa snapped.

"I've put on twenty pounds and the camera adds another ten, so—"

"You were in a life-threatening accident. It's a miracle you're not in a wheelchair. And you're going to walk in there tonight like the badass you've always been. Besides, the focus tonight is the charity, not the celebrities who are going to be there."

"I bought the table in your name," I said. "So maybe no one even knows I'll be there."

Vanessa rolled her eyes. "Would you stop it? It's going to be a blast. It's a freakin' bachelor auction of professional athletes! I've got a thousand dollars put away for Nash Riley from the Mavericks."

I laughed, relaxing for the first time all night. "I thought you were hot for that new pitcher for the Cardinals?"

"We'll see which one strikes my fancy." She arched her brows and grinned. "Maybe I'll take both."

"I could use a little fancy-striking myself." I sighed. "It's been more than a year since I've had sex."

Vanessa shuddered. "Jesus, woman, that's a streak that needs to end right fucking now."

"I know." I turned back to the window. "But what guy is going to want to hook up with the fat chick with the cane?"

"Same guys who wanted to hook up with you

before? And anyway, the cane is temporary. You've come so far and it's time—"

"Sheridan, do you want me to take you right up to the front?" My driver/bodyguard, Flynn, opened the partition. Though I didn't own the limo, we'd rented it so he could drive Vanessa and I to this event since I never went anywhere without him these days. He was an employee but also a friend and my full-time bodyguard. The only person I trusted more than Flynn was Vanessa.

"If we go right up to the front, that's where the bulk of the press will be," I protested.

"But that's where you have the shortest distance to walk," he pointed out.

I loved Flynn ninety-nine percent of the time. Right this minute, I hated him.

Mostly because he was right.

"Okay. The front it is." I stiffened my spine and sat up straighter.

I could do this.

I'd been through worse and wasn't going to let one broken back derail the rest of my life. Even though it was turning out to be harder than I'd ever imagined.

He pulled up to cones directing which lane the VIPs were supposed to use and flashed our pass to the security guard who waved him through. Then he stopped and a few dozen reporters surged forward, anxious to see who was getting out.

"Let's go," I told Vanessa. "But you first, okay?"

"I'm all about the attention!" she laughed, holding out her hand to Flynn, who helped her out of the car. A few flashbulbs went off but no one recognized Vanessa Cruz, my best friend since we were fifteen, the CTO of my new plus-size lingerie company, and the smartest woman I knew.

Flynn reached out a hand to me.

"You got this," he said in a tone so low only I could hear.

I took a breath before letting him help me out of the limo. I tested my footing, since I was wearing the highest heels I'd worn since the accident—rhinestone covered sandals with two-inch wedge heels—and straightened up. I smiled as the first flash went off and then I heard the whispers.

"Holy shit, it's Sheridan Lee!"

"Hey, Sheridan, look over here!"

"Sheridan, you look amazing!"

I smiled and waved, walking slower than I would have a year ago but with an even, steady gait, the way my physical therapist had taught me. Learning to walk again as an adult was hard.

"Are you coming back to modeling?" someone called out.

"Sheridan, how's your back?"

Luckily, we got inside before I had to answer and I exhaled heavily.

Okay, the first hurdle was done. Now I could sit in a chair, have a glass of wine, and enjoy the auction. Which I was actually looking forward to. I didn't plan to buy myself a date, but I'd donate a few thousand to the cause. Anything to do with helping pediatric cancer patients was right up my alley.

The room was beautiful, with tablecloth-covered tables, a huge T-shaped stage that jutted down the middle of the room, and two huge bars and buffet tables set up on each side of the room. A DJ was playing dance music and for the first time in thirteen months, my body itched to move. Really move. God, I'd loved to dance BA.

BA and SA.

Before Accident and Since Accident.

That's how everything was classified in my life right now.

"Here we go." Vanessa put a glass of white wine in front of me and sank down beside me. "The party starts now. You hungry?"

"Famished," I admitted.

"I'll get us plates and then we can look through the program, see what else is on the menu." She chuckled as she walked away and I shook my head fondly.

We'd been through a lot together over the last thirteen years, but nothing as traumatic as my accident. And Vanessa had been at my side every step of the way, holding my hand, encouraging me, and kicking my ass when necessary.

I took a sip of wine and looked around, wondering how many familiar faces I'd see.

Coming in on her husband's arm was the owner of the small, local modeling agency where I'd gotten my start and I resisted the urge to wave. Though I loved Delia Hammond, I didn't have it in me to retell the story of the accident, my recovery, physical therapy, and of course, answering the number one question on everyone's mind: Are you going back to modeling?

I had no idea.

"Yum!" Vanessa put a huge plate heaped with what appeared to be every item on the buffet down in front of me and sat down again. "And for dessert, they have salted caramel chocolate mousse or white chocolate raspberry cheesecake. Want to share both?"

Vanessa weighed a hundred pounds soaking wet but ate like a freakin' NFL linebacker. I hated her sometimes, but I just smiled and shook my head. "I'll have a bite of each, but I need to lose the next ten pounds."

She rolled her eyes. "Fine." She popped a bite of prosciutto-wrapped mozzarella in her mouth and then opened the evening's program on the table between us.

"There's your boy." I pointed out the Cardinals' new pitcher, Scotty Dominguez, on the first page. He was five-eleven with long-lashed dark eyes and short, dark hair cropped close to his head. But man, he had the world's best lips. Between the lashes and the lips, he could be on magazine covers.

Vanessa cocked her head. "He's sexy. But let's see what else is out there."

We flipped through the pages, checking out each bachelor that would be available tonight and I paused toward the back. "Now that's a guy I could climb like a tree," I murmured.

"Who is he?" Vanessa frowned.

"Defenseman for the Mavericks," I said thoughtfully.

"Hockey?"

I nodded absently, reading the short blurb about him. "Holy shit, he's six-six, two-fifty."

"And you love that long-haired Viking look," Vanessa said, peering down at his photo. "He looks spectacularly underwhelmed in this picture."

I chuckled. "I'm sure the single guys were forced into this."

"Oooh, he's Swedish. He's younger than you too, only twenty-six."

I grinned. "I'm only twenty-eight, but I can cougar that boy all night long."

We laughed together and it felt good to enjoy some sort of normalcy after the year I'd had. Vanessa had spent a lot of time with me, but being out at a big event like this was different, and I allowed myself to get into the spirit of the evening's festivities. It was all for a good cause—children's cancer—and if we could joke and laugh about hot guys and sex for a couple of hours, all the better.

The auction started promptly at nine and though I'd told myself I wasn't buying myself a date, my glance kept dropping to the picture of Lars Jansson. Physically, he was my fantasy man, but obviously I didn't know him. He was probably a womanizing jerk—a lot of athletes were—and that wasn't my thing at all. Even before the accident, I'd been careful about the men I dated.

As a plus-sized woman, I was used to comments about my weight. As the most well-known plus-sized supermodel in the world, I was used to men "settling" for my body type because I was beautiful, wealthy, and successful. And I would never, ever settle for a man who didn't love all of me. I'd done it once and it took me a long time to get past the humiliation. Now, I held the reins when it came to relationships, dating, and even one-night stands. Not that I'd had any of those lately. I hadn't had sex in thirteen months, which was the longest I'd gone since losing my virginity at fifteen.

Gazing down at Lars' picture, I wondered if he looked as good in person as he did on the page.

Vanessa nudged me back to the present. "Your boy is up soon."

The last guy had been auctioned off for four hundred dollars, which didn't seem like a lot, but I'd also never heard of the rookie running back for the city's newest football franchise, the St. Louis Sentinels. The most well-known players were being saved for last, and Lars was somewhere in the middle, so I figured he'd go for a little more.

You know you want to bid, Sheridan.

The devil on my shoulder seemed to be speaking directly to my libido.

"Too young, right?" Vanessa was asking me, motioning to the baseball player who'd just flexed his muscles on the stage. He was laughing, obviously having a good time with this, pulling off his dress shirt and waving it around as a bunch of barely twenty-somethings started bidding.

"He's probably not old enough to drink," I told her, laughing.

"Probably not. And I'm torn between Nash and Scotty anyway."

"Take them both," I teased her.

Her eyes gleamed. "Damn, I would if I thought I could get away with it!"

Three more guys were auctioned off and then they announced Lars. I sat up straighter, trying not to look too interested, but holy hell, he was even hotter in person. He was big all over. Not just tall, but muscular and broad-shouldered. His thighs flexed as he walked across the stage, muscles bulging even beneath his dark gray dress slacks, and his shoulders seemed to take up the whole room.

"Here." Vanessa pretended to hand me her napkin. "You're drooling."

"Two hundred!" One of the twenty-somethings sitting near the stage jumped up, waving the card with her number on it. We'd all gotten them when we arrived, and everyone's information was already on file, so the purchase process would be seamless.

"Two twenty-five!" One of her friends stuck her tongue out at her as they laughed.

"Two fifty!"

"Oh, for fuck's sake," I muttered under my breath.

Lars did *not* look happy to be there and each

time someone called out a bid, he jumped a little. Not only did I want to jump his bones, I also had the most irrational need to protect him. Which made no sense for a big professional hockey player like that.

"Three forty!" The first young woman yelled out.

Lars was simply standing at the bottom of the stage now, and while the other guys had laughed, flirted, and had fun with it, he was somewhat wooden, the smile on his face obviously forced. But he was beautiful. His long, blond hair was parted down the middle and fell to his shoulders, curling the tiniest bit on the bottom. His eyes were electric blue, even from ten or fifteen feet away, and when we made eye contact, I almost spontaneously combusted. Those high cheekbones were the final nail in the coffin of my self-control and I slowly got to my feet.

"Three fifty!" One of the other ladies called out.

I smiled at Lars and held up my card. "Ten thousand dollars."

"Excuse me?" The emcee paused. "Number twenty-four—did you say ten…*thousand*?"

I smiled at the three young women who were now shooting daggers at me with their eyes before I turned to the emcee. "I did."

"Now that's what I call donating to charity!" The

emcee was pleased as punch. "Lars Jansson goes for ten thousand dollars! Do we have any other bids?"

I sat down with a smug smile.

The emcee grinned as he spoke. "Number twenty-four takes Lars Jansson for a whopping ten thousand dollars—the rest of you boys have some work to do!"

Everyone laughed, but my eyes were on Lars. And then his met mine. For the first time since he'd come out on stage, I saw a glimmer of his personality as he took a moment to study me. Mostly, I saw curiosity, but there was also a hint of annoyance with a dash of…interest?

Before I could figure it out, he was gone, striding to the back.

"This right here is why we're besties." Vanessa dissolved into laughter and I joined her, my eyes never leaving Lars' retreating back.

I'd either done something really cool or incredibly stupid. Either way, I'd just won myself a date with a professional hockey player who looked like a Nordic god, and for the first time in thirteen months, I was excited about something.

ACKNOWLEDGMENTS

Our villages expanded by a lot while writing this book. Everyone on our individual teams huddled up and worked hard to make this book a success, and we are grateful! We truly can't list out everyone who helps us on a day-to-day basis, because that would take pages and pages, and we'd still probably forget someone. But know that if you're a blogger reading the ARC for this book, an author friend to one or both of us, a reader who never misses one of our hockey books, or a really hot hockey player, we are grateful for you.

Special thanks to Renita McKinney, who worked us in for a developmental edit at the drop of a hat while she was traveling. Renita, your encouragement and sound advice gave us everything we needed to finish this book in the way we wanted to. Our publicists, Heather Roberts, Jessica Estep and Jenn Gaffney are our promo Dream Team. Thanks, guys, for handling so much of the non-writing work so we can stay lost in the St. Louis Mavericks world. Line editor Taylor Bellitto polished this book until it shone, and we dig her a whole lot. Rosa Sharon is our sharp-eyed, awesomely talented proofreader, who helps us rest easy and not feel like we have to read through the book several more times when our eyes are already burning. Our cover photo is by Rafa Catala, and it so perfectly captures our Wes. Lori Jackson put the perfect touches on it with her design work, and the cover was a huge part of our inspiration as we wrote.

This was fun, you guys! Maybe we should do it again...like soon?

Writing books is a lovely, frustrating, draining, exhilarating experience for me. After I finished my first book, I was hooked. I've crafted stories, both in my head and on paper, since I was a kid. This career is a dream, but it can, at times, be lonely. The opportunity to write this book with Kat came at a time when I was experiencing some personal issues that left me unable to focus on anything else. But then Kat and I started talking about this idea, and our enthusiasm snowballed by the day. We didn't just love these characters and this story—we *felt* them deeply. And as I wrote, I escaped my worries for a few hours at a time. I got to experience that incomparable feeling of a new chapter from Kat showing up in my inbox. Co-writing with Kat came to me when I needed it most, and she has become a dear friend in this process. Hard Fall is more than a book to me. When I look back on it, I'll remember the friendship that started and grew out of it. I'll remember that when I was feeling lost, this book was there to remind me that I had a place I could go for a little break—the Mavericks world.

My greatest hope is that Hard Fall can be for readers what it was for me: an escape from real-life stresses and worries, and that after that time away, readers will feel just a little bit recharged and ready to take on the world again. Even if we never meet in real life, having that connection with a reader is a precious gift that I'm forever grateful for.

~Brenda

When I first started publishing my fiction five years ago, I never imagined I'd want to share my characters and ideas with anyone else. The stories we create are so incredibly personal, it's hard to invite someone into that process. And yet, from our very first phone conversation, Brenda and I found kindred writing spirits in each other. The storyline for Hard Fall grew quickly, and we started putting words on paper within a few days of discussing the project. Having someone to bounce ideas off of, and developing these characters together, made the process both painless and unforgettable. Usually, I'm ecstatic when I finish a book, but I felt an equal amount of sadness with this one because I didn't want it to end. I hope you, the wonderful readers out there, feel the same way.

It's an honor and a privilege knowing you're out there reading my words, and I appreciate each and every one of you.

~Kat

ALSO BY BRENDA ROTHERT

Chicago Blaze Series

Book 1 - Anton

Book 2 - Luca

Book 3 - Victor

Book 4 - Knox

Book 5 - Alexei

Book 6 - Easy

Book 7 - Jonah

Book 8 - Kit

Book 9 - Olivier

Sin city saints Series

Book 1 - Maverick

Fire on Ice Series

Book 1 - Bound

Book 2 - Captive

Book 3 - Edge

Book 4 - Drive

Book 5 - Release

ALSO BY KAT MIZERA

Las Vegas Sidewinders:
Dominic
Cody's Christmas Surprise
Drake
Karl
Anatoli
Zakk
Toli & Tessa
Brock
Vladimir
Royce
Nate
Sidewinders: Ever After
Jared
Dmitri's Christmas Angel
Ian

Sidewinders: Generations:
Zaan
Tore
Anton (coming 2022)

Alaska Blizzard:
Defending Dani
Holding Hailey
Winning Whitney
Losing Laurel
Saving Sara
Chasing Charli
A Very Blizzard Christmas
Tending Tara
Calling Cassie

St. Louis Mavericks (with Brenda Rothert)
Hard Fall

The Royal Trilogy:
Nowhere Left to Fall
Nowhere Left to Run
Nowhere Left to Hide

Royal Protectors:
Sandor

Cocky Protector (book 1.5, part of the Cocky Heroes Club series)

Xander

Axel

Dax (*A Royal Protectors/Sidewinders crossover novel*)

Rock Hard:

Play

Pause

Rewind

Fast Forward

Inferno:

Salvation's Inferno

Temptation's Inferno

Redemption's Inferno

Tropical Inferno (formerly "Tropical Ice")

Romancing Europe:

Adonis in Athens

Smitten in Santorini

Lucky in Lugano

Other Books:

Special Forces: Operation Alpha: Protecting Bobbi (Susan Stoker's Special Forces World)

Special Forces: Operation Alpha: Protecting Delilah (Susan Stoker's Special Forces World)

Brotherhood Protectors: Catching Lana (Elle James's Brotherhood Protectors World)

View Kat's entire collection of books at
www.KatMizera.com

ABOUT THE AUTHOR

USA Today Bestselling author Kat Mizera was born in Miami Beach with a healthy dose of wanderlust. She's lived from coast to coast, and everywhere in between, but home is wherever her family is.

A devoted mom and wife to her wonderful and supportive husband (Kevin) and two amazing boys (Nick and Max), Kat loves to travel the globe with her adventurous, hockey loving family. Greece is at the top of that list. She hopes to one day retire there, spending her days writing books on the beach.

Kat is former freelance sports writer who now writes steamy hockey romance about her favorite fictional teams, the Las Vegas Sidewinders and the Alaska Blizzard. The library of novels she's penned also include sexy contemporary stories about baseball stars, alpha sex club owners, special forces heroes, rock stars and royalty. Regardless of genre, her books about bad boys with hearts of gold will steal your breath, rock your world and melt your heart.

WHERE TO FOLLOW KAT:

WEBSITE
FACEBOOK
TWITTER
INSTAGRAM
BOOKBUB
KAT'S PRIVATE FACEBOOK GROUP

ABOUT THE AUTHOR

Brenda Rothert lives in Central Illinois with her husband, children and two dogs. She loves to hear from readers through her website or her Facebook Group, Rothert's Readers.